TALENTED
AMATEUR

About the Author

Maryn is blessed to have retired young after thirty years in public education. Writing is her second post-retirement hobby. Her first hobby, upcycling furniture, was great until the basement and garage overflowed with finished projects. When not busy with hobbies, Maryn and her partner like to travel to warm places and sip umbrella drinks by the pool.

TALENTED AMATEUR

MARYN SCOTT

BELLA
BOOKS
2021

Bella Books, Inc.
P.O. Box 10543
Tallahassee, FL 32302

Printed in the United States of America on acid-free paper.

First Edition - 2021

Editor: Heather Flournoy
Cover Designer: Kayla Mancuso

ISBN: 978-1-64247-236-3

Dedication

To my love.
I hold your words in my heart: always, all ways.

CHAPTER ONE

Peel Primm was stretched out on her couch drifting to sleep when the pop of something hitting the window caused her to sit bolt upright. She knew that sound. At a sprint she ran to the sliding glass door and looked out to her newly potted flowers. She groaned at what she saw. Hail. Little balls of icy destruction hit her patio, her plants, and her house. In no time, the ground was covered with white marbles and shredded leaves. Then things picked up.

The pops against the windows changed to a steady barrage of dime-sized stones hammering the glass. She stepped back as the intensity of the storm increased and the amount of hail doubled. The sound was deafening. For a full minute ice poured into her yard, blanketing everything. She watched until at last the hail changed to heavy rain, then barely a drizzle.

That's when she heard it. Draining water. Inside the house. "No, no, no," she cried as she chased the sound down the stairs to the unfinished basement. It'll be okay, she told herself. Everything down there was in plastic bins. Everything except the corner containing the last of her mother's boxes.

Which was exactly where the water was coming in. The long window had broken near the top, allowing water to pour in but holding back the hailstones and debris that filled the window well. All of the boxes were wet, but none appeared to be soaked through. Peel ran back upstairs, found a plastic painter's tarp to lay on her kitchen floor, and carried the boxes up.

The heaviest box had been on the bottom of the pile, the crisscrossed flaps smashed down to form an open square. Now that the box was in bright light, she could see it contained old photo albums. The label wasn't her mother's handwriting but her grandmother's: "Grady Family Photos." Was it even worth looking at? The Gradys were her grandfather's adopted family. They'd already raised a family when two-year-old Charles came to live with them. She doubted there would be any pictures of interest to her. Still, her mother had kept the albums. The least she could do was look before throwing them out.

With a deep breath, she pulled the flaps open. One by one, she pulled out the broken albums and loose pages and stacked them on the plastic. Plopping down next to the pile, she paged through the Grady albums. After twenty minutes of looking at the faces of strangers, she was ready to discard the lot. When she got to the last album, she could see that it was the most recent. The children in the earlier photographs were grown, and the couple had aged considerably. She flipped through the pages until one of the larger photographs caught her eye. It was a family portrait, but there was a face she hadn't seen in any other of the photographs. She picked at the edge, trying to get the photo to lift off the black paper. Once she peeled the first corner, the rest lifted easily. Only the edges had been glued, and when she pulled the photo, she saw why. A neatly folded piece of paper had been hidden behind the portrait. She opened it and gasped.

It was her grandfather's birth certificate: Jared Charles Devin, born September 19, 1931, to Charles and Elizabeth Leary Devin. Devin. No one had known his real last name. His father had abandoned the young family. Elizabeth Leary's dying wish was his last name would be changed to Grady. Her heart ached. In the years since her mother's death, there had been so many things she wished she could have shared, but none bigger than this, her family name.

Myra Primm lost a short battle with lung cancer when Peel was still in college. Although she'd had a persistent cough throughout the summer, no one imagined her ailment was cancer. She'd never smoked and had always been healthy. By the time it was diagnosed, Myra only had a couple of months to live. Peel was twenty when she died.

Her mother's death brought Peel and her father even closer, if that were possible. She came home from college every chance she got. They talked on the phone often, critiquing movies they'd seen and TV shows they were watching together. Peel's grades suffered a little with her viewing schedule, but it was worth it to know she was keeping her father busy. His death from a heart attack when she was twenty-five left her devastated. With no siblings, no aunts, uncles, or cousins, she was completely alone. There was no one left who would understand the significance of the paper she was holding.

* * *

The next morning Peel didn't have to be at the library until midday. She was the youngest of the full-time librarians at their large suburban library. Her day started with lots of book returns and the regular Monday crowd, but by midafternoon the library was quiet. Peel grabbed a cart of returns and made her way through the stacks shelving books. As she worked, she tried to remember the stories her mom had shared about her own father and his childhood. There wasn't much. She knew he'd been born to a father who didn't want a family and to a mother who died way too young. His adoptive family had been kind, if not distant. They were in their fifties when they took him in and didn't give him much attention. It was hard not to draw parallels to her own loneliness.

Fortunately, Monday evenings she sponsored the high school Anime club. It was usually the highlight of her week.

This evening, though, the Anime kids were antsy. When Peel joined them, Jenn, their leader, was brainstorming shows for them to watch. Peel eyed the list on the board while Jenn cajoled, "Come on you guys. Somebody has to have a new idea."

"There's nothing good out right now. Everybody's waiting for the new *Samurai Ghost Fighter* to come out," one of the boys complained.

A girl in the front threw a look of disgust over her shoulder. "That's just a rumor. They killed off the main character Seri Sujimoto. The series is over."

Loud protests came from other areas of the room. "Hello, Ghost Fighter? Of course, they killed off Seri. He's coming back to fight in another realm." Peel tuned out the bickering, used to the rhythms of the group. If they stayed true to form, the bickering would go on for ten minutes, then Jenn would get exasperated and pick a show. Lost in her thoughts, she didn't notice when the argument stopped.

"Peel, hello, Peel?" Jenn was waving a hand in front of her while Kenton dragged a tall chair to the front of the room.

"Yeah, you promised us a long time ago, you'd explain." Uh-oh. Tuning out was bad, but what could she have possibly agreed to explain? They'd all had sex education, right?

Her panic was short-lived. "That's right. We want to hear how you went from being a super spy to a librarian," one of the kids teased.

Oh, that. Crap. She wondered if she offered details on conception if they'd let her off the hook. "It's a boring story. Nothing dramatic like how I got my name." She was pleased at the laughter. "See, you still think it's funny. This story is not funny."

"That's okay. If we can't watch a Samurai decapitate ghosts, we might as well listen to you."

"Ouch." Peel grabbed her heart. "Now there's no way I'm telling you." They laughed again, and Peel conceded. "Okay, but I'm warning you. There's nothing to this story." She took a seat in the center chair and hooked her heels on the crossbar. "All right, you know I was obsessed with spy movies and the TV show *The Avengers*…"

"What? You mean the movie franchise? Was that even out when you were little?"

Peel was saved from answering by Rachel, a girl she was pretty sure was gay. "No. That's the name of the TV show with Mrs. Peel." The girl looked at Peel. "I watched it after you told us that's how you picked your name. It's a little cheesy, but her leather catsuit was hot."

Peel blushed, unsure of how to answer. The leather catsuit had done it for her, too, but there was no way she was going to admit that to a high school student. "Um, okay." She brushed her hair back off her face. "Anyway, I didn't tell people I wanted to be a"—she waved her hand—"spy or secret agent, whatever the term is." She took a breath. "You know when you have career days at school? I couldn't say, 'Yeah, my goal is to be in MI6.'"

"Especially since you don't have an accent," one of the kids pointed out.

Rachel spoke again. "Steed was the spy. Mrs. Peel was just a 'talented amateur.'"

"She was not!" Peel exclaimed. "She was as much of an agent as he was."

"Huh-uh. It's in the opening credits of the early black-and-white episodes. You know, the ones with the chessboard? He's a 'top professional' and she's a 'talented amateur.' The one who replaced her, Tara King? She was a spy." Rachel looked around the room. "What? I told you I watched it."

Peel groaned, only half in jest. "Are you telling me my whole life has been a lie? I've been aspiring to be a 'talented amateur?'"

"She was just as good as he was. If Diana Rigg stayed on the show, they would have made her an agent." Rachel was trying to salvage her childhood dream. Peel decided to let her.

"You are absolutely right. Plus, she was too busy fencing and sculpting with power tools to have a full-time job."

"Come on, back to the story," Jenn demanded.

"Okay. So, when it was time to go to college, my mom was worried. She told me she thought I was using the idea of being a spy to avoid making a real decision about my life." Peel shrugged. "I probably was. I had no idea what I wanted to be when I grew up." Peel stopped. "No one's a senior, right?"

"We will be in a couple of months." One girl pointed to the boy next to her.

"Do you have any idea what you want to do for the rest of your life?"

"I don't, but Jeremy wants to design video games."

"Do people take you seriously, Jeremy?"

"My computer programming teacher does, but my parents think it's a waste of time."

"Parents," she commiserated. "My mom told me to enter school with an open mind and concentrate on doing well in my general education classes. She told me that I would discover a career if I let myself be open to the possibilities. I did what she said, but I kind of cheated, too. Not cheated in college." She held up a hand to clarify. "Cheated on my promise to my mom. I did the gen ed courses, but when I had a choice, I picked classes I thought would attract the attention of the CIA."

They laughed. "You think the CIA watches certain classes?"

Jenn was kinder. "Like what?"

"I always liked to analyze things. I took technology, statistics, logic, lots of research, and," she added with a little smile, "literature classes. Obviously, I like to read." She gestured around her. "I also watched for recruiters." When she saw the puzzled looks on the kids' faces, she explained. "At most universities, businesses and government agencies make campus visits to recruit potential employees. The FBI came a couple of times, so did several police departments, but never the CIA." She made a face. "Honestly, in the back of my mind, I thought if I just took the right combination of classes, they would find me."

Some of the kids laughed. Others looked at her sympathetically. Jenn was one of the latter. "That's sad, Peel."

"I know. I was immature." She took a deep breath. "Then my mom was diagnosed with cancer and died the summer before my junior year." The room was silent. "I went back to school and met with an adviser. Turns out, I'd been on a degree path all along." She spread her arms wide, gesturing around her. "Library Science and Information Technology. And here I am."

Jenn crossed the room. She wrapped Peel in a side hug, resting her head on Peel's shoulder. "We love you," she said.

"Hey, Peel," one of the boys called. "What if you're a new kind of sleeper agent? You know how Russia plants agents in the US and then activates them years later?"

"Yeaahh." Peel stretched out the word.

"What if you don't even know you're a sleeper agent? What if they've been monitoring you all this time waiting to call you up?"

Peel widened her eyes, happy to be able to lighten the mood. "I can only hope."

* * *

Mondays and Tuesdays, Peel worked late. Her usual routine was to sleep in, catch the end of a morning news show, then head to the rec center to work out. Tuesday morning she woke early. When she turned on the television, the anchors' chatter only irritated her. After a quick breakfast of cereal and toast, she drove to the rec center. Running helped clear her head, and today her mind was clogged. She programmed the pace and plugged in her headphones, allowing the familiar playlist to ease her into the workout. After the third mile, an idea formed.

As part of her graduate work, she'd researched her ancestry. Because she was the only child of two only children, her family tree was barely developed. Her father's side yielded a few results, but her mother's dead-ended at her great-grandmother's death and her grandfather's adoption. What would the name Devin add? It would be fun to see how much further back she could go.

Showered, she sat at her computer with a fresh cup of coffee and accessed the genealogy site she'd used previously. After reactivating her account, her family tree appeared onscreen. She added Charles Devin's name. In no time, an entire new branch appeared. Peel sat back, amazed. Her great-grandfather had been born in Pennsylvania, one of seven children. Along with the names of these new ancestors, she also found several primary source documents. Most were census records, and she used them to trace Charles Devin's path west, ending in her grandfather's hometown. Unfortunately, that's where they ended. There was no record of him after that.

The last documents were marriage certificates. She opened the first. Charles Devin and Elizabeth Leary, her great-grandparents, were married in Colorado. She already knew that. She clicked on the second document expecting to see the same copy, then froze, staring at the screen. The bride in the second marriage certificate wasn't Elizabeth Leary. Four years after his marriage in Colorado, Charles Devin moved to Tierra de Oro, Mexico, and married Louisa Sanchez. She was surprised by the anger she felt. "Asshole," she said aloud. "You abandoned your family and orphaned Grandpa, and then remarried? Asshole," she repeated, and slammed the laptop closed.

At the library, Peel was still fuming when she told her supervisor, Sheryl, the story. "I was excited to find the birth certificate, but all it really gave me was confirmation that Charles Devin wasn't a good man."

Sheryl patted her arm. "But your great-grandmother was a strong woman. You've got to respect what she did to protect her baby."

"I know," Peel said. "She protected him, but he was raised by this older couple. Mom said he had a lonely childhood." She crossed her arms. "At some point Charles had to find out Elizabeth had died. Otherwise, he wouldn't have been able to remarry."

"Maybe he didn't know. He moved to Mexico. I'm sure no one checked to see if he was married previously. Why would they?" Sheryl's logic made sense.

"Then he's an even bigger asshole than I thought. I'll bet his second wife had no idea he had a child."

"Are you going to keep searching? Do you want to know if he had children with her?"

That was the question Peel had been pondering all day. She wondered if she had other relatives out there, but it seemed disloyal to Elizabeth Leary to search for them. She said as much to Sheryl.

"Well, look at you. I didn't realize you were sentimental," Sheryl said.

"Hey," Peel protested. "I've got depth." She blew out a breath. "I don't know, Sheryl. Her dying wish was to keep him away from that family."

"Since I'm sure he's long gone, I don't think you'll betray her. There's no harm in getting information."

"I do like a good research challenge."

Sheryl laughed. "Then consider yourself challenged. How's your Spanish?"

"Borderline awful." Peel moaned. "I took two years in high school, and then repeated the same two years in college. I'll have to hope for a sympathetic English speaker."

Two hours later, that's what she found. After checking the time zone—central standard—she found the number to a local library and dialed. "*Tierra de Oro Biblioteca.*"

"*¿Lo siento, hablas inglés?*" Peel had looked up how to say, "I'm sorry, do you speak English?"

"*Un momento.*"

Within minutes, a second voice came on the line. "Hello, are you looking for an English speaker?"

"Yes, thank you. I'm sorry, my Spanish is very poor."

"That's fine. I like to practice my English. How can I help you?"

Peel summarized the discovery of the birth certificate and a little of her family history. "We don't have a lot of records here at the *biblioteca*, but there are a few. Who are you researching?"

"Charles Devin is my great-grandfather. He married Louisa Sanchez." When Peel heard a sharp intake of breath, she asked, "Do you know them?"

"Um, no. No." The woman was fumbling with something in the background. "Sorry, I dropped something. Devin is the family name?"

"Yes. D-E-V-I-N. He married Louisa Sanchez. How much do you charge for research? Is it an hourly rate?"

"Don't worry about money. I can look for you. You say you work in a *biblioteca*?"

"Yes, in Colorado. But I don't want you to go to any trouble."

The woman ignored her. "Tell me your name, again? And where are you located?" Peel repeated her name and the library's information. The line was silent while the woman wrote. "I'll call if I find anything."

"You don't have to do that. I can call you," Peel said.

"No need. We'll be in touch."

It was a prophetic statement.

CHAPTER TWO

A week later, Peel finished shutting down the computers and checked that everything was in order for the next morning. She was looking forward to winding down with a glass of wine on the deck and finishing her novel. With a contented sigh, she walked out the back door.

She had just turned from checking that the door had latched when a man stepped out of the shadows. Startled by his sudden appearance, she jumped. "Hello…" she started to say, but a hand clamped over her mouth, smothering the words. He wrapped a second arm around her chest and pulled her against his body. The hand over her mouth and the pressure on her lungs made it hard to breathe. She struggled against his grip, but he leaned back, lifting her until her feet barely touched the ground. Instinctively, she started swinging her legs wildly trying to get some power to connect a kick. From his grunts, she knew that she made contact a couple of times. He tightened his hold and she sucked in hard, trying to get air.

He turned and dragged her backward toward the parking lot. In the moment before they turned, she saw a white panel van idling, door open, waiting. She struggled harder against his hold. As long as she was out in the open she had a chance, but if they got her in the van…She wouldn't finish the thought. The lack of oxygen was weakening her, but she couldn't give in. Peel tossed her head, trying to free her mouth to scream. In the struggle, his hand slid down, fingers pressing between her lips. It was the opportunity she needed. She opened her mouth, allowing the fingers inside, then bit.

Shouting in pain, he let go of her chest and used his free hand to club Peel on the side of the head. Even though he didn't have much leverage, the blow stunned her. As she fell, he ripped his fingers free. He towered above her, rage in his eyes as he clutched the injured hand to his chest. She tried to stumble away but was dazed and out of breath. He lifted a foot to kick her when suddenly the night was filled with a cacophony of screams and yells.

"Get away from her, asshole."

"We've already called the police, so you better run."

Peel could see the shock and confusion on his face. He looked at her, but when another, deeper voice yelled, "We're going to kick your ass if you don't get out of here," he sprinted for the van. Peel rolled to her hands and knees, taking in deep breaths. Her chest hurt and her mouth felt bruised where the hand had pressed against her skin.

"Peel, are you okay?" Jenn slid onto the ground next to her, followed by ten wide-eyed teenagers.

Peel looked up in disbelief. "That was you guys?" She rolled to a sitting position, looking at the circle of faces around her. Their expressions reflected the terror Peel felt. She swallowed as the reality of the situation hit her. "You saved my life," she said, her voice trembling. "I can't believe you did that. How did you know? What are you doing here?" They talked at once, pointing in different directions. Peel didn't bother to decipher their words. "Thank you." Her voice was quiet. She spread her arms wide and pulled them into a group hug. The smell of sweat and foot odor was both strong and comforting. "Did you really call the police?" she asked. Her answer was the sound of a siren approaching.

"The police are here." Courtney held a phone to her ear, light bouncing off the piercings in her eyebrow. "Yes, we're in a group on the back side of the library. He's not here anymore." She pulled her phone away and told the group, "911 operator. She stayed on the line with me." She put her phone back to her ear. "Thanks, Amy. I think everyone is okay, but he punched Peel. You should probably send an ambulance."

When the police arrived, the kids explained how they happened to be there when Peel needed them most. As usual, Jenn spoke for the group. "It was a nice night, so we decided to play ghost in the graveyard in that field over there." She pointed. "Dashawn is the one who noticed the van pull into the parking lot and turn off its lights. It was a white panel van, so we were all a little scared," she admitted. "We crouched down in the field for a while, then army-crawled closer to the library." She made an awkward, elbows-out crawling motion with her hands. The other kids nodded.

"When that big guy got out of the van and walked to the back of the library, we didn't do anything right away. We thought he was a friend here to pick up Peel." She turned. "Sorry, Peel." Peel gave her a half hug. "That's why we didn't call 911 right away. Even when he grabbed her, we weren't sure. But then you could tell she was trying to get away from him. That's when we started running and screaming."

"They were amazing," Peel said to the officer. "They came out of nowhere and made so much noise." Then she remembered something. "Hey, whose deep voice?"

Kenton raised his hand and boomed out, "That was me." In his normal voice he added, "I have Intro to Acting this semester."

"Can anyone give me a description of this guy?" the officer asked.

Jenn called over her shoulder, "Deshawn!"

A skinny boy stepped forward. "Jenn told me to start recording as soon as we saw the van. I got a good shot of the license plate before we ran to save Peel." He looked to his leader—Jenn, not Peel. "I think I have a video of him grabbing Peel, but I put my phone down when I thought we were going to fight." Peel looked at the tiny freshman and her eyes welled up. They had all been willing to fight to protect her.

The officer looked at Peel. "Can we go in the library?" Then he turned to Deshawn. "I'll need your phone, and we'll need to get information from all of you, and call your parents."

Peel expected a groan at those words but was surprised when Jenn said, "We'll call our parents now, so they know we're here with the police. Can we tell what happened?"

"If you don't, I will," Peel replied. "You saved my life," she said again. She hoped her tone conveyed her sincerity. Not for the first time tonight, she looked at her motley crew and wanted to cry.

While the officers were busy with the kids, Peel went into the staff bathroom to wash her face. She brushed her teeth over and over and over. She couldn't erase the thought of those fingers in her mouth and between her teeth. She worried that she'd drawn blood when she bit down, so she scrubbed her gums and tongue. She finished with a gargle of the baking soda they kept in the back of the refrigerator. Normally, that would have grossed her out, but her gross-out spectrum had changed drastically in the last hour. When she was done, she inspected her face in the mirror. She pushed her curly hair away from her temple. It was red where he'd hit her, but she didn't think it would bruise.

Two men in suits arrived fifteen minutes later and introduced themselves as Detectives Bellamy and Jorgenson. Bellamy was bald and had a bushy gray mustache. Jorgenson was clean-shaven, his thinning hair parted on the side. They could be anywhere between forty and sixty, Peel thought. The bald one, Bellamy, started. "Can you tell us what happened?" His voice was kind.

She blew out a breath. "Of course. It was all really fast, and because of the kids, it was over quickly." She told them what she remembered.

When she finished, he asked, "Do you have any idea who this guy is?"

"No," Peel said. "I think it was just a random attack. He saw the opportunity to grab a woman and took it."

"We don't think it was random," the detective said. "He was at the library." He gestured around him. "This isn't the kind of place random attacks happen. Also, you exited out a back door. He was waiting there, not at the front of the library. This is someone who knows your movements" He tapped his pen on the table. "Could it be a boyfriend?"

She shook her head. "I don't date men."

"Oh." He was taken aback by her answer. "Well, could this be related to a relationship? Angry girlfriend?"

"My exes aren't like that."

"Like what?" Detective Jorgenson spoke for the first time.

"Interested," Peel said.

He chuckled. "Neither are mine. So, you're not in a relationship, currently?"

"No."

Bellamy looked at Jorgenson and then back to her. "Can you think of any reason why someone would want to hurt you?"

Peel sighed heavily and rubbed her eyes with the tips of her fingers. The relief she felt when the police arrived was giving way to reality. She had been moments from being kidnapped, possibly raped and murdered. How did she answer his question? "I can't. I'm a librarian at a suburban public library. I'm nobody. I don't have money. I don't have wealthy relatives. I really don't even have relatives. I don't argue with my neighbors or suffer from road rage, or…or, anything."

"We're going to have the patrol officers take you home," the detective said. "They'll check out your house and make sure everything is safe."

"What do you mean? Do you think he might be at my house? He knows where I live?" Her voice rose.

"We don't know." The detective gentled his voice. "But let's just be sure. Do you have someone you could stay with for a couple of days while we investigate? The officers will wait while you pack a bag, and then take you to a friend's house."

Her mind was blank. She couldn't think. She raked her fingers through her hair, tugging at the tangled curls. Would she have to move? Leave town? Go into witness protection? Don't you have to be a witness to be in witness protection? She moaned out loud. "Do you really think this is necessary?"

"Yes," he said. "You're going to have to be very cautious from now on. Who can we call for you?"

She picked her phone up and handed it to him. "Linda."

He handed it back. "Can you unlock it?" She pulled up Linda's name, pressed the number, then gave him the phone. She couldn't talk. Tears were too close to the surface.

She could hear Linda's worried voice when she answered, "Peel, are you okay?" How did Linda already know? She looked at the clock. Midnight. Of course. She would wonder why Peel was calling this late.

"This is Detective John Bellamy with the Hawk Ridge Police Department. Ms. Primm was attacked tonight while leaving the library." He took a breath, which gave Linda a chance to react. Peel heard the sound of fear in her voice as Linda asked about her. "She's fine. She's sitting here with me now." He paused. "No, we're at the library. We'd like Ms. Primm to stay with someone for a few days. She gave us your name." Another pause. "No, we'll have an officer bring her to your house. It should be about an hour from now." He pulled out a notebook and wrote something on a blank page. "Thank you." He hung up, then tapped her phone screen. "I'm going to program my number into your phone. Call me tomorrow. You'll need to come in to make a formal statement." She nodded.

After an uneventful trip to Linda's house and a long, hot shower, she sat in the living room drinking a glass of wine. Linda lived in a home like so many others in the community: relatively new construction with an on-trend floorplan where the kitchen was open to the family room, a huge island separating the two. They sat side by side at the island facing each other.

"Thanks for the shower. I had to scrub that man's hands off of me."

"Better now?"

Peel did feel better physically, but emotionally she was raw. "I don't think it's a good idea for me to stay with you. They seem to think the guy was after me specifically, which means anyone with me could be in danger, too."

"Don't worry, they're outside tonight and promised they would be on this street regularly until he's caught."

"Maybe a hotel is a better idea. They have security. Well, at least they have a front desk you have to walk by."

"Really?" Linda asked. "You're going to stay at a chain hotel and think you're secure? Will the front desk person drink wine with you? Where are you going to wash your clothes? Will you be safe eating out every meal?" Linda's list was in order of her personal priorities.

"It doesn't matter tonight," Peel said. "I'm supposed to go to the police station tomorrow to do an official statement. I'll ask them how long they think I should be out of my house." She took a sip of wine, trying to hide her fear. "Can't he get me here as easily as my house?"

"Don't say that. There'll be no 'getting you.'" She looked at the clock. It was nearly two thirty. "Are you going to work tomorrow?"

"No, I already talked with Sheryl. She called when all of the social media alerts started. She told me she'd take me off the schedule for a couple of days, but I think I'll just take tomorrow to meet with the detectives."

"Are you okay if I go to bed?" Linda asked as she swallowed down the rest of her wine. "I've got to work tomorrow, and I have a class tomorrow night. But, I'll stay up with you if you want to talk."

"No, I'm tired, and there's nothing else to say."

"Do you want to sleep in my room tonight?"

Peel hugged her. "You're so good to me. I'll be fine. Thank you for taking care of me."

Linda kissed her cheek. "Try to get some sleep." They headed to their respective rooms, Linda to sleep, Peel to stare at the light playing across the ceiling. She thought about her work at the library. She did spend a lot of time online searching through databases, archives, public records, and all manner of web pages. She was careful about where she searched and what links she clicked, but that didn't mean she hadn't stumbled into something. It was possible. No one was completely safe online. Her mind spun, and at four thirty she finally gave up. She went out to Linda's kitchen and started a pot of coffee.

She found her computer bag near the door and pulled her laptop out of the case. If she was going to be awake, she might as well see if she could find anything strange in her recent browsing. She copied her search history and pasted it into a Word document. Methodically, she worked through the list of searches and websites. Even though she knew most of the sites she'd visited, Peel still went through each one. It was an eclectic mix. She'd been watching old nineties television shows, but all those were through a subscription service. Clothes shopping featured prominently, but each site she checked was legitimate. Recently there was her genealogy research and book reviews for work. Nothing questionable. There wasn't any site she hadn't been on before or didn't trust the source of.

By the time she finished, Linda had showered and joined her in the kitchen. "Did you sleep at all?" The concern was evident in her voice.

"I couldn't. I just kept thinking about him and wondering why it happened." Peel slid her cup across the table for Linda to refill.

"Is that what you're working on?" she asked.

"I thought maybe I got into something online, but there's nothing here." Peel gestured to the document on the screen.

"Maybe it was random. Could it have been whichever librarian was there last night?" Linda handed her the cup and sat down next to her.

Peel perked up at that thought. "You're right. Maybe it's not me they were after. Maybe they thought I was someone else."

"Possibly, but you're the youngest by far. It would be hard to confuse you with one of the other librarians. And let's be honest, you're the most likely to have stumbled into a shady website."

"Thanks," Peel muttered.

"Tell me I'm wrong."

"No, you're right," Peel admitted.

Linda walked to the window. "Did you check to see if they're out there?" Before Peel could reply, Linda answered her own question. "Yep, right in front of the house. I'm probably the headline in today's cul-de-sac gossip. I'm surprised my neighbor hasn't walked her dogs to get a better view of what's going on."

"It's early yet." Peel chuckled. "Give her time."

"When are you going to the police station?"

"I don't know. I thought I'd wait until midmorning to call Detective Bellamy."

"I've got to get going. Do not go out without letting those guys know what you're doing. It may be random, but don't take any chances." She looked hard at Peel. "Don't get antsy. There's lots of food and plenty to watch on TV."

"Don't worry," Peel assured her. "I have no interest in seeing the inside of that van."

CHAPTER THREE

Peel fell asleep watching morning television and woke around noon. She'd turned off her phone the night before, knowing as news got out that something happened at the library, friends would start texting. "Only five texts?" she muttered. Quickly, she composed a group text letting everyone know she was okay and staying with Linda for now. She ended the text with, "We'll all do happy hour soon, and celebrate my Anime kids!"

Within seconds her phone sounded with replies. Good, she thought. That would hold them off for a week or so. She really didn't want to see people when she wasn't sure what was going on. If she had been the target of the attack, she could be risking the safety of her friends just by going out for lunch. Her phone rang in her hand, startling her. The readout said: "Detective John Bellamy."

"Hi, Detective."

"Ms. Primm." He sounded more formal than he had the night before. "The officer out front is going to give you a ride to the station. Are you ready to leave now?"

"Um, I guess I am. I haven't eaten. Should I eat first?"

"We'll get you a sandwich here," was the clipped reply.

"Okay." His tone made her nervous. "Has something happened? Did you catch him?"

"We'll fill you in when you get here. The officer is at the door now." As if he was talking to the officer at the same time, the doorbell rang.

"Okay," she said again. "I'll see you in a few minutes."

She looked through the peephole and saw a female patrol officer reach to ring the doorbell again. She opened it. "One second, I just need to grab my bag." She reached for her purse and, by habit, her computer bag, locked the door, and followed her to the car.

The officer opened the back door of the patrol car. "Can I ride in the front with you?" Peel asked.

"It's not allowed," the officer answered. Her tone was neutral.

Peel climbed in, her feeling of unease growing. When the door closed, the stench of unwashed bodies hit her. She looked around the small space trying to decide where to sit. Was one seat cleaner than the other?

"Buckle up," the officer said. When Peel met the officer's dispassionate eyes in the rearview mirror, she hurried to comply. Hands clasped tightly in her lap, she sat forward, trying to limit her contact with the seat. The notification of a new text distracted her. It was Sheryl. "Call as soon as you can. It's urgent." Peel pulled up her name and called. Sheryl answered on the first ring.

"Thank God you called," she said, forgoing a greeting.

"What's wrong? Did someone else get attacked?"

"I'm walking into my office. Give me one second."

As Peel waited, she caught the eye of the officer in the rearview mirror. The officer held her gaze for a moment, then looked back at the road. What was going on?

Slightly out of breath, Sheryl said, "Peel, those detectives were here this morning asking a lot of questions about you."

"Me?"

"They wanted to know if you have many visitors during work. I told them the only visitors you have are Linda and the

Anime kids. They wanted to know if you get many packages. I told them we all do, especially at Christmas time. The bald detective got a little snippy at that. 'Does Peel get regular deliveries?' he said. I told him whatever he was thinking was wrong. You don't get any more deliveries than the rest of us." Sheryl took a breath. "Peel, they wouldn't let it go."

"Why are they asking that? I got attacked, and I'm pretty sure the guy did not work for UPS." Peel was incredulous. Stupidly, her mind flashed to what she remembered of her attacker. No, he was wearing jeans, not brown shorts.

Sheryl continued. "When I told them you don't get deliveries, they wanted to know who unpacks shipments of books for the library. I told them we all do. Something is going on, Peel." She whispered, "Are you in trouble?"

Peel's stomach hurt. "I don't know. I haven't done anything. Why do they care about deliveries? It's a misunderstanding. It has to be." She was talking fast because the car had stopped at the police station. "I have to go, Sheryl, I'm actually going in to see the detectives right now. Thanks for the warning." She hung up without waiting for a reply. It was clear the detectives had more information about the attack, and it wasn't good.

She wondered if she needed a lawyer. She didn't even know how to get a lawyer. She walked alongside the officer in a daze, her hands jammed deep in the pockets of her jeans. Is this how people ended up in jail? She decided to stay quiet and just listen. She had the right to remain silent. That's what she'd do—remain silent.

The officer took her into a room with a table and two chairs. She looked up to see if there was a mirror and made eye contact with her reflection. Shit. They were serious. She was in an interrogation room. The officer gestured for her to sit and said, "The detectives will be with you shortly." True to her new silent self, Peel said nothing.

She busied herself on the phone. Of course, there was no signal. She wondered how they blocked it. Concrete walls? Probably. She'd play Scrabble. Although she couldn't concentrate on the game, she wanted to look unconcerned to the people behind the glass. Finding it hard not to look in the mirror, she turned sideways, one arm on the table, the other on the back of the chair. Hopefully, her feigned nonchalance was convincing. It might have been if she hadn't jumped when the door opened and the two detectives entered the room. "Ms. Primm, I'm Detective Bellamy and this is Detective Jorgenson," the bald one began.

Peel looked at him, confused by the introductions. "I know," she said. "I met you last night."

"That's right. You were pretty shook up, so we wanted to reintroduce ourselves." This was positive. He knew she wasn't faking her fear last night. She stayed quiet. "We have a few questions that have come up in the course of our investigation." He paused, giving her a chance to speak.

"Am I under arrest?" Damn it, she cursed inwardly. Already she'd forgotten to stay quiet.

"No. Why would you ask that? Is there something you need to tell us?" Bellamy leaned toward her.

"Well, I'm sitting in an interrogation room with a mirror. It feels like I'm under arrest."

His tone was serious. "You're not under arrest, but there are some peculiarities we'd like you to clear up for us." Her hands were sweating and starting to shake, so she slipped her phone into her back pocket and clasped her hands in her lap.

Bellamy opened a file folder and flipped through a couple of eight-by-ten photographs. "We managed to get a good likeness from the video." He slid a photo across the table. "Do you recognize this man?"

In the time it took to spin the picture around and look down, Peel had an internal debate. Should she look quickly and say a firm no? Or, pore over the picture, seeming to take a lot of time to consider? She knew the answer. She'd never seen the man before last night. She looked anyway. He was facing the kids looking malevolent. She caught her breath when she saw his eyes. Peel covered her mouth.

"Do you know him?" Bellamy leaned forward.

"No, but look at him. He could have killed those kids." She looked up, all pretense gone. "Do you know who he is? Why did you ask Sheryl if I take deliveries at the library? What's going on, Detective?"

The two men exchanged looks and then Bellamy tapped the photo. "Look closely. Do you see the tattoo on his neck?" He traced the image with the tip of his finger. She leaned closer rather than picking up the picture. Squinting, she could barely make out a circle with a center dot and a crown. "That's an alchemist symbol for gold. It's a tattoo for the Mexican drug cartel, de Oro."

Once Peel heard "drug cartel," the questions made sense. "You think I'm getting drug deliveries at the library? How would that even happen? We get our deliveries through the post office, UPS, and FedEx. Surely, you can't just ship drugs through the mail? It's a public library, for God's sake," she finished in a rush.

Detective Bellamy folded his arms and leaned back. "Can you explain why someone from a Mexican cartel would come to Colorado and attempt to kidnap a librarian?"

"No," she said miserably. "Maybe it's a case of mistaken identity." She didn't want to suggest they were looking for one of the other librarians. No one was getting drug shipments at Plains. "Wait. Peel isn't my given name. It's Esther. Esther Primm." There was a pause, and then the other detective snorted a laugh. "I know. That's why I don't use it, but maybe someone else with that name is a drug dealer."

For the first time Detective Jorgenson spoke. "Have you ever googled your name?" She nodded. "And? Find any likely drug dealers with the name Esther?" he asked.

"There are a few other Esther Primms, but they're on genealogy sites and are long dead." She froze, her mind whirling. She stared hard at the floor as pieces came together. "A Mexican cartel?" She grabbed her laptop out of the bag and quickly booted it up. The document she needed was on the desktop. "What did you say the name of the cartel is?"

"De Oro. Why?" Bellamy asked.

"Because." She paused. "I just spoke to a librarian in Mexico." She pointed to the document on her screen. "Tierra de Oro, Mexico."

Bellamy clicked his pen and started writing. "You called a library in Tierra de Oro? When was this?"

"Last Tuesday."

"Was this to arrange a shipment?"

"No!" Peel was outraged. "I found out my great-grandfather lived in Tierra de Oro. I was calling to find out if he had a family."

Bellamy's eyebrows raised. "You have relatives in Tierra de Oro, the center of the de Oro cartel? Do you think you should have told us this last night?"

She didn't bother to hide her exasperation. "I didn't know the man who attacked me was in a cartel. How would I know that?" She took a deep breath to steady herself, then proceeded to tell the story of finding the birth certificate and calling the librarian in Mexico.

"You speak Spanish?" Bellamy had his pen ready.

"No, not really. I asked for someone who could speak English. I talked with a really nice woman who said she'd call me back in a couple of days."

"When was that?"

"I told you. It was last Tuesday. I was thinking about calling her back but decided maybe it was fate."

"Fate?" Bellamy looked at her suspiciously.

"Yeah. My great-grandmother wanted her husband out of her son's life. Maybe I wasn't meant to find out about him either."

Bellamy looked skeptical. "You're saying you called a library in Tierra de Oro Mexico, last week, to find out about your grandfather? Then when you don't get a call back, you think it's fate?"

She glanced between Bellamy and Jorgenson. "This doesn't make sense to me either, and I know it seems unlikely that last night was connected to that phone call, but believe me, it's more likely than me dealing drugs."

"We'll see." Bellamy sniffed. He looked at Jorgenson. "Do you have any other questions?" Jorgenson shook his head. Bellamy turned back to Peel. "We'll have the officer take you home."

"You believe me?" she asked, not bothering to hide the desperation in her tone.

Bellamy answered, "We'll check it out," but she saw Jorgenson give a slight nod in her direction.

Forgetting about the germs in the squad car, Peel rested her head on the seat during the ride home. She hadn't slept much, and the last hour had exhausted her. She was sure Bellamy didn't believe her, and she felt paralyzed by the uncertainty of her situation. It seemed she would either end up in the back of a van or in prison.

At Linda's, she decided to take a nap and literally bury her head under the covers. Before she did, she sent a quick text to Sheryl. "It's all a misunderstanding. I'm going to lie down for a while. I decided I will take tomorrow off after all. Thanks for arranging it." Then she turned off the phone and fell asleep.

It was late afternoon when she awoke, disoriented and groggy. Hunger sent her to Linda's kitchen, where she made a peanut butter sandwich and poured a glass of milk. While she ate, she checked the windows facing the street. It was empty. No police bodyguard this evening. Did it mean they didn't believe her? She shook her head. It was time to start figuring out how to prove her innocence.

At the table, she opened her laptop. She'd already searched for "Charles Devin in Tierra de Oro" and gotten nothing. She tried "Devin de Oro cartel." Plenty of hits on the de Oro cartel came up, but none included "Devin." She selected an article published in an online encyclopedia and started to read.

De Oro Drug Cartel

The de Oro drug cartel began in the mining town of Tierra de Oro, Hidalgo, Mexico. Although it is one of the smaller Mexican cartels, de Oro maintains a lucrative drug trafficking operation led by Sebastien Gutierrez, grandson of founder Francisco Gutierrez.

Francisco Gutierrez—Gutierrez Mining Company-1930s-1967

In the 1930s the town of Tierra de Oro (Golden Land) rose up overnight when Francisco Gutierrez discovered gold in an abandoned mine shaft. Within a few years, the Gutierrez Mining Company was one of the richest in Mexico, employing hundreds of workers. Although the original gold mine appeared to have deep veins, that proved to be untrue, and profits from the mine gradually decreased by the start of World War II. As his mineral fortunes faded, Gutierrez sought new sources of revenue. Other Mexican entities were growing illegal drug crops at the time, but few had the resources of the Gutierrez Mining Company. To transition from mining to farming, Gutierrez offered his workers plots of land in exchange for cultivating poppies. Within two years, the Tierra de Oro valley was transformed from a mining town to one of the largest poppy-growing regions in the world. At the same time, Gutierrez fostered partnerships with organized crime syndicates in the United States to build Mexican facilities for processing opium into heroin.

Eduardo Gutierrez—de Oro Drug Cartel-1967-2006

The 1970s were the golden age for what had become known as the de Oro cartel. Recognizing the booming market for marijuana in the United States during the 1960s and '70s, Eduardo Gutierrez changed from producing heroin to growing marijuana. With ruthless efficiency Eduardo Gutierrez eliminated any competition in the Hidalgo region by recruiting men from the Mexican army trained in weapons, explosives, and intimidation.

In early 1970, Eduardo Gutierrez sent his younger brother Carlos to Chicago to establish a drug distribution network. The chaos created by the end of the Vietnam War and the return of thousands of soldiers allowed Carlos to follow the de Oro business model and recruit from the military to form the Chicago street gang

Disciples of Gold. With Carlos Gutierrez in Chicago, de Oro could now traffic marijuana directly to their users. It was a lucrative time for the cartel.

Arrests

In 1987, Eduardo Gutierrez, his sons Francisco and Alejandro Gutierrez, and other high-ranking de Oro leaders were arrested. Over 100 million dollars in cash and drugs were seized at the time of the arrests. Despite being sentenced to twenty years, Eduardo only served two. However, his sons Francisco and Alejandro were killed in prison riots.

The 2000s—Sebastien Gutierrez

The de Oro cartel officially remained under the control of Eduardo until his death in 2006, but it was widely believed that Sebastien Gutierrez, his only surviving son, was running the day-to-day operations.

Under Sebastien's leadership, the cartel regained much of the power lost during the 1980s and 1990s. Gutierrez has fostered alliances with other cartels and Mexican crime families by ostensibly selling access to the de Oro drug routes and distribution to US markets.

Peel finished reading and leaned back. While this was all good information, she was no closer to finding a connection to Charles Devin, and she was at the limit of what an Internet search could provide. She needed access to a larger database of magazine and newspaper articles. She needed to be at the Denver Public Library. Again, Peel looked out the window. No patrol car. Rather than being a deterrent, the lack of police presence gave her the impetus to move. She sent a quick text to Linda. "I'm going to the downtown library. Don't worry, I'll stay in crowds." Avoiding the scolding she knew Linda would send back, she turned off the phone and headed for the car.

Throughout the forty-minute drive, Peel obsessively checked her mirrors. There were plenty of white vans on the road with her, but most had business logos on the sides. Heavy traffic kept her from knowing whether she was being followed. That, and she had no idea how to identify a tail. The car behind her all the way down Speer Boulevard—was she being followed, or was someone heading in the same direction? In her rearview mirror, she saw a tired-looking woman staring out her windshield. To her right was a man with a loosened tie and an open-collared shirt. Neither paid her any attention. Both were gone before she reached the library.

It was after six when she pulled into the parking garage. The May evening promised a couple more hours of sunlight, and she'd make sure she was back in the car before dark. She drove around the garage for a few minutes, passing open spaces as she contemplated the safest place to park. The garage was fairly busy so there were few close-in spots.

She chose a spot farther from the entrance than she liked but compromised when she saw it was under a light. She kept her door locked and checked the mirrors. There was no one around. She planned to wait until someone else was in the garage, but after several minutes, she grew restless. Another check of the mirrors and a minute of craning her neck in all directions, and she opened the car door and stepped out.

She had just clicked the lock button on her fob and dropped the key in her purse when she heard the rapid acceleration of a truck. She fumbled in her purse, but the key had somehow slipped to the bottom of the bag. The sound of screeching tires echoing through the garage magnified her alarm, but there was nothing she could do. They were on her before she found the key.

Once again a hand clamped over her mouth and an arm tightened across her chest. This time a second man reached for her legs. She kicked at him. He punched her in the stomach. She tried to double over, but the man behind her held her upright and dragged her to the open van door.

The van sped off before the cargo door slammed closed. Despite the blow to her midsection, she struggled to her knees and launched herself at the door. Someone behind her grabbed her upper arms and snapped her back to the middle of the van. She used her legs to try to scramble away, but the hands gripped her tighter. She screamed, loud and long. The man facing her hit her with a quick backhand, snapping her head to the side. He followed with a hard slap. The men laughed. Then she was pulled back sharply and shoved hard toward the far side of the van. As she stumbled, he held her arms long enough that she couldn't stop her head from connecting with the steel wall. She crumpled to the floor. For several minutes, she lay still, dazed. Her face burned and the sharp pain where her head hit the steel was making it hard to catch her breath. When the pain eased a little, she got her hands under her and lifted to a sitting position.

She looked around her and saw nothing but white steel. No seats, no carpet, no helpful carpenter's tools she could grab to bash into the head of the guy who hit her. Her gaze landed on the two men who leaned against the other side of the van—the door side. One wasn't looking at her, the other sneered when she met his eyes. He looked at her reddened cheeks, then back to her eyes. Hot anger surged through her, and before she could get herself under control, she taunted him. "You're such a tough guy. You hit women a lot? Are the men too much for you to handle?" She didn't think he understood her words, but he must have understood her mocking tone.

He stood up, showing her bruised fingers, presumably from her bite. Her gaze dropped to his neck and the tattoo. The alchemist symbol for gold. Because of that distraction, she didn't react fast enough when he drew his fist back. When she saw the movement in her peripheral vision, she tried to angle her face away, but that caused her to be off-balance when he connected. The pain of the blow intensified when once again she hit the steel wall of the van. She lost consciousness.

Sometime later, she awoke. Her face and head pounded. Disoriented, she rolled to her back and was hit with a wave of dizziness. Her stomach roiled, and she tried to swallow back her nausea. It was no use. She turned her head and vomited. Voices protested in Spanish as she emptied the contents of her stomach. She slid away from the mess, rolled to her back, and gently touched her face. One eye was swollen. Her face and hair were sticky. She closed her eyes to the pain and nausea.

The next time she awoke it was to the sound of the cargo door sliding open. The van shifted as men climbed out. She shut her eyes but opened them again when the back door was flung open. Four hands grabbed her prone form and pulled her out until her heels hit the ground. She moaned at the pain. "I'm going to be sick." She started retching and they dropped her. On her hands and knees she continued to retch, bringing up only bile. When the heaving stopped, she crawled a few feet and collapsed.

It was less than a minute before rough hands grabbed her arms and she was pulled to standing. The vertigo came again, and she collapsed in their arms. Someone said something in Spanish, and she was dragged away from the van. Each step caused the pain in her head to intensify. She began to cry. Whether it was the tears or something else, they let go of her, stepping away as she dropped to the dirt. More laughter. She curled into a ball, desperate to ease the pain.

Someone knelt beside her and made a disgusted sound. A light shone in her face and then down her body. "You stink," he said in English. "You are not flying in my plane smelling like vomit." He turned away and spoke to the other two men. They laughed and started ripping at her clothes. She tried to struggle but was too weak to fight. She was soon stripped of all but her bra and underwear.

The man with the light looked down at her. "There are tarps in the back you can cover yourself with." With those words, the light was out of her eyes and she was again lifted, only this time the hands didn't stay at her arms and legs. Despite the pain and her grogginess, she screamed and struggled against their wandering hands.

One sharp word and the men stopped their groping. They tossed her into the cargo area of the plane and let her drop. Her head slammed into the floor, and she passed out.

CHAPTER FOUR

Anna woke to the sound of footsteps outside her door. Carefully she reached under her pillow, searching for her gun. Her right hand closed on the grip just as she heard a soft knock and an even softer, "Anna."

Anna left the gun where it was and jumped up to answer the door. In front of her was a small woman, her face creased with age and worry. Seeing the look, Anna asked in Spanish, "Rosita, what is it?"

"Anna." Rosita grasped the taller woman's hand. "They brought a girl here. She's hurt. I need you."

Anna looked at Rosita. Her tidy gray hair was flattened where it had recently rested on a pillow. "Take me," she said.

Together they walked the path from Anna's casita to the pool, climbed the stairs to the upper terrace, and crossed the expanse of lawn and gardens to the main house. Anna checked the walls as they walked. Two dark shadows moved. From experience she knew each was carrying an automatic rifle.

French doors led them through a solarium filled with lush greenery casting eerie shadows in the light from the gardens.

Anna followed Rosita up the staircase and down the long hallway to a closed door. "They just brought her." Rosita opened the door and whispered to another woman standing by the bed. "Thank you, Elena. Please wait outside." The woman nodded, glanced at Anna, and left.

Anna took a long look at the woman lying on the bed. Despite being covered in a blanket, she was shivering. One side of her face was a deep reddish purple and her eye was swollen shut. Her brown hair was matted with blood and some other substance that, as she got closer, Anna realized was vomit. She leaned over the girl. "Has she been awake?"

"When they brought her in."

"Did she say anything? Was she talking?"

"Yes, but she spoke English," Rosita said.

Anna pulled the blanket down as she asked, "Is she hurt anywhere else?"

"I don't know. She was shaking so much, I thought we should warm her up."

"That was the right thing to do. She may be in shock." She looked up at Rosita as the woman's bare arms and torso were revealed. What must have once been a white bra was filthy, as were black boy shorts. Anna exchanged a look with Rosita. "Where are her clothes?" Rosita shook her head.

"I will kill them if they did," Anna muttered as she ran her hands over the woman's arms and legs, checking for injuries. Rosita didn't need an explanation. The men they worked with saw women as property and thought nothing of using them for whatever pleasures they wanted. Anna breathed a sigh of relief as she moved the waistband of the briefs and saw the grime was confined to the cloth. Gently, she reached between the unconscious woman's legs. No blood. No fluids. It didn't appear she'd been raped.

Anna covered her and turned to Rosita. "Ask Elena to get more blankets and call the doctor. Tell him we need him here right away. I'm sure she has a concussion. Let's hope her skull isn't fractured."

Rosita stepped out of the room. A few moments later, Elena returned with an armful of blankets, which she gave to Anna.

"Thank you," Anna murmured. She opened two blankets and placed them over the unconscious woman. "Could you get me a warm washcloth?" Elena hurried to the adjoining bathroom and Anna heard water running in the sink.

Anna looked at the woman again. She didn't look Mexican. Her hair was brown, but not a deep glossy brown. Anna lifted the eyelid of the uninjured eye. Blue. She let the eyelid close as Elena returned and handed her the washcloth. Covering two of her fingers, she began to wipe the woman's face. This close, the smell of vomit and blood was strong. "We'll get you bathed as soon as the doctor looks at you," she said in English. There was no response.

Rosita returned. "He's on his way."

"Did he give you any trouble?"

"No. He would not risk angering Sebastien." Rosita took the dirty washcloth from Anna. "I'll rinse this off and get another. Has she stopped shaking?"

"Yes, I think she's finally warming. We'll need to bathe her if the doctor says she can be moved. Can you find some clothes for her?"

"She is tall, no?" Rosita asked.

"Taller than you are," Anna teased.

Rosita smirked. "She won't fit in my clothes. Do you have something she could wear?"

"I suppose that would be best. When the doctor comes, I'll get something from the casita."

They worked together in silence as Anna gently wiped the woman's face and arms. Rosita exchanged cloths as one got dirty or cold. Eventually, Anna told her they would have to wait for the doctor to do more.

When they heard the sounds of a car pulling up the long drive and stopping in front of the house, Rosita left the room to greet the doctor. "You're safe now," Anna whispered in English. "The doctor is here to take care of you." She brushed the filthy hair away from the woman's face.

Rosita returned with a small man carrying a medical bag. The man's broad, flat face spoke of native ancestry. He was in his fifties, but his hair was completely silver. Anna wondered if it was from the stress of being at the beck and call of Sebastien Gutierrez. Without speaking, he walked to the bed and looked down at the injured woman. He pulled out a penlight, lifted her eyelid, and quickly moved it in front of her eye and away again. He repeated the motion several times before he seemed satisfied. He put the light in his shirt pocket and used both hands to feel the woman's head through her matted hair. The woman moaned as he probed a spot on her temple. His hand came away bloody. "Did she walk in here?" Elena handed him one of the washcloths and he wiped his hands.

"No. They carried her."

The doctor nodded. "What is her name?"

"We don't know." Anna answered this time.

"Has she been awake?"

"Yes, briefly. She spoke English," Rosita added.

The doctor bent down and spoke to the woman in English. "I'm Doctor Aguilar. Can you open your eyes for me?" He waited a couple of seconds and then spoke again, this time checking her pulse. "Miss, can you open your eyes and tell me where you are hurt?"

The one blue eye fluttered open. The doctor smiled down at the woman. "Can you tell me your name?" The eye blinked rapidly. "Do you know what your name is?" he asked again. Anna leaned in to hear.

The woman focused her eye on the doctor. "Peel," she said in a low voice. An American accent.

He leaned closer to her and repeated the question. "Do you know who you are?"

"Peel Primm," she said.

He made eye contact with Anna. She shrugged. "See if she knows where she lives."

He looked back. "Where do you live?"

She licked her lips. "Denver," came the weak voice. "Was I in an accident? Am I in the hospital?"

The doctor straightened, reverting to Spanish when he spoke to Anna. "I'm going to give her an IV. She's dehydrated and has a concussion. I'd also like to get a better look at that cut. She may need stitches, but I'm not going to move her until I check her extremities."

He pulled back the blankets, exposing one arm. "Can you move your fingers for me?" She lifted her arm and wiggled her fingers. Anna was relieved to see the movement. Without prompting, she moved her legs back and forth under the covers like a snow angel. This time the doctor chuckled. "Good. I'm going to check the cut on the side of your head now. Do you feel able to sit up?" Dr. Aguilar reached behind the woman and gently lifted her. In Spanish, he asked Rosita to prop the pillows behind her. When he caught sight of Peel's expression, he asked, "Feel sick?" She nodded, then moaned, reaching for her swollen face.

"I'm going to lay you on your side while I clean this cut. It doesn't look like you'll need stitches." He turned and spoke rapid Spanish to Rosita. She left the room only to return moments later with towels, which she spread in layers on the pillow. Together, they guided her down, making sure there was no pressure on her bruised face and blackened eye. After a few minutes of attempting to clean the wound, he sighed and turned to the woman next to him. "She needs to be bathed and her hair washed. I can't get this wound clean when there is so much dirt and vomit in her hair. Is there someone here who can help her?"

Anna looked at Rosita. "We can help her. Do you think she can walk?"

They were all surprised to hear the injured woman answer. "Yes." Her voice was weak but determined. The doctor looked at Anna and shook his head.

Anna bent over the bed. "I'll help you up and into the bathroom. I don't think you should shower, but the bath has a handheld nozzle you can use to wash your hair. If you're fine by yourself, I'll leave you alone."

The blue eye looked at her. "Okay. I can't stand this smell anymore."

"Tell me your name."

"It's Peel."

"Your name is Peel, as in banana?"

The one eye frowned at her. "No, my name is Peel as in Mrs. Emma Peel."

"Your name is Emma?"

"No." The injured woman was insistent. "My name is Peel Primm."

"Who's Emma Peel?"

The woman closed her good eye. In a resigned voice, she said, "Never mind. My name is Peel, like banana."

Anna abandoned their circular conversation and pulled the covers back to expose Peel's legs, then she and Rosita turned the woman until her feet were touching the floor. For a long minute they stayed like that. Anna didn't say anything, just waited.

Peel inhaled deeply. "Okay, I think I'm ready."

Anna gestured to the older woman. "Rosita is going to stand on the other side of you. Whenever you're ready, let me know."

Peel said, "Ready," and got to her feet. Neither Anna nor Rosita expected her to move so quickly. Anna just managed to catch her arm before she fell to the floor. Peel cried out. Too late, Anna noticed bruises on her upper arms.

"This isn't going to work," Anna growled. She bent down and lifted the woman into her arms, ignoring the feeble protests. Rosita scurried ahead into the bathroom.

"Fill the tub?" Rosita looked back at Anna.

"I'm not sure. The water will be dirty as soon as we put her in, but she will get too cold if we put her in the bottom of the bathtub."

Rosita nodded. "She needs to be warm." She plugged the drain and turned on the water.

"I can stand if you help me." Peel looked up at Anna. "You can put me down."

"Your color is back." Anna lowered Peel's feet to the floor but kept an arm around her back.

She was trembling and unsteady, but said, "I got this now."

Anna lifted her eyebrows. "Really? You don't look strong enough to do this on your own." Peel blushed. At least Anna thought she was blushing. It was hard to see her natural coloring under the dirt and bruises. "Look, I know you're uncomfortable, but I don't think you can do this without help. We'll make sure the doctor doesn't come in, but Rosita and I are staying."

The blue eye looked back at her. "Fine. I guess I really don't care as long as I can wash the puke out of my hair." With that she slowly reached around her body and unhooked her bra. It fell to the floor. Nobody moved for a moment, then the woman closed her eye and said, "I don't think I can take my underwear off without falling over." Now there was no doubt her face was fiery red.

Anna nodded to Rosita, who had already reached for Peel's bra. She tutted and pulled the waistband of Peel's boy shorts down. "I'm so embarrassed." Peel moaned, then looked at Rosita holding her filthy undergarments. "Thank you."

Rosita smiled and gestured to the bath rapidly filling with steamy water. Peel lifted her foot and tentatively put it in the water. After a couple of seconds, she said again, "Thank you." Then, she looked to Anna. "I think I need your help to sit down."

Anna nodded. "Turn your back to me. I'll support you while you sit."

Peel turned and Anna and Rosita held her by her forearms as she lowered herself into the water. Once she was sitting, she turned and slid to the back of the tub. "Do you know what happened to me? Was I in a car accident?"

Anna busied herself gathering shampoo and soap from the cabinet. Finally, she looked at Peel. "We don't know what happened to you. Lean back. I'll help you wash your hair." Peel leaned back and closed her eye as Anna turned the handheld nozzle on and gently wet Peel's hair. Then, she reached for Peel's hand and turned it over, squirting shampoo into it. "Be very careful with the side of your head." Peel lifted her palm and slowly began massaging the shampoo into her scalp. When she got to the back of her head, she hissed in pain and let her hands fall heavily back into the water.

"I need help," she whispered, her eye tearing.

Anna reached for the shampoo bottle and squirted a generous amount into her own palm. "Can you turn around and lean against the side of the tub?" Peel did. Anna took a few seconds looking over the woman's scalp before she started to work shampoo into the matted hair. She gently massaged the woman's head and felt two large lumps, one at the back and one near the cut, which was oozing blood. There was so much blood and vomit in her hair, the shampoo hardly lathered. "I'm going to try to rinse it all out now. Keep your eyes closed." She turned the water back on and gently washed the soap away. Peel flinched and jerked her head away when the soap hit her open wound. "I'm sorry," Anna said. She reached behind Peel and grasped her neck to support her head. When the water ran mostly clean, she reached for the shampoo bottle. "I need to do it one more time," she said. The slight nod she got in reply told her that the woman was fading. "Rosita," she said over her shoulder. "Get the soap and wash as much of her as you can reach while I finish her hair." Together they washed the injured woman, revealing more bruises as the grime disappeared. At last, Anna pulled the drain and used the handheld nozzle to rinse away the soap just as the water emptied.

"Can you stand?" Anna asked. Receiving no answer, Anna looked at her. Peel's eyes were closed and her face was pale under the bruises. She called louder. "Peel, it's time to get out." Peel opened her eye and closed it again without focusing on anything. Anna couldn't tell if the woman understood her.

Swearing, she removed her shoes, reached for a towel, and climbed into the tub. She placed one foot on either side of Peel's body, bent down, and draped the towel over the inert woman's chest and thighs. She reached around Peel and eased her to a sitting position. Now she was straddling the lap of the naked woman. "Peel, I need you to tuck your feet under and help me get you up." Peel opened her eye and started to close it again. Anna grabbed her under the chin, forcing Peel to make eye contact. "No!" she said sternly. "Put your feet flat on the ground and help me stand you up." The command didn't register at first, but then Peel bent her knees, dragging her feet along the edge of the tub until they were underneath her. "Good. I'm going to lift you on three. You have to try to stand. One, two, three!" Anna grunted with the effort of deadlifting the woman, but she managed to get her into a standing position.

Rosita waited with another towel, but Anna said, "Let's just put her in the bed." Rosita nodded, and Anna lifted the woman and carried her out of the bathroom. Elena had changed the soiled sheets and replaced the towels on the pillow with fresh ones. Anna laid her gently on the bed and pulled the covers up to her chin.

"Where is the doctor?" Anna asked after settling Peel on the bed.

"I'm here." The doctor walked into the room carrying a stand with a hanging IV bag. "I'll give her some fluids and something to help with the nausea." Quickly he untangled the tubing and inserted the IV into Peel's hand. When the bag was hung, he set to work probing the cut and dabbing it with gauze. "It doesn't need stitches. I'll bandage it and stay with her until the bag is empty."

"Thank you." Anna walked into the bathroom to retrieve her shoes. She heard Rosita ask the doctor if he wanted a breakfast tray brought up. With his affirmative response, Rosita walked out of the bedroom with Anna.

Anna looked over her shoulder to make sure no one was close. "She'll have a lot of questions when she wakes up. Maybe it's best if one of the maids who doesn't speak English stays with her."

Rosita reached up to touch Anna's cheek. "Thank you for your help. Do you want breakfast, too?"

Anna covered her hand with her own. "No. It's early. I'm going back to sleep. I'll check with you later this morning to see how she is."

Anna's cell was ringing when she got back to her casita. "Shit," she muttered when she saw the caller ID. "Hello."

"Where the fuck you been? I been trying to call you all night."

"I was—"

"I don't care. We delivered a package to Sebastien last night. Who is she?"

"I don't know."

"The fuck you don't know. What did he say?"

"He's not here."

"Don't act like a dumb bitch. You talk to him. What did he say about her?"

"I haven't talked to Sebastien. I don't know anything about this situation."

"Bullshit. He wanted her bad. You covering for him now, Anna? It'd be a big mistake if you forgot who you work for."

"I don't know what to tell you. The housekeeper woke me up when she got here. Your guys beat her up."

"Bitch bit one of the guys. She had it coming."

Anna was now past irritation, but she knew better than to show Ojos he was getting to her. "What can I help you with, Ojos?"

"I want to know who she is and why he wanted her so bad. You find out and call me back." He hung up.

Anna threw the phone on her bed.

CHAPTER FIVE

Peel woke, disoriented and in pain. Her confusion wasn't helped when a man stepped into her line of sight and bent over her. "Do you remember me?"

Peel blinked a few times trying to bring her eyes—wait, eye—into focus. She did remember him. "Doctor?"

"That's right. I'm the doctor. I'd like to check your head and see how you're feeling."

"Crappy. My head hurts."

"I am sure it does. You have a couple of nasty bumps and a black eye. You will have a headache for at least a week."

Peel groaned. "A week?"

"Tylenol will help. So will sleep. Stay in bed for a couple of days and let your brain rest."

"Can I get up to use the bathroom?"

"Yes, but while you have this headache, someone needs to be with you. How is the nausea?"

Peel paused for a moment. "Right now, my stomach feels fine."

"Good. I'm going to give you something for the headache and another dose of anti-nausea medication. Drink as much as you can and eat something."

"Was I in a car accident?"

The doctor looked away, busying himself in his bag. "I don't know what happened to you, señorita."

Señorita? The doctor had an accent, but that wasn't unusual in Colorado. "Am I in a hospital?"

The doctor's eyes looked everywhere but at her. "No."

"Then, where am I?" She was frustrated by his evasiveness.

"It is best if you ask someone in the household. I will leave your medications with Rosita, but take these now." He reached across the bed and grabbed two pillows. "Let me help you sit up."

The pain in Peel's head intensified as he lifted her. When she was settled back on the pillows, he handed her a glass of water and four tablets. Peel swallowed them down with a drink of water, then leaned back against the pillows. "Thank you." She felt cool air on her skin and touched her chest. Her eye flew open as she ran her hands down her body. She was naked.

The doctor seemed to misunderstand her alarm. "Do you want me to get someone to help you go to the bathroom?"

"Are the nurses still here from last night?"

The doctor paused for a moment. He looked at the open door. "I will get someone for you." He walked out. Peel closed her eye and tried to breathe through the headache.

She heard soft footsteps on the carpet and opened her eye to a young Hispanic woman. The woman smiled. "*El baño?*"

"Do you speak English?" The smile remained, but the woman shook her head no. Peel closed her eye and tried to recall her college Spanish. "*La ropa?*" she asked, pointing to herself.

The young woman picked up an oversized T-shirt and sweats from the bureau. Relieved, Peel sat up, moaning as a sharp pain stabbed at her temple. The woman reached a tentative hand to support her while she pulled the T-shirt over her head and down over her breasts. Instantly, she felt better. The shirt was big enough it would fall to mid-thigh when she stood. She looked at the sweats and sighed. "*El baño* first," she said.

The pain intensified when she stood. She shuffled to the bathroom while the young woman held her arm. At the toilet, she turned and attempted a smile. "*Gracias.*"

The woman backed out, closing the door behind her. Peel sat on the toilet and cautiously looked around the room. When she caught sight of the bathtub, she closed her eye. "Oh no," she said aloud. "That's why I wasn't dressed."

She finished and flushed the toilet, slowly standing and shuffling to the sink to wash her hands. A quick look in the mirror took her breath away. One side of her face was purple and her eye was swollen shut. Her hair was matted, but at least it was clean. There was a bandage near her hairline on the bruised side of her face. What had happened to her? Why couldn't she remember anything? She washed her hands. When she looked up again, the young woman was behind her. Together they shuffled back to the bed. Within minutes she was asleep.

The clatter of silverware and dishes woke her. The same woman mimed helping Peel sit up. Peel was having trouble understanding through her fog. "*La cena,*" the woman said and put her arms behind Peel to lift her up. Peel didn't protest, nor did she offer any help, but soon she was sitting up. Her helper retrieved the tray and gently placed it across her lap. "*Sopa de pollo.*"

With effort, Peel focused on the food in front of her. Chicken soup. It smelled delicious. "*Gracias,*" she whispered. When the woman left the room, Peel laid her head back against the pillows. She could hardly keep her eyes open, but the doctor's words came back to her. She needed to try to eat. With a sigh, she reached for the soup spoon and dipped it into the bowl. It took effort to lift it to her mouth, but when she did, she was pleasantly surprised. This was no canned chicken noodle soup. Nor was it hospital food. Accompanying the soup were warm tortillas and a bottle of water. She took a long drink of the water and ate all of the soup and two tortillas. When she was done, she lifted the tray off her lap and placed it on the other side of the bed.

For the first time, she looked around the room. One wall was covered with floor-to-ceiling drapes. Light leaked out at the top and bottom along the length of the wall. She stared at it, contemplating getting up and looking outside. That thought didn't last long as the bright light shot arrows of pain into her brain. She turned her head and saw two pills in a small dish beside the water. She took them both. Although she felt marginally better, the effort of sitting up and eating had exhausted her. She closed her eyes.

* * *

It was evening by the time Anna returned to the kitchen to talk with Rosita. "Any better?" she asked.

"The doctor was here. He left medication for her headache and something to settle her stomach. She ate a bowl of soup for dinner."

Anna nodded. "Do you know why she's here? Or what we're supposed to do with her?"

"Sebastien called this morning. He said she is to be treated as a guest and given anything she wants except a phone or computer. I told him she has many questions. He said we could tell her she is a guest of Sebastien Gutierrez and will be staying indefinitely."

"Indefinitely? Who is she?" Anna asked.

Rosita shook her head. "He didn't say, but he said he would call you later today."

Anna nodded. It was evening, but it wasn't unheard of for Sebastien to call her in the middle of the night. His schedule was their schedule. As if reading their minds, her phone rang. Anna retrieved it from her pocket and showed the display to Rosita, who walked away.

"Hello, Sebastien."

"Anna, how are things at the estate?" As always, his voice was low, soothing, and his words unfailingly polite.

"Everything is fine. I'm working on finalizing the plans with Chicago. They're having some problems procuring what we want in the quantity we need. They want to know if you're interested in partial shipments."

"What did you tell them?"

"That I would speak to you. I mentioned that you were contacting Phoenix."

"Their response?"

"Ojos was angry."

"Ojos is always angry. He's becoming tiresome." Sebastien paused. "How is the girl?"

Anna took a breath. This was new territory, and she wasn't sure how to approach it. Hearing her hesitation, Sebastien said, "Tell me why Rosita sent for the doctor."

Keeping her tone level, she replied, "She has a concussion. When she arrived, she was bleeding from a wound to her head and had been vomiting. Her eye is swollen shut and one side of her face is bruised. She was wearing only her underwear."

"Hmm. Was she raped?"

"No, just beaten."

"I told Ojos to do what was necessary to bring her here. She either forced his hand or he took his anger out on her. How is she now?" The polite tone belied the casual cruelty of his words.

Anna controlled her anger and kept her voice even. "I don't know. Elena has been taking care of her." There was silence on the other end of the line, and Anna rushed to fill it. "That was my decision. Elena doesn't speak English, and since we didn't know your wishes, I thought it best for language to be a problem."

A pause. "Fine, but from now on you and Rosita are in charge of her."

Anna couldn't mask her surprise. "Me?"

"As you said, Chicago is a few weeks out. She is an American. Make her feel comfortable and get her whatever she needs. Be her friend. Go to Mexico City and buy her clothing and cosmetics. Whatever she needs."

I don't want a friend, Anna thought with a sigh.

"What was that?" Sebastien asked sharply.

Did she say that out loud? She paused, afraid she'd angered him. "What do you want me to tell her about her injuries? She thinks she's been in a car accident. She's also been asking where she is."

"Tell her she is my guest, nothing more. If she continues to push, be sure she understands that her injuries could have been worse." He let the words sink in. "I will explain everything to her when I return sometime next week. For now, make sure she is better by the time I arrive. Rosita said she is not very clearheaded." He paused, and Anna wasn't sure his next words were intended for her. "I have waited a very long time for this opportunity." The phone went dead.

CHAPTER SIX

The headache was still there. This morning she knew where she was, or more accurately, where she wasn't. She wasn't at home, nor was she in a hospital. For a couple of minutes, she lay looking up at the ceiling blinking away the sleep. Why was she so groggy? She knew the concussion would make her tired, but she felt completely out of it. Peel pushed the covers back and slowly started to raise herself up in the bed.

"Whoa, wait a second," a woman's voice came from the doorway. This was not the same voice from yesterday. Peel let her head drop back to the pillow. Soon, dark brown eyes appeared in her line of sight.

"Hey, I remember you!" Peel smiled. "You're the nurse, aren't you?"

The woman shook her head, "No, I'm not a nurse, but I can help you sit up. Do you need to go to the bathroom?"

"Desperately."

"Hold on to my arm and I'll lift you up."

Peel widened her eye. "Wait, you're not going to pick me up, are you? Because I think you already did that. Didn't you lift me out of the bathtub? God, that's mortifying." Peel's words came out in a rush as the memory of her bath flooded back.

"I was hoping you'd lose that memory in the fog of your concussion." The tall woman grinned back at her. "And, no, I'm just going to help you sit up."

"I think I remember more than I want to." Peel blinked. "Let's just get this all over with. You carried me to the bathroom, undressed me, put me in the tub, and washed my hair, right?" At the woman's nod, she continued. "Then you lifted me out of the tub and carried me back to bed." Peel felt her face grow hot. "And I think I was naked when you paraded me through the bedroom. Did I miss anything?"

Now the woman was laughing. "Just one thing."

Peel covered her face. "God, I'm afraid to ask."

"You're wearing my shirt."

Peel looked down. She rolled her eye. "Of course I am."

"Come on," the woman said. "Let's get you to the bathroom."

She helped Peel to her feet, and Peel leaned on her as they moved slowly into the bathroom. When she reached the toilet, she looked back at the woman, who seemed unsure what to do. Peel pointed to the door. "Your nurse duties end here. Leave me some dignity. Out."

The woman bowed slightly, backed out, and closed the door. Peel's head ached from the movement, and she stayed on the seat longer than was necessary. When the pain subsided, she used the nearby counter to pull herself up. She flushed the toilet and turned to the sink to wash. She leaned closer to the mirror, inspecting the swelling and deep purple bruises on her face. What happened to her?

She jumped at a knock on the door behind her. "Okay?" the woman called.

"Do you think I could brush my teeth? And my hair?" Peel called back.

The door opened and the woman stepped into the expansive bath. She opened a couple of drawers, pulling out items. "Rosita keeps these rooms stocked with anything a guest would need."

Peel picked up the brush and started working on the tangles in her shoulder-length hair.

"Careful. You have a cut on the side of your head."

Peel paused in her movement and met the woman's gaze in the mirror. "I'm Peel."

The woman laughed. "Yes, I know. Peel. But, I don't think it's like banana peel. Who's Emma? Your mother?"

Peel groaned. "No. Mrs. Emma Peel is a character from a 1960s British TV show. That's where my name came from." Peel didn't have the energy to explain further. "I'm sorry, I don't remember your name."

"Anna. Back to bed?"

"I'd rather not. I feel like I've been in bed for days." She looked at Anna. "Have I been in bed for days?"

Rather than answering, Anna pointed to the foot of the bed. "I brought you clean clothes. I thought sweats and a T-shirt were best." She paused. "Do you need help?"

"I think I can do it."

"Okay," Anna said. "I'll go get your breakfast while you dress."

"Wait!" Peel called out as Anna started to walk away. "No one will tell me where I am or what happened to me. Can you? Do you know?"

Anna turned back. "I'll tell you what I can. But first you need to eat something. I'll be back in a few minutes."

Peel shuffled into the sitting area. At the window, she pulled a drapery back, then flinched as the bright light pierced her brain. She shaded her eyes and moaned softly, the headache pain intensifying. Collapsing into a chair, she leaned back against the cushion. There were so many questions, but the pain made it difficult to think. She turned her head carefully and looked at the bed. It was king-sized, covered with luxurious white bedding. The room resembled an expensive hotel suite, but she didn't think she was in a hotel.

Anna returned with a tray and walked over to the seating area. "Do you want to eat here?" When Peel nodded, she put the tray down and walked over to the window. "Would you like the drapes opened?"

"No!" Peel said sharply. Anna turned to her with a raised eyebrow. "Sorry. My head is killing me. I looked outside and made it worse."

"Light sensitivity. The doctor said you might experience that. I'm sorry, I wasn't thinking. Do you want coffee?"

Peel thought for a minute. "I'll try some. I feel like my stomach is better." Anna poured from a carafe and handed Peel a delicate white cup and saucer. The cup rattled and coffee sloshed over the side. Anna put a steadying hand over hers. "Do you want me to take it?"

"Maybe I'm not ready for coffee."

"Eat something," Anna urged.

Peel reached for a pastry and took a bite. "What is this? It's good."

"Rosita made it for you. It's a pasty. Black currant and cheese. They're famous in this area. When Cornish miners came to work the gold mines, they brought them from England. Now, it's a specialty of the region."

Peel put the pastry down and swallowed hard. "Are we in Colorado?"

Anna leaned back in her chair. "You're in Mexico. Outside of a small town called Tierra de Oro."

Peel couldn't swallow her gasp. "Mexico? Oh no, no, no." She leaned forward, covering her face. The pressure on her swollen cheek and the sudden movement intensified the pain in her head. "Shit," she breathed out. Slowly, she raised up and leaned against the cushion. Her mind flooded with memories of Monday night outside the library. The men must have come back. Had they broken into Linda's house? Was Linda okay? She started to cry.

Through her tears, she heard Anna say, "You are a guest of Sebastien Gutierrez."

"A guest?" Peel choked out, raising her head. "He kidnapped me! I got away the first time he tried, but obviously he succeeded the second time. Did he do this to me?" She gestured to her face.

"No, it wasn't Sebastien. One of the men did it. I'm sorry that you were hurt."

Peel snorted, anger surging. "You're sorry? Is he sorry?" Peel wiped the tears off her cheeks, then groaned when she rubbed the bruises.

Anna hesitated. "He told me he regrets it."

"Wow. I feel so much better." She narrowed her eyes. "Does it bother him?"

"What?"

"This. What they did to me. If I'm his guest, does he care that they beat me?"

"No." Anna hesitated again, then seemed to make up her mind. "Look, these are violent men. You need to be careful."

Peel took a shuddering breath. "I read about him. He runs the de Oro drug cartel, right?" Anna didn't speak but held her gaze. "Never mind. I know the answer." She laid her head back, staring at the ceiling. "Why did he do this? What does a Mexican drug lord want with a librarian from Denver?"

"I don't know."

She lifted her head. "Is he going to kill me? Will I just disappear?" A thought crossed her mind, and it terrified her more than the thought of dying, "Will he torture me for information I don't have? I swear to you, I don't know anything about drugs!"

"Peel, he told me to treat you as a guest. He suggested I take you shopping for clothes and cosmetics. Does that sound like he wants you tortured?" Anna gave her a half smile. "It sounds like he wants me tortured."

"Are you fucking kidding me?" Hot rage filled Peel. "He wants to buy me clothes? He takes me from Denver so I can go clothes shopping in Mexico? What the fuck?" Peel put her hand on her forehead. "Shit," she moaned.

"I don't know anything else," Anna said. "Do you think you can eat a little more?" When Peel picked up the pasty, she said, "I'll get you some Tylenol. Maybe you should take something for your stomach too."

Peel was silent as Anna got up and found the bottles on the bedside table. She shook out two tablets. "Why are these blue?" she asked Peel.

Peel rolled her head toward Anna. "I don't know. Maybe they're nighttime. That would explain why I feel so groggy."

Anna looked at the pills in her hand. "Probably. Do you want to take these, or do you want me to find some others?"

"What day is it?" Peel asked.

This time, Anna answered the question. "It's Friday morning. You've been here since very early Wednesday morning."

"I've been sleeping for two days?"

"Basically. The doctor said it's the best thing for you."

"Are you American?"

If Anna was surprised by the non sequitur, she didn't show it. "I am."

"You work for him?" Peel asked.

"Yes."

"By choice?"

"Yes." Anna didn't look away, but a mask dropped over her face. When Peel opened her mouth to ask more, she held up her hand. "No more questions."

"But, you seem nice," Peel whispered, feeling like a child desperate for a new friend.

Anna looked at her for a long moment. "Sleeping pill or not?"

Peel closed her eyes. "Sleeping pill."

* * *

Anna eased the door shut behind her. She didn't need the complications the sudden appearance of the American had created. She didn't want the responsibility, and she definitely didn't want her questions. In truth, the question had thrown her. The easy answer was, yes, she was here by choice, but sometimes the choices weren't good. She took her cell phone from her pocket, went to "favorites," and pressed a name.

"Hey, sis." She relaxed at the friendly voice. Her brother Miguel was a couple of years younger, but they'd always been close.

"Hey there. Busy?"

"Nah, not too bad. Never too busy to talk to my favorite sister."

"You know how old that is, don't you?"

"Doesn't change the fact you're my fave."

"How's Mom? Is she following her diet?"

He made an exasperated sound. "Right. Like that's going to happen. Dad says she does okay for a while and then loses her mind and deep fries everything she sees."

Anna laughed. "Does she smother it in cheese?"

"I see you've met our mother." They laughed together. There was a short pause when their laughter faded.

"You should visit," Miguel finally said. "Can you?"

Anna's sigh answered his question. "I don't know. Maybe if it was an emergency. I guess empanada binges don't qualify as an emergency."

"Are you homesick? Is that why you're calling in the middle of the day?" he teased.

"A little. I wanted to hear a familiar voice."

"Should I come to Mexico?" It was a question to which they both knew the answer.

Anna forced a laugh. "Who will check on *los padres*?"

"Please. Do you think they let me take care of them?" He took a breath and changed the subject. "Anna, what's going on down there? Ojos is pissed about something with you and Sebastien. He went off on me yesterday."

"Yeah." Anna blew out a breath. "He's even more pissed today."

"Why is he so mad? Are you okay?"

"I think it's time, Miguel."

She heard his sharp intake of breath. "Now?"

"Yes. Do you think they're ready?"

"We've talked a lot about it. They know what has to happen."

She thought for a moment, then said, "Do it. Tomorrow."

In the background, a voice called out. Miguel said something unintelligible, then spoke to her. "I need to go."

"Send them. Tomorrow," she emphasized.

"Yeah," he muttered. "You're right."

"I love you, little one."

"I love you, too." He hung up.

Anna stared at the phone, melancholy washing over her. She crossed the lawns and walked down the steps of the terraced hillside to the pool. Lounge chairs lined the pool deck. She sank into one and closed her eyes. Her family was always at the forefront of her thoughts. Tonight, her brother would help her parents pack a few belongings. In the morning, they would leave Chicago. For months they'd been telling their friends they were moving to south Texas to live with relatives. There weren't any Texas relatives. Instead, they would drive to Texas, sell their car, then fly to Miami, where they would disappear into the Hispanic community.

After tomorrow, Miguel would be her only worry.

CHAPTER SEVEN

The next morning, Anna tugged on her swimming suit and headed to the pool. Growing up in Chicago, a pool was a luxury she could only dream about. Now she could swim whenever she wanted. There were advantages to living in Mexico on the estate of one of the wealthiest men in Hidalgo.

Even though this part of Mexico was mountainous and the weather was mild, Sebastien's pool was always warm enough to use. Only the coolest days kept her from a morning swim. She dove in, and after a few cursory stretches fell into an easy rhythm. She loved swimming. The rhythmic pattern of breaths cleared her head and gave her the only peace she'd had since coming to Mexico. But today the swim wasn't helping. Her mind kept flashing back to her parents, Miguel, and the American woman.

Anna took a breath just as her own wave washed over her face. She choked and stood, swearing at herself. She rolled onto her back and swam to the side of the pool. Lifting her goggles off her face, she looked up at the beautiful landscaping all around her and wondered if she was ever going to get out of Mexico.

The ringing phone shook her out of her reverie. She lifted herself out of the pool, dried her hands, and answered. "Good morning, Sebastien."

"You sound out of breath. Were you swimming?"

"Just finishing."

"I've found a buyer for the shipment."

This was news. He had been gone several weeks meeting with other cartels and the heads of organized crime families. "Are they okay with the delay?"

Anna heard Sebastien's frustrated sigh. "They weren't happy," he admitted, "but they don't have another source, so they're willing to wait for us. This will be the last time."

Anna waited. When he didn't say anything else, she asked, "Phoenix?"

Sebastien addressed the silence rather than her question. "I know you're loyal to the Disciples, but they aren't reliable anymore. In fact, they haven't been reliable for a long time."

"I could go back to Chicago," Anna began.

Sebastien silenced her. "I thought you understood your role, Anna. You don't work for the Disciples. You work for me." His voice was quiet, but there was no mistaking the power in his words.

"Yes, I understand that." She kept her tone businesslike. "Do you want me to start reaching out to Phoenix?"

"Just make inquiries. We'll use them if Chicago can't meet deadlines."

"I'll get on it," she said, preparing to end their conversation.

Sebastien surprised her. "How is our guest today?"

"She is improving. I imagine she'll be ready to get out of bed today."

"Good. Allow her to use the amenities of the estate and provide her whatever she needs. Is she compliant?"

Anna didn't know how to answer this question. What did compliant mean in this context? Peel certainly wasn't happy, but she was polite to Anna and the staff. "Um, she's polite, but confused and a little angry."

Sebastien chuckled. "Only a little?"

"Well…" Anna hedged.

"Tell her all will be explained soon." There was a pause on the line. "Have you spoken to your brother lately?"

Her breath caught and she took a moment to make sure her voice didn't betray her concern. "Yes."

"And Ojos?" Sebastien let his question hang. "I understand he has been asking about the woman. Why have you not told me about his questions?"

Anna's heart rate accelerated. Her only defense was the truth. "My brother is at his mercy. He can get to him any time. I can't make Ojos angry."

"You're willing to risk making me angry?" His voice was still polite.

"Sebastien, you know how he is. I'm in an impossible situation."

"I realize that, Anna. I'm making arrangements to take this pressure off you."

"Thank you," she said.

"You're very valuable to me. I want you to be happy here in Mexico." A pause. When he spoke again, there was an edge to his question. "Are you happy?"

"Yes."

"Good. I'll see you very soon." With that, he hung up.

Anna stared at her phone. The answer to Peel's question from yesterday had never been clearer. She was not here by choice. Reaching for the towel she'd discarded during the conversation, she headed back to her casita for a shower.

Thirty minutes later, her hair braided down her back, she walked into the main kitchen. As usual, Rosita was bustling around preparing an array of breakfast pastries. She smiled when she saw Anna. "Did you swim?" she asked, reaching for Anna's damp braid.

"Yes, but not very far."

"How would you know?" Rosita teased. It was familiar ground for the two of them. Rosita couldn't understand why Anna would swim back and forth in a pool day after day. For a woman who'd worked long hours all her life, taking time to exercise was ridiculous.

Anna laughed and helped herself to coffee. "Do you know if she's awake?"

"No. No one has been upstairs today."

Anna looked at her watch. "Could you make me a tray with some coffee and fruit? I'll check on her." Rosita pulled some fruit out of the giant refrigerator and made up a plate while Anna gathered coffee supplies. Tray loaded, she climbed the stairs. When she reached the room at the end of the hall she placed the tray on the table, but before she could knock a voice called, "Come in."

Anna opened the door and turned back to collect the tray. "Good morning. How are you feeling?" She made sure her voice was friendly, but her manner remained reserved.

Peel reclined against the headboard, her answer automatic. "I'm fine, how are you?"

Anna placed the tray on the table in the sitting area, then looked back over her shoulder. "Really? You're fine?"

"Well, I have two working eyes."

Stepping closer to the bed, Anna saw the swelling had receded some. "It looks more like one and a half to me. How's your head?"

"It's not nearly as bad as it was. I really do feel better. Enough to crave some coffee and that amazing pastry-thingy you brought me yesterday."

"Uh-oh." Anna looked at the tray. "I only brought fruit this morning. Rosita was just pulling fresh pasties out of the oven. I'll be right back."

When Anna returned, Peel was sipping a cup of coffee, some of the sleepiness gone from her face. "You don't need to knock every time," Peel told her.

Rather than answer, Anna displayed a plate of pasties. "Fresh. Rosita is very happy you like them. Now you'll get them every morning."

Peel stared at her. "And how long will that be, Anna?"

Anna looked away. "I'm sorry. That was thoughtless."

Peel leaned toward Anna. "Do you know anything else? Have you found out what he wants?"

"No," Anna answered. "And I won't."

"What does that mean? You won't ask him?"

"No, I won't."

"Are you afraid of him?"

Anna paused, contemplating how best to answer the question. Her relationship with Sebastien was complex. He was always polite and even thoughtful, yet the fact that he ran a cartel was never far from her mind. She suspected that was intentional. When she answered, she made sure her face betrayed no emotion. "How I feel about Sebastien is not up for discussion."

Peel stared at her for a long minute. When she looked away, Anna could barely hear her question. "This isn't going to end well, is it?"

After her conversation with Sebastien, Anna felt trapped, and she let some of her frustration seep into her reply. "Look, Peel, I don't know anything. I can't tell you what he wants. I don't know why you're here. I work for him, I'm not his confidante."

"Will you help me?" Peel asked quietly.

Anna should have expected the question. She stood. "I'll get you some clothes for today."

"Anna," Peel called after her. Anna considered ignoring her, but stopped in the doorway and turned back, her expression stony. Peel made eye contact but couldn't hold her gaze. "Could you get me some regular Tylenol?"

"Of course," Anna said and left the room.

* * *

Peel cursed herself for asking for Anna's help. Would Anna tell Gutierrez? So far, she had been treated like a guest, not a prisoner. But if Anna reported back to him, he might be angry that she was trying to turn his employees against him.

If she was going to survive this situation, she was going to have to be smarter. To do that she needed a clearer head, which meant no more sleeping pills. She leaned her head against the cushion and thought about Anna's reaction to her question. Anna hadn't said she was afraid of Sebastien Gutierrez, but Peel had seen the shadow cross her face.

She was convinced Anna was the key. She needed to befriend the woman, to get her to care enough that she wanted to help. Peel figured her chance of survival was better if Anna and the staff liked her. Maybe if they thought of her as a friend, they would be willing to help her escape.

Again, she heard footsteps outside the door. Anna was returning with the Tylenol. Peel stood and walked toward the door. She opened it to a startled Anna, whose fist was raised. "I told you, you don't have to knock every time."

Anna met her eyes briefly, then looked at the bottle in her hand. "Regular Tylenol and a couple bottles of water." She extended both hands toward Peel.

Peel reached for the bottle with her right hand and wrapped around Anna's hand with her left. "I'm sorry," she whispered. "I should never have put you in that position. I can see you are afraid of him."

Anna's eyes widened. She slowly withdrew her hand from Peel's grasp and took a step toward the dresser. "I'll just put the water here. I'll get some clothes for you and then leave you alone." She was clearly uncomfortable.

"Do you think I could leave this room today?" Peel asked. "Maybe you could show me around a little?" At Anna's silence, she tried a more cajoling tone. "C'mon. You're supposed to treat me like a guest."

"All right. Are you going to take a shower?"

"I was planning on it."

"I'll leave some shorts and a T-shirt here." She pointed to the dresser where she had placed the water. "I'll come back in an hour or so?" It was a question.

"Perfect," Peel said. "Thank you."

* * *

Back in the casita, Anna searched through her drawers for clothes that would fit Peel. The other woman was thinner and shorter than Anna, so Anna chose athletic shorts with an elastic waistband. They were too short for Anna's comfort, so they might be just right for Peel. She found an old university T-shirt and added it to the pile. She was going to have to make a trip to Mexico City to buy the visitor some clothes.

Anna thought about Peel's question and subsequent apology. She had frozen when Peel asked for her help, panicking. What if someone had overheard them? Was her response enough to show loyalty to Sebastien? She hadn't said no, nor had she chastised the other woman, but her message must have been clear or Peel wouldn't have apologized. That's what she would say if Sebastien asked.

Anna once again knocked on Peel's door. Getting no answer, she cracked it open, listening for the shower. She placed the clothes on the dresser, grabbed the breakfast dishes, and headed back downstairs, making note of the time. She'd return in an hour to take Peel on a tour of the house. She'd also have the woman list her clothing sizes and preferences.

This situation was so different from anything Anna had experienced since she came to work for the cartel. Who was this woman? Sebastien had gone to a lot of trouble to have her grabbed, including incurring a debt to Ojos. Sebastien was ruthless in business, but he wanted Peel treated as a guest. None of it made sense.

Thus far, Anna's role in Sebastien's organization had been clear. She was here to facilitate an expansion that could prove to be extremely lucrative. Peel Primm was a distraction from that task, and Sebastien never tolerated distractions from business. Yet he'd said on the phone that Peel represented an opportunity he'd been waiting on for a long time. As much as Anna wanted to know more, she knew curiosity could be very dangerous.

CHAPTER EIGHT

Peel walked over to the large wall of windows covered by gray curtains. Being careful not to look directly outside, she pulled them back, allowing bright sunshine to fill the room. It was the first natural light she'd seen in days. With a sigh, she squinted and looked out the window. The light still hurt her eyes, but the pain wasn't as intense as it had been just yesterday. She turned her back to the window and sat in the sitting area.

Now that her head was starting to clear, the reality of the last three days settled on her. She was a prisoner. No matter how nice the accommodations were, no matter how kind the staff had been, she had been taken against her will by a drug lord. She was being held in Mexico. She felt a burning anger starting to creep from her chest into her throat. What right did he have to kidnap an American citizen, beat her, and take her to Mexico? She slammed the side of her fist on the chair and let out a frustrated wail. The frustration gave way to despair, and tears filled her eyes and spilled over. She leaned her head back and let herself cry.

After several minutes, she stood and walked to the bedside table. Of course there was a box of tissue there, she thought. She blew her nose and took in a shuddering breath. Returning to the chair, she thought about Linda. Peel couldn't remember being taken, but she remembered Linda's schedule. She was at work, then at class. Knowing Linda was safe provided a little peace, but her friend must be frantic with worry. No matter what the police department thought about Peel, Linda would know better. And Sheryl. Sheryl had been indignant when Detective Bellamy suggested she was shipping drugs through the library. She could count on the two of them to defend her and make Bellamy listen to the truth.

But what could he do? No one would ever guess she was in Mexico, and even if they did, the Hawk Ridge Police Department couldn't come to Mexico to rescue her. What about the FBI? It was a kidnapping, so the FBI got involved in those, right? At least Bellamy knew the de Oro cartel was behind her attack. Maybe he'd figure out she was in Tierra de Oro. Or not. Why would he believe she was staying in the home of Sebastien Gutierrez? How improbable was that? Did they even know where this place was?

A knock startled her. "Come in, Anna," she called out. She sat upright in the chair and pasted a smile on her face. She was going to make this woman like her. "Thanks for doing this. I'm sure you're busy, but I can't stand being in here any longer."

"My only responsibility right now is you." Anna's tone was formal, distant.

Peel held her smile, trying to break through Anna's wall. "Really?"

"Yes, Sebastien has given me explicit directions to make you comfortable. How do the shorts fit?" She pointed to Peel's outfit.

Peel stood up and straightened the shirt and shorts. "Not bad," she said.

Anna looked her up and down, then pulled a notepad and pen from her pocket. "Okay, first things first. I'll go to Mexico City tomorrow. Let's make a list of the clothes you need and your sizes."

Peel tried to choke it back, but the rage rose up, again. "You're joking, aren't you? I'm a prisoner, here. Since when do prisoners get a new wardrobe?"

Anna winced. "Let's just make you comfortable, okay? You'll feel better with clothes that fit and underwear that's yours."

Peel breathed deeply, reminding herself she needed Anna's trust. She took a deep breath and forced a smile. "No offense, but wearing my own underwear is a big deal to me."

"None taken. Let's start with underwear, then. What size bra do you wear?"

Peel blushed. "No way. Give me that. I'm not having this conversation with you."

Anna slid the pad and pen across the table to her. "While you're at it, do you want shorts, jeans, T-shirts, dresses?"

"No dresses. I assume the weather is warm. Just T-shirts and shorts. And underwear," she added unnecessarily.

"Do you swim? There is a beautiful pool and spa."

"Really?" Peel looked up from the paper. "You know this is crazy, right?"

"I know. Try to just go with it for now. Bikini?"

"Never. One piece. Or, even better, boardshorts and a tankini."

"What SPF on your sunscreen?"

Laughing, Peel responded, "As high as you can go." Then she looked speculatively at Anna. "Could I go with you? It would be easier for me to just pick things out for myself."

Anna rubbed her eyebrow. "I don't think that's a good idea." She started to say more, then just shook her head. "Anything else?" Her tone was back to being businesslike.

"No, let's just go with that. Hopefully, I won't be here that long, right?"

Once again, Anna appeared uncomfortable with the direction of the conversation. She tore the list off the pad and looked toward the door. "You know, I think I should go shopping today. You'll be more comfortable if you're wearing clothes that are yours." Anna stood. "The drive to Mexico City is about two hours, but traffic in the city is horrible. I'll be gone for the rest of the day. If you need anything, Elena and Rosita will be around." She said the last words as she walked out the door.

Peel watched Anna's retreating form, surprised. What just happened? She'd been looking forward to taking a tour of the house, anything to get out of this room. She hurried to the bedroom door.

"Anna," she called as she rushed down the wide hallway. "Anna," she called again, this time louder. She hurried toward the staircase visible at the end of the hall. Anna was on the bottom stair. "Please," Peel called out to her. Anna stopped and turned to look up the staircase. "Anna, please don't go today."

Anna stared at Peel for a long minute and then nodded her head. "All right," she said.

The relief Peel felt seemed out of proportion to the circumstance, but she didn't question it. She wouldn't be alone in that room all day. Letting out the breath she'd been holding, she smiled. "Thank you."

Anna gestured to her. "Come downstairs."

Worried that Anna would change her mind, Peel hurried down the steps. "I'm sorry," Anna said when Peel reached her. "I shouldn't have changed plans like that. That was thoughtless of me."

Peel was touched by the apology. She reached for Anna's forearm. "Thank you," she said again. "I just couldn't stand the thought of being up there another day."

"Well, now you don't have to be. Where would you like to start?"

"I don't know." A pause, then an idea hit her. "The kitchen. I need to see where Rosita creates those wonderful pastries."

"They're called pasties. Rhymes with nasty."

"The pastries are pasties? I thought you were mixing up your words. I guess pasties are something you wear if you work in a strip club."

"Hmm," Anna said. "Would you like me to tell Rosita that's what you think of her pasties?"

"No! Definitely not. Take me to Rosita, so I can show her the proper respect."

"Follow me." Anna walked toward the back of the house. When she reached a large wooden door, she turned to face Peel and pushed her back against it. The door swung open. "Welcome to Rosita's domain." She held her arm out in a flourish.

Peel was hit by an intoxicating variety of scents—coffee, bread, and spices she would never be able to identify. The mix delighted her, and she breathed deeply. "It smells so good in here." She looked around to see what was cooking, but the stove was empty.

Rosita looked up from her place at a long, rectangular table pushed up against a wall of windows. Sunshine spilled across the table, lighting the newspaper and the empty dishes in front of her. When she saw Anna and Peel, she started to get up. Anna held up a hand and spoke to the woman in Spanish. Rosita's smile broadened and she sat back down. To Peel, Anna said, "I told her I wanted to take you on a tour of the house, but all you wanted to see was the kitchen."

Peel looked at Rosita. "I had to see where you make those delicious…" She hesitated for a moment, looking at Anna. "Pasties."

Anna translated, then walked over to the coffeepot on one of the long counters. "Do you want some?" she asked Peel as she carried the pot over to Rosita and refilled her mug.

"That sounds great. May we join you?" Peel asked Rosita, gesturing to the table. Rosita looked between the two women and smiled. She nodded, gesturing to the two chairs beside her at the table.

Anna reached in a cupboard, pulling down two earthenware mugs and filling them with coffee. "I know you use cream, but do you take sugar, too?" she asked Peel.

Peel looked at Anna in surprise. "No, just cream. Thank you."

The two women pulled out chairs at the table. Peel was drawn to the view through the large windows and couldn't help staring at the expanse of gardens. It was a mistake. The bright sunlight was too much. She blinked several times and looked down. "Should we sit at the island?" Anna stood. "Is the sunlight bothering you?"

Once again, Peel was surprised that Anna noticed. She stood, too. "Thanks. It does seem to shoot daggers into my brain. It's beautiful out there."

Anna looked over to a confused Rosita. She explained the problem, gesturing to the island. Rosita shook her head no, said a few words to Anna, and picked up her paper and dishes. Anna's words took on a wheedling tone, but the other woman shook her head and left the room.

Peel took the opportunity to look around the large room. Unlike the style in American homes, the kitchen was its own room, not open to the rest of the house. Peel liked the separation. The big room was oddly cozy. Even though the appliances were of restaurant size and quality, the kitchen was warm and welcoming. She looked at Anna. "It's nice in here. Homey."

"That's all Rosita. The house has been in the Gutierrez family for generations, but Sebastien renovated a lot of it. When he started on the kitchen, I guess he had a design, but Rosita overruled him. She made sure he didn't turn it into a cold restaurant kitchen." She gestured to the old farm table and the wire baskets of fruit and vegetables on the counters. There were brightly colored pots of herbs growing on a baker's rack in the corner. The mismatch of colors and sizes added charm to the room.

"Does she live in Tierra de Oro?" Peel asked.

"She lives here. She has a suite of rooms adjacent to the kitchen." Anna pointed in the direction Rosita had gone.

"Does her family live here, too?"

"Rosita doesn't have a family."

Peel raised her eyebrows. "Is that not allowed?"

"She could have a family if she wanted. She told me she moved around with Sebastien so much that she never met a 'nice boy.'" Anna ended her sentence with air quotes.

Peel looked at Anna over her mug of coffee. "She moved around with Sebastien? Does that mean what I think it does?"

"It depends. If you think it means she has been his cook and housekeeper for most of her life, then it does. She is a very respectable and religious woman." This time Anna pointed to the crucifix over the door they entered.

"Oh." They sat silently for a few moments. "Can I ask more questions?"

"As long as you don't insult my friend."

"I'm sorry. It just seems a little *Downton Abbey*, you know? It's hard to understand."

"It's hard for an American to understand, but not for Mexicans. Don Eduardo offered her an incredible opportunity, and she was smart enough to take advantage of it."

"Don Eduardo? I thought she worked for Sebastien. Who is Don Eduardo?" Peel wrinkled her brow in confusion.

"He was Sebastien's father. Rosita's parents both worked for the Gutierrez family. They lived here on the estate. Rosita grew up here."

"What did her parents do?"

"Her mother was one of the cooks and her father was a driver for Don Eduardo. Rosita played in the kitchen when she was little, and all of the staff looked out for her. When she was old enough, her mother put her to work helping prepare the meals and wash dishes."

Peel was fascinated. Rosita's life had been so different from her own mother's. "Did she go to school?"

"Yes, in Tierra de Oro. After she finished school, Don Eduardo gave her a job working with her mother in the kitchen, but he wouldn't officially hire her until she had finished school." At Peel's questioning look, she said, "Kind of like a vocational high school." Anna sipped her coffee. "When Sebastien went to university, Don Eduardo decided he needed a staff. He asked Rosita's mother who he should hire, and she convinced him to choose Rosita. From that day on Rosita has worked for Sebastien."

Peel looked at Anna in surprise. "Really? Her mother sent her daughter to live with a college boy? What did her father think?" Afraid her question would be perceived as an insult, she added, "My parents would never have allowed that."

"No, neither would Rosita's. She wasn't the only one hired. Don Eduardo sent an older woman to be the housekeeper and the woman's husband was Sebastien's driver. It was all chaperoned and dignified, very *Downton Abbey*." Peel searched her face, looking for any sign that Anna was teasing. When Anna's stoic resolve was broken with a quirked eyebrow, Peel laughed out loud. Was it possible that she was honestly enjoying the woman next to her?

After they finished their coffee, Anna took Peel on a tour of the main floor. The house was sprawling and showed signs of additions and renovations throughout. Although the actual items decorating the home were vastly different from her own, Peel recognized the style. She said as much to Anna. "This reminds me of my house. I live in the house I grew up in, so nothing is really a reflection of my taste. It's more a combination of my style and those things of my parents and grandparents that I can't bear to get rid of."

"I'm going to give you a peek of the best area of the house, but I think a peek is all you'll be able to stand with your light sensitivity." She entered a small sitting room and flipped a switch on the wall. Peel turned at the mechanical sound and watched in awe as a wall of glass doors was revealed. Behind the glass was a beautiful garden room. Sunlight filtered through tall palms. Flowering plants and shrubs surrounded a stone seating area.

"It's gorgeous." She put her hand above her eyes to block the light. Even so, she could only look for a moment before turning away. "Wow, that's incredible. If this were my house, I'd never leave that room."

"I know. I'm from Chicago. I keep thinking how much a place like that would make the cold winters bearable." Anna sighed.

Peel grabbed that small piece of information. "You're from Chicago?"

Anna's mouth tightened. She walked over to the wall switch and closed the shades. "I really need to do some work, and I'm sure you must be tired. I'll walk you to your room." They made their way silently through the house back up to the second floor. When they reached the door to Peel's room, Anna said, "I'll have Elena bring you a lunch tray. Have a good afternoon." With that, she was gone.

Peel watched her retreating form, then opened the door to her room. Once inside, her shoulders slumped. The little bit of exercise had exhausted her, and the sharp pain in her head was back. Still, she smiled. There had been a tiny crack in Anna. She'd let down her guard enough to let a piece of personal information slip out. That crack gave Peel hope.

* * *

Anna had followed Sebastien's orders to treat Peel like a guest. That was becoming a problem. Anna was finding it hard not to like the woman. From the first night, the combination of vulnerability and playfulness she had seen in Peel caused Anna to lower her guard. She needed to be more cautious when she was with their visitor. She knew better.

When she first arrived at the estate, Anna made the mistake of casually smiling at a man as Sebastien introduced them. The visitor greeted her with a leer and made a show of slowly looking over her body. His eyes never returned to hers. When he finished his perusal, he gave Sebastien a satisfied nod. Anna was infuriated and started to say something, but one look from the cartel leader told her it would not only be futile but also foolish. Crude words and laughter followed her as she hurried from the room.

That night she locked her door and stayed awake. Around midnight she heard him stumbling on the step leading up to the tiny porch. The doorknob rattled when he tried to turn it against the lock. He didn't knock or call out, but instead walked away. She sighed, releasing the tension she'd been holding. She should have known better.

She was in the bathroom when she heard the scrape of the lock cover and a key slide into place. Panic rose in her throat. She reached for the bathroom light, turning it out just as the door opened. In the dark, she tried to recall what was on the counter. A hair dryer, deodorant, lotion bottles, brushes, a comb. Nothing of any use against an attacker. Under the cabinet were cleaning supplies in various spray and aerosol forms. She listened, desperately hoping her eyes would adjust before he reached her bedroom and found the bed unoccupied.

It was strange what crossed her mind while she was waiting in the dark. Maybe it was because her senses were heightened, but the mint of her toothpaste was sharp in her mouth, and that made her angry. She regretted brushing her teeth. He would assume she did it for him. The sound of a body part colliding with something solid propelled her to action. When he cursed, she surged forward, opened the cabinet door, and lightly slid her fingers across the plastic bottles. She stopped when she felt the cool touch of an aerosol can. She grabbed it and wrestled with the plastic cap, fearing it would come off with a loud pop. Finally, it gave, and she reflexively shook the can. At the sound of sloshing liquid she stopped, irritated at her stupidity.

Her bedroom was just off the living room, and she kept the door open at all times. That was another habit she was going to change. She positioned herself just slightly behind the open door of the bathroom and watched. He walked into her room and approached the bed, unfastening his belt as he got closer. Without another thought she strode into her room, letting her fury rise in full force. "What the fuck are you doing in my room?" she screamed at him.

He jumped and turned to her, hand still on his belt buckle. She lifted the can and sprayed. The smell of bleach hit her before the sound of his screams and curses. Ah, scrubbing bubbles, she thought, continuing to spray. With rage she didn't realize she possessed, she emptied the can in his face and at his retreating back, screaming obscenities. When the can sputtered, she dropped it and sprinted past the staggering man, not stopping until she was in the kitchen pounding on Rosita's door.

The older woman took one look at her, grabbed her forearm, and pulled her into the room. She locked the door and pushed Anna into the bathroom. "Lock the door," she ordered. Anna did as she was told. Sebastien would be furious with her. There was a pecking order in this world, and women were at the bottom. Anna took off her shoes, wrapped herself in a towel, and climbed into the empty bathtub. She spent the night there.

At breakfast, Sebastien's only comment was, "You made a dangerous enemy last night."

She looked at him and knew her response was vital to her future safety. "So did he." Nothing else was said, but she thought she saw a flicker of amusement in Sebastien's eyes.

The next day a locksmith arrived while Sebastien was in town. That afternoon Rosita pressed two silver keys into her hand. Anna returned to her casita to find a new deadbolt and a heavy-duty swing bar lock installed.

Since that day, Anna had worn a mask. It was the perfect balance of indifference and disdain with everyone except Sebastien and Rosita. Now when she entered a room, she met the eyes of the other occupants, held their gazes for mere seconds, and then deliberately slid her eyes away, communicating how little she thought of them. More than a few times she heard men call her a bitch or a cunt under their breaths. Never again did one try to enter her room.

She'd made a couple of other changes, too. Now her style of dress mimicked that of the men who worked for Sebastien: black tactical pants and a black T-shirt. Her only deviation was black Nike tennis shoes in place of their boots. Her hair was pulled back in a tight, high ponytail, and she never wore makeup, at least not at work.

The final change was more difficult than visiting an army/ navy surplus store. She needed a handgun. In some ways, guns were impossible to get in Mexico. There was only one gun store in the country and it was run by the military. It took months of background checks to even get in the door.

But Anna didn't need a legal firearm. She took a chance and asked Rosita. When the older woman walked away without a comment, Anna was afraid she'd made a grave mistake. But minutes later, Rosita returned with one of Sebastien's men. He named a price in dollars more than double the cost of a firearm in the US. She merely nodded and went to her room for the money. Two days later, she found the gun under a pillow in her bedroom. Rather than feeling safer, panic set in at the thought that once again someone had access to the keys to her casita. She hurried to the kitchen, and the fear must have shown on her face. Rosita patted her arm, then walked over to her large ring of keys. She flipped through several, then held up a shiny silver key matching the two she'd given Anna. "In case I need you," she said simply.

Anna had smiled in relief. She had a gun and a friend.

CHAPTER NINE

During her early morning swim, Anna solidified her plan for the day. As soon as she showered, she would take the breakfast tray up to their guest and make sure Peel understood the danger of asking too many questions. Then she would follow Sebastien's directive: drive to Mexico City and buy Peel the clothes she needed. She had no intention of returning tonight.

After showering, she dried her long hair and left it hanging loose around her shoulders. With a quick glance in the mirror to set her stony look, she headed to the main house. Rosita looked up from the island when she entered the kitchen, a broad smile on her face. The smile dimmed slightly when she saw Anna's expression.

"What is it?" she asked gently.

"Nothing," Anna said. "Just lost in thought." Before Rosita could say more, she continued. "I'll take the tray up, then I'm going to Mexico City for the day."

Rosita's eyes twinkled and she touched Anna's loose hair. "And the night."

Anna should be used to Rosita's teasing, but she felt her face grow warm. "I may stay overnight. I'm not sure yet."

Rosita chuckled and patted her arm. "The tray is over there. The pasties are warming in the oven."

"Thank you," Anna said as she bent to kiss the woman's cheek.

Walking up the long staircase, Anna once again steeled her expression. She set the tray down and knocked. There was no response. She knocked again and gently turned the handle. The room was dark and silent. "Peel?" she called. Still no reply. Anna listened for sounds in the bathroom as her eyes adjusted to the dark room. It was quiet. For a brief moment, her heart stopped. Had Peel managed to escape? As soon as that thought crossed her mind, a darker one replaced it. Was the woman's head injury more serious than they realized? "Peel?" she said again, much louder. A small answering moan came from the bed.

Anna crossed the room in long strides. "Peel? What's wrong?" Worry made her voice sharper than she intended.

"My head," came the faint reply.

"Can I turn the light on?" Anna was already reaching for the switch.

"No, please. My head is pounding."

"Okay, I'm going to turn the bathroom light on so I can see you better." Anna crossed to the bathroom and flicked the switch inside the door. She turned back to the bed and could just make out the pale figure. "How long have you been like this?"

"Don't know. Last night."

"Last night?" Anna's voice rose on the last word. "Why didn't you tell someone?"

Peel opened her eyes and looked wearily at Anna. "Who?" she asked quietly before closing them again. Guilt stabbed at Anna. She had deliberately stayed away from Peel after the aborted house tour. With the maids' limited English, she was right. There hadn't been anyone to ask for help.

"I'll have Rosita call the doctor. Have you taken anything?" Anna picked up the pills on the side of the bed and shook the bottle.

"I threw it up."

Anna couldn't help herself. She bent down and brushed Peel's cheek with the backs of her fingers. "I'm so sorry," she murmured. "I'll be right back."

Anna ran down the stairs calling to Rosita and Elena as she went. Just as Rosita appeared in the kitchen doorway, Elena rushed from the back of the house holding a dusting cloth. Quickly, Anna explained Peel's worsened condition. "Elena, call the doctor and see if he can come right away." Elena hurried off and Peel turned to Rosita. "She threw up the pills Dr. Aguilar gave her. I think she needs something in her stomach." Rosita nodded and turned back to the kitchen. Anna followed. "Do you think ice would help? I'll make her an ice pack. Maybe some tea?"

Rosita looked at Anna with an odd expression. "Why don't you make an ice pack and sit with her until the doctor comes? I'll bring tea and a little soup to settle her stomach." Rosita patted her hand when she seemed to hesitate. "Go, now."

Anna nodded, filled a towel with ice, and ran back up the stairs. When she reached the door to Peel's room, she slowed and took a deep breath. In a calm, quiet voice she said, "Peel? I brought some ice. Do you think that would help?"

Peel opened her eyes. "My whole head is pounding. I don't know where I would put it."

Anna eased down on the side of the bed. "What if we put it on your forehead and eye?"

"Okay." Peel reached for the ice pack, but Anna took her hand and placed it back on the covers.

"Let me do it," she said. Gently, Anna brushed the hair away from the other woman's face and placed the ice pack low on her forehead and brow. "It isn't very cold right now, but the ice should start to melt soon." Peel said nothing, just closed her eyes.

They sat like that for several minutes before Anna heard Rosita at the door. If Rosita was surprised to see Anna sitting beside Peel and holding the ice pack, she didn't comment. She placed the tray on the low coffee table, turned on a lamp in the sitting area, and walked to the bed.

"The light was too much for her," Anna said. Rosita nodded and went into the bathroom, returning with a towel. She draped it over the lampshade, immediately muting the brightness of the light. Anna grinned. "Why Rosita, I think you might have done this before."

Rosita sniffed. "I watch American movies, too."

Anna laughed softly. She looked at Peel, who had opened the eye not covered by the ice pack. "Is that light okay?"

"Yes."

"How about the ice? Is it helping?"

"Yes, but it's dripping all over the bed. It will make a mess."

"Are you too cold?"

"It's cold, but it helps. At this point, I'll do anything."

"Rosita," Anna called. "Can you grab a towel from the bathroom? And maybe another blanket?"

Rosita went back into the bathroom, returning with a large towel, then left the room. Anna rolled the ice pack off Peel. Her face and hair were wet, and when Anna slid her hand along the pillow she could feel wetness there, too. "Can you roll toward me? I can put this towel under you so you don't have to lay on a wet pillow." She said all of this while wiping the moisture off Peel's face.

With a moan, Peel rolled toward Anna, who supported her back with one hand while she used the other to spread the towel over the pillow. When she was done, she gently rolled Peel back on the pillow and placed the ice pack back on her face. They stayed like that until Rosita returned with a blanket, laying it over Peel. "I think I can hold it now," Peel said to Anna.

"Are you feeling any better?"

"A little."

"Do you think you can sit up? If you eat something, you might be able to keep a pain pill down. Do you want to try?"

"Okay." Peel started to roll to her side and lift her head.

"Wait, wait. Let me help you." Anna moved the ice pack to the bedside table. "Do you want to sit up in bed or can you walk over to the table?"

"I don't think I want to stand up. Last night when I got out of bed, I had terrible vertigo. That's when I got sick."

Anna looked around the room. "In here?"

"No, I made it to the bathroom. I spent some time in there last night," she said.

The guilt was back, and it was keeping Anna from creating the distance she needed. Tomorrow. If Peel was better tomorrow, Anna would be more professional and make sure she knew her curiosity wasn't wise.

With a nod and a few quick words to Rosita, the two of them propped Peel up in bed. Anna backed away. "I'm going to wait for the doctor. Rosita will help you eat."

Peel looked at Anna, the pain clear in her eyes. "Thank you," she whispered. Anna ran from the room. The sight of Peel in such obvious pain troubled her more than she wanted to admit.

An hour later, she met with the doctor at the door. "I've given her another IV," he said. "She was dehydrated. I also gave her stronger pain medication. She will sleep most of the day."

Anna crossed her arms and looked at the doctor intently. "She was better yesterday. She even came downstairs. What happened?"

"That's the way it is with concussions. I'm sure she's had a constant headache. The vertigo she described is not unusual. She should be better tomorrow, but she has to stay hydrated and rested. I'll come back this evening and give her another IV and something to help her sleep through the night. Make sure she takes it easy for the next day or two, and you should be seeing improvement soon."

Anna nodded and walked him out of the house. Should she call Sebastien and update him on Peel's condition? She took out her phone but changed her mind. Anna needed to leave the estate this afternoon, and she was afraid Sebastien would order her to stay. She needed time away from this woman. Peel was a distraction, and Anna couldn't afford to be distracted. There was too much at stake.

She returned to her casita and changed out of the black uniform and into jeans and a tank top. She put on makeup, adding earrings and a long necklace. Shopping was just an excuse to visit Mexico City and her favorite bar. She planned to relax with several beers and a hot tourist.

That was the only kind of distraction she wanted.

CHAPTER TEN

The drive to Mexico City took just under two hours, but traffic congestion often meant Anna spent another two hours driving through the city. Usually she spent the time listening to an audiobook getting lost in the happier lives of other people. She looked forward to this time, a time when she could stop worrying about her parents, her brother, and the reach of the Disciples. But today she couldn't concentrate on a book. The sight of Peel in the darkened room brought back memories of Anna's mother and her heart problems. There'd been many nights when she sat on the side of her mother's bed soothing her worries and pain.

Anna had been a couple of months from graduation when Miguel called telling her their mother suffered a heart attack. When Anna arrived, her brother stopped her before she went into the hospital room.

"She needs surgery," Miguel told her.

"Okay," Anna said, her mind in turmoil. "When can they do it?"

"They can't. They won't let her stay here."

"What? Why?"

"They have no insurance. They said she has to go to Chicago Public."

"Chicago Public? No, she needs better care than that. I'll talk to them. Maybe they can work out a payment plan with us. I'll be able to afford it when I get a job." Anna met with the billing office, then an administrator. They were all kind, but unmoving. They couldn't help her mother unless she had insurance. That's why Chicago Public Hospital existed, they told her.

Miguel was gone when she returned to her mother's room. "He's going to ask Ojos for the money," her father told her.

Anna sank into a chair by the bed. "Oh, Papa, no."

Her father shrugged. "He's a man now. It is his decision to make."

"Papa, the gang will own him."

He looked at the still figure in the bed. "Our luck ran out, Anna."

Even though the Disciples of Gold ran her neighborhood, they never bothered Anna. They were looking for girlfriends, and Anna wasn't girlfriend material. She dressed in baggy sweats, never wore makeup, and tied her beautiful, long hair in a ponytail. While the other girls flirted and teased the boys, Anna barely noticed them, and they returned the favor. That left her free to escape into her classwork. She excelled in school.

Life wasn't like that for her brother Miguel. He didn't want to escape into school. He loved cars. At fourteen, he had the choice to attend a regular high school or a vocational school. He happily chose the vocational school and auto body technology. Like Anna, he was smart, and now that he had a passion for what he was learning, he quickly became a top student. By his sophomore year, he was working for a local body shop and helping his friends fix up their cars. Even though Miguel's skills were valuable, for some reason the Disciples left him alone, too. Maybe Papa was right. Maybe Ojos had just been waiting for their luck to turn.

The summer between her freshman and sophomore year in college, Anna had returned home to a shocking change.

Her parents had aged. Her mother had always worked six days a week cleaning houses in the suburbs. Her father, now in his mid-fifties, still did construction. It was backbreaking work, and he suffered in the hot summer sun and the frigid winter temperatures. They were tired. Her mother came home at night too exhausted to do anything other than shower and collapse into her chair. Her father came home bent over and sore. He was too old to do the physical labor required and lacked the skills to do anything else.

Anna watched helplessly as they became shadows in her life. It would be years before they could retire, and even then, she knew they couldn't live off their meager Social Security benefits. She took over all the cooking and cleaning, but that did little to ease her mother's burdens. For the first time, she realized how desperate their existence was. Her minimum wage job added a little relief, but it didn't give her mother an extra day off.

In the fall, she got some good news. Her financial aid included a work-study job on campus. She could take a full schedule of classes and still earn money to send home. When she met with the financial aid office, though, she was surprised that the only available position was secretarial support in the business college. "My major is criminal justice. I thought I would be working in that department," Anna said carefully.

"I got an unusual request from the business college for a bilingual student," the adviser explained. "They're willing to pay an additional dollar an hour to a qualified student. One of your professors heard about the opportunity and recommended you."

"Really?" Anna's voice went up an octave. "Who?"

He shuffled through the papers on his desk looking, then shrugged. "I don't remember. Someone who was impressed by you in class."

She started the next day. The business college had a different energy from the criminal justice department. There was an intensity and a professionalism that she found fascinating. Wealth and success were expected; so were hard work and intelligence. Like she had all of her life, Anna watched and learned. One afternoon in October, she was surprised when one of the younger professors turned from her mailbox and regarded Anna. "I teach most of the Intro to Business courses and haven't seen you in class. Did you transfer from another university?"

Anna widened her eyes, surprised to have been noticed. The woman laughed. "You think you're hiding, but you do know that most of the professors save their work for the days you're here, don't you?" Anna shook her head. "Well, we do, and sometimes we fight when someone monopolizes your time."

"Professor Dabney?"

The woman laughed delightedly. "You don't miss much, do you?"

"I try not to, Dr. Reynolds."

The use of the professor's name earned Anna a bright smile. "Good for you. Now why haven't you been in my class?"

"I'm a criminal justice major."

"Good God. Why?" Apparently, Dr. Reynolds wasn't big on tact.

"I really didn't know what else to do." Anna wasn't sure what it was about the professor, but she found herself being honest. "I didn't want to be a teacher or a social worker, so…"

"So, you thought that was the only other option? To be a cop?"

"Yes."

"What year are you?"

"Sophomore."

"Plenty of time. Do you know when my office hours are?" When Anna nodded, Dr. Reynolds continued. "I'll expect you tomorrow." Without waiting for an answer, she turned and walked out.

By the time Anna returned home for Christmas, she was an accounting major. She continued to watch the attitude and posture of the students and professors around her and learned to carry herself with the same confidence they did. The shyness that kept her safe in her neighborhood stood in the way of her success, so she forced herself to interact with other students and even started going out with her roommate. To her surprise, she found she enjoyed the nights out. A new love for beer didn't hurt, either.

With Dr. Reynolds's help, she had internships in large accounting firms the next two summers. This was a different Chicago from the one she knew. Women and men in expensive suits rushed from one towering building to another. What had been an intense focus in the business college was a cutthroat play for power in the accounting firms. She tried to talk to Dr. Reynolds about it, but the professor brushed off her concerns. "You don't need to worry. You'll learn fast, and soon you'll be comfortable in that world." Anna wasn't convinced, but she didn't argue with her mentor.

The summer internships kept Anna away from home. The university was closer to downtown, so she stayed in student housing. While she was gone, Miguel became the man of the family. The owners of the shop he'd worked in throughout school were thrilled to hire him full time when he graduated. With his income, her parents finally had breathing room. Her mother no longer worked Saturdays and her father was able to leave construction and worked for Miguel's boss. That was why her father had so easily accepted Miguel's right to make the decision to go to Ojos for the money for their mother's surgery.

After graduation, Anna had offers. The internships she hated, loved her. What wasn't to love? She was smart. She worked hard. She was Latina. They tiptoed around her, always careful about what they said, yet eager to point out the diversity she brought.

Then her mother's illness and her brother's actions took those choices from her. While her fellow graduates submitted their résumés to the big firms in downtown Chicago, she went to see Ojos.

Ojos Gutierrez, grandson of Carlos Gutierrez, ran the Disciples of Gold. The story of Carlos's immigration from Mexico and creation of the gang were legend in her neighborhood. Carlos never married, preferring to have a series of women at his command. He'd had several children, but only Ojos's mother had mattered to him. She was the daughter of the one woman he had loved, a woman who had been killed in an attack meant for him. Their daughter was the only child he raised and the only child he allowed in his life. She was sixteen when her mother was killed. Within a year, the girl was a pregnant addict. When Ojos was born, she took him to Carlos, then disappeared.

Ojos claimed to have gotten his name from his grandfather, given as a sign of affection for the young boy who followed him around watching his every move, but everyone knew that was a lie. The real story was shared among the Disciples as a cautionary tale. The nickname came when the youngest Gutierrez argued with Carlos over an order to act as a lookout during a drug deal. When Ojos protested he was too important to be merely a lookout, that he should be the brains and not the eyes, his grandfather sent him out of the room. Later Carlos Gutierrez told him that until he learned respect, he would remain the *ojos*. As a reminder of the lesson, the old man called him Ojos from that day forward. Everyone knew he hated the nickname, and so the older members of the gang made sure it was the only name he was known by. By the time his grandfather died, it was a symbol of the powerlessness he felt under the old man's thumb. It was also impossible to change it.

This was the man Anna had to meet with in order to pay her family's debt. When Ojos finally consented to the meeting, he barely spared her a glance. "Why do you think I want to do business with you?"

She knew she didn't have much time to convince him. He was volatile and would become violent at any perceived disrespect. "You saved my mother's life. I would like to pay our debt."

Ojos was not stupid, but he was vain. Those two traits worked in Anna's favor. He paused for a few moments, looking her up and down. "You are a college girl. An accountant? Why do I want an accountant?"

She'd taken time to study how money was laundered in organized crime. One afternoon, she'd dared Dr. Reynolds to come up with a "hypothetical" money-laundering scheme. Her professor was smart and her idea was good, so Anna proposed the plan to Ojos.

Ever since that day, she worked for the Disciples. She was scrupulously honest, knowing her brother's life depended on it. Together they repaid the money for the surgery along with an outrageous interest charge. That night, the two celebrated their freedom with cheap beer and a Cubs game. But Ojos had other ideas. The day after the final payment, Ojos drove a car to Miguel's shop for modifications. When Miguel protested, Ojos draped an arm around his shoulders. "Don't worry, you'll get paid for your work."

"Um, we're pretty busy at the shop. I was doing all of your work at night. I don't think I can fit it in, Ojos." Miguel was careful to stay respectful.

Ojos moved his arm so it was around Miguel's neck. "I wasn't asking. Have this ready by tomorrow." He took an envelope of cash out of his pocket and gave it to Miguel. Ojos patted Miguel's chest just over his heart. "How's your sister doing?" he asked.

She'd been working for Ojos for four years when she came across the newspaper article. She was stunned when she read it. It was so easy. She could set up a new revenue source and use it to bargain for her family. After putting a plan together, she went to see Ojos.

Anna started by laying out what she'd learned. "Mexico only has one gun store in the entire country, and it's on a military base. It's almost impossible to buy guns legally there. Most of the guns the cartels are using come from the US. They are purchased legally here, shipped across the border, and sold for three times the cost.

"There are other gangs in this business, but I think there's room for us to get into the market. Most of the gangs work directly with one cartel, just like we have with de Oro, but those gangs are all in southern border states. Those states have laws requiring dealers to report anyone who purchases more than a couple automatic weapons. We don't have that issue in the north," she explained.

Ojos stared at her. She could tell he was intrigued but didn't want to show it. "That easy huh? You want me to just send the guys out to Walmart and start buying AKs? Look around you. You think any of these guys is going to pass a background check?" He turned to the man seated next to him and laughed.

Before either could answer, she spoke. "There are hundreds of gun shows around us every year. Not every seller is a licensed dealer. Only dealers have to do background checks. If some guy has a table and wants to sell his gun collection, all we have to do is walk in with cash and walk out with untraceable guns."

Ojos scratched his chest. "How the fuck are we going to get AKs over the border? They'd be too heavy to fly ultralight from New Mexico." He was referring to the small aircraft the cartel used to transport marijuana.

"We don't have to fly them. We can drive them over. The Border Patrol isn't as concerned about what goes in to Mexico as they are about what comes out. The guns can be broken down and hidden in the same cars the mules have been using. Even better, dogs can't sniff guns."

Ojos kept his gaze fixed on Anna while she talked. She was careful not to hold his eye contact for long, so she looked down as she took a breath. When she looked up, he was still scratching, but now he seemed less interested in the opinions of his men. "How much?"

She had him. "You can make up to two to three thousand on every semi. If you add magazines and ammunition, a shipment of a hundred guns could bring four hundred grand. The gangs at the border are selling to the cartels at the border. Your connection is in Hidalgo, further south. There's a big untapped market in the south."

Ojos didn't blink or look away. His expression never changed.

"I have an idea about getting the money back, too." When he nodded, she continued. "The Caymans. You never have to bring money back to the States. You open accounts in the Caymans."

Now he laughed. "We just gonna fly money to the Caymans?"

"You can, or once the accounts are set up you can just deposit the money in Mexican banks and have them transfer to the Cayman accounts."

"And the money is clean."

"Exactly."

"What's in this for you, little girl?"

"Gratitude." This time she held his gaze.

"Bullshit. Who the fuck you think I am?"

"I need you to guarantee my brother's safety. And I need to get paid enough so my parents can retire and move out of the neighborhood."

"Why do you want them to leave our neighborhood?"

Anna was ready for this question. "Since Mama's heart attack she can't take the cold. I want to buy them a house in Texas and make sure they have enough money to live."

"You expect me to pay for that?"

"No, I expect you to pay me enough to take care of my family. I'm no different than anyone else. *Mi familia* comes first."

Ojos looked her up and down. "You know I can just take this and pay you nothing."

Anna anticipated this challenge, too. "You know anyone else who has the skills to organize the buyers? You know another accountant who can set up your accounts in Mexico and the Caymans? You need me, and you know you can trust me."

"I can, can't I? I own you and your brother." He turned to the man next to him and gestured with his head. The man immediately stood and walked toward Anna. The meeting was over.

Eight months later, she was in Mexico.

CHAPTER ELEVEN

Anna arrived in the Zona Rosa neighborhood of Mexico City in the early afternoon. It didn't take her long to buy clothes for Peel. She consulted the list of sizes and smiled to herself when she looked at the handwriting and thought of the woman's refusal to let Anna write them down. She also found herself choosing clothing she would like to see Peel wear. Rather than question her motives, she decided to just enjoy herself. More button-down shirts and low-cut tanks were in the bags than Peel requested. The bras were sexier than the one Peel had been wearing when she arrived. If she had any complaints, Anna could tell her Mexican women liked to look sexy. She grinned. This shopping spree was turning out to be a lot of fun.

By three she was ready for a beer. After locking her purchases in the SUV, she walked to her favorite bar in the middle of the gay-friendly area. Stepping into the dark room, she exhaled deeply and let her shoulders relax.

"Anna!" Smiling in greeting at the call of her name, she strode over to the bar just as her usual beer slid across the top.

"Juanita! Miss me?" she asked.

The bartender, a short, round woman, laughed delightedly and stepped around the bar to give her a hug. "Where have you been? You missed a lot of hot women last night. There was this one girl…" She waved her fingers to fan her face while she let her words trail off.

"American?" Anna asked.

"Another *turista*, just like you like 'em."

"She go home with anyone? You maybe?" Anna teased.

"You know better than that." Juanita sniffed. "I don't bring home strays." Juanita and her girlfriend had been together fifteen years. Even with all the girls who flirted with her, Juanita was never tempted. Anna wondered if it was love or fear that kept her friend in line. "She danced with a lot of girls but left alone. Maybe she's just waiting for a big girl like you."

Anna feigned outrage. "You have to say 'tall' to the *turistas*! If you say '*grande*,' they all think I'm fat. Did you tell her about me?"

Juanita flicked water at Anna. "Do you think you are my only sexy customer?" A group of women walked in through a door on the opposite side of the room and headed for the bar. "Go on," she told her as they walked up. "See if there's anyone for you to play with on the patio."

It was unusually warm for late May, so the place was more crowded than usual. A few women nodded at her when she stepped outside. A couple of others who obviously had been at the bar for a while looked her up and down. Anna ignored them. She had a type. Gay American tourists flocked to Amberes Street, many looking for an evening of fun on their vacation, and Anna was happy to provide it. She was exotic enough to make the fling exciting, but her American accent made the tourists feel safe. All she had to do was mention she was from Chicago, working in Mexico, and she had her pick of women. Sometimes, if she was really homesick or really liked the woman, she would spend the entire weekend in Zona Rosa.

Anna found a table in the corner of the patio and settled in to people watch. Now that she was seated, no one paid her any attention. She turned her face up to the bright sun and let out a deep breath. This was just the break she needed. She was definitely going to get a room for the night. Draining the last of her beer, she left the glass on the table to mark her place and stood to go inside. "Hey," she said in Spanish to a woman at a nearby table. "Could you make sure no one takes my table?"

The woman nodded. "You waiting for someone?" Anna knew it was an innocent question, but the woman's girlfriend didn't. She uncrossed her legs, leaned forward, and scowled at Anna.

This was why Anna didn't make friends in the local community. It was too easy to be misunderstood and get caught in lesbian drama. In her business she had to remain as unobtrusive as possible. To defuse the situation, she gave all her attention to the scowling woman. "I haven't decided yet. Let me know if you see someone." She winked.

The woman chuckled and said, "We'll watch the table."

The bar was more crowded than it had been, and Juanita was busy. With barely a glance at Anna, she reached for a glass and flipped the tap. She deftly filled the beer and slid it across the bar top. "I was just going to send someone out for you." She tilted her head to the side and Anna caught sight of three women leaning against the bar waiting to be served.

"Nice," Anna murmured as she brought her beer to her lips. "Let me buy their round."

Juanita poured tequila into three margarita glasses lined up on the bar. She huffed. "Since when do you pay for a drink? You want shots, too?"

Anna reached into her pocket and made a show of dropping twenty US dollars into the tip jar. "Of course. I don't have to get up early tomorrow." Juanita reached below the bar and set up four shot glasses. After pouring the clear liquid, she speared limes and placed them across the rims. Anna gathered the shot glasses in two hands. On her side of the bar Juanita picked up the margaritas, and the two made their way to the women.

An athletic-looking blonde tapped her credit card on the bar as Juanita approached. The bartender placed the margaritas in front of the three women and nodded over their shoulders to Anna, who was standing behind the group holding the shots. "Anna bought this round." To Anna, she said, "I'll bring your beer over."

Anna set the shot glasses on the bar and extended a hand to one of the women. "I'm Anna. Juanita said you're visiting from the States. She knows I get a little homesick," Anna explained with her best sheepish expression. The women all smiled back and introduced themselves—Deb and Carla were the couple, Jamie was the blonde.

"Where you from?" she asked.

"Denver," Jamie answered.

Anna flinched, and before she could catch herself, said, "I just met someone else from Denver."

"Here?" Jamie looked around the bar.

"No, she's staying nearby."

Deb or Carla asked, "Where are you from?"

"Chicago."

"You live in Mexico now?" At Anna's nod, Jamie asked, "What do you do here?"

Anna always answered these questions as close to the truth as possible. "I'm an accountant. Our company has a branch in Chicago and one a couple of hours from here. Since I'm fluent in Spanish, they sent me to Mexico."

Deb/Carla asked, "Do you like living here full time?"

"I do. The weather is much better than Chicago. When I first came, I thought it was going to be tropical, but it's really more like spring temperatures all year round. I love it. Plus, our offices are in a mountain valley, so the views are incredible." She reached for the saltshaker and offered it to the other women. Deb and Carla both licked their hands and sprinkled salt on the spot. Jamie just shook her head. Anna picked up one of the shot glasses. "To Mexico." The others picked up their glasses and echoed her toast.

After a sip of beer, Anna asked, "What do you guys do in Denver?"

Deb's answer helped Anna distinguish the couple. "Carla is an insurance agent. She won a trip anywhere in North America. We've always wanted to visit the Aztec and Mayan ruins, so we chose Mexico City."

Anna was impressed. "Don't most people choose a beach destination?"

Carla laughed. "We did that the last couple of years. It was time to do something different."

Anna turned to Jamie, who explained her place in the group. "They're my best friends, and I'm their designated third wheel. Pretty much wherever they go, they take me along."

Teasingly, Anna cleared her throat. "Well then…" she said, looking among the three of them. They all laughed.

Jamie playfully slapped her arm. "Get your mind out of the gutter. We are not sleeping together. That would be like sleeping with my sisters. They just think if they don't get me out of my house, I'll become a hermit." She looked affectionately at the couple next to her. "They're probably right."

"A hermit, huh?"

"It's not as bad as that. I'm just not big on going out."

"You're out now."

"And that's why they bring me. For some reason, when I'm on vacation I become the party girl. I drag them out to bars and clubs every night."

"Jekyll and Hyde," Carla said dryly.

"I can understand that," Anna said. "Why sit around in a hotel room? It's not your home, so you might as well go out."

"Exactly!" Jamie gripped her arm playfully. "Finally, someone who gets me."

"Oh, God." Deb groaned. "Unless you're going to move to Denver, don't encourage her."

Anna laughed and made eye contact with Jamie. "Well, since I can't move to Denver, what if I only encourage her a little?"

"Perfect," Jamie said.

The four women laughed and drank the rest of the afternoon. They sat on the patio enjoying the sunshine and gossiping. When the dance music started, they made their way inside where Jamie grabbed Anna's hand and led her out onto the dance floor.

She pulled Anna close and whispered in her ear, "I hate this kind of music."

Anna leaned her head back. "Then why are we dancing?"

Jamie pulled her in tight. "You know why."

They danced for a few songs, getting progressively closer and more sexual in their movements. When Anna leaned down to kiss Jamie, she was stopped with a hand to her chest. "We could make out here on the dance floor, or you could just walk me to my hotel."

"What will Carla and Deb think?" Anna didn't care, but she was curious about the answer.

"They'll wonder what took me so long." She grinned, then grabbed Anna's hand. Making eye contact with Deb and Carla, Jamie waved and they nodded their approval. Anna laughed.

The two wandered out into the cool night. Now that the sun was down, the temperature dropped into the sixties, and Anna's sweat cooled on her skin. She shivered a little. "Where are you staying?"

"It's close," Jamie said. "Do you think you can make it? Here." She pulled Anna tight against her body.

"Much better." Anna leaned down to kiss Jamie's cheek close to her ear. "But we should hurry," she whispered.

This time, Jamie shivered.

CHAPTER TWELVE

It was late morning by the time Anna arrived back at the estate. She stopped at the main house and unloaded her purchases for Peel, then headed to her casita for a shower. Rosita was in the kitchen when she returned. The older woman looked her over with a sly grin. "You look tired. Did you have trouble sleeping last night?"

Anna gave Rosita a wicked grin. "I didn't have trouble with anything last night." Rosita tutted and swatted at Anna with a dish towel. Anna leaned down and kissed the older woman's cheek, then asked, "How is she today?"

"She has only just gotten up." Anna glanced at the clock on the wall. It was nearly noon. "The doctor gave her a strong sleeping pill last night," Rosita explained. "He said it would help her feel better."

Anna reached for the tray Rosita was loading with silverware. "I'll take it up and see how she's doing." Anna picked up the tray and made her way up the stairs. Outside of Peel's room, she could hear movement behind the door. She set the tray down and knocked softly.

"Come in." Peel's voice was strong. Anna was surprised at the relief she felt at the sound. She turned the knob, picked up the tray, and pushed open the door.

Peel's smile was bright. Anna had to work to fix her face in an expressionless mask. "You must be feeling better," she said.

"Much. My headache is barely there. I think if I take the Tylenol, it will go away completely." Peel continued to smile.

"Good. The swelling seems to have gone down as well." Anna kept her tone businesslike with just a hint of ice.

Anna watched as a series of emotions crossed Peel's face— confusion, hurt, and finally, fear. "Is he here?" Peel asked, her voice a whisper.

"No, he's not here. I don't expect him for another day or so."

Peel exhaled and reached a shaky hand toward Anna. Anna sidestepped and walked to the sitting area. "You slept through breakfast. Rosita has some soup and tortillas for you. And water. The doctor said no caffeine until you're better." Anna didn't look at Peel as she placed the tray on the table.

"Anna, what's going on? Why are you angry? Why won't you look at me?" Peel stepped toward Anna.

Her resolve weakening, Anna looked into Peel's blue eyes and felt guilty. She felt guilty for being cold, and she felt guilty for being part of whatever Sebastien had planned. In the months she had been in Mexico, she'd heard stories of Sebastien's brutality. His cultured veneer barely covered the psychopath underneath. He was a man motivated entirely by greed and family loyalty.

"Anna?" Peel said again. When Anna didn't respond, she sank into a chair. "Oh my God. You know something, don't you? Is he…Did he tell you…" She couldn't get the words out. She struggled to catch her breath, then buried her head in her hands and started to sob. Anna's heart broke at the sound. She dropped to her knees in front of the chair and put her hands on Peel's thighs.

"Peel, I haven't talked to Sebastien in days. I don't know anything." She gently shook her thighs. "Peel, look at me, please."

Peel looked up. "I let myself think that everything would be okay, but it's not, is it?" She choked out the words. "How can it be? I'm being held prisoner by a Mexican drug lord. When he gets whatever he wants, he'll kill me." Sobs wracked her body, and she covered her face with her hands.

Anna went in search of tissues. She grabbed a box from the bedside table and placed it on the arm of the chair, then went into the bathroom and wet a washcloth with cool water. She looked at her reflection in the mirror, deciding to give the other woman privacy as she cried. Even though Peel had misread Anna's distance, her conclusions were not wrong. Sebastien had brought this woman into his home. He would never allow her to return to the US. She sighed heavily and looked back down at the water running into the sink. Her own eyes started to well with tears.

In many ways, Peel's experience mirrored hers. When she talked with Ojos all those months ago, she never dreamed she would end up here. She'd agreed to come to Mexico to set up their accounts. After the first shipment of guns had been sold, Sebastien flew her in his private jet to the Cayman Islands. She was accompanied by four of his men and a quarter of a million dollars. Once those accounts were opened, she returned to Mexico to set up transfer accounts in Mexican banks. Eventually, the cartel would deposit the cash from the gun sales into several different banks, always staying below the federal cash maximum. After a few days, the money would be transferred into the Cayman accounts and out of reach of the Mexican and American governments.

Anna spent a month at the estate. Sebastien was a gentleman and a thoughtful host. She enjoyed getting to know him and listening as he recounted the archaeological digs he had been on. When he told her the history of the native peoples of Mexico, his passion was contagious. She could see the teacher he once was. Her last night, she said as much. "You are an excellent teacher. Do you miss the university?"

"Every day," he answered. "But, my family needed me to return, and family comes first."

The next day her bag was packed when she joined him for breakfast. "Sebastien," she began. "I can't thank you enough for your hospitality." Whenever she talked with him, she found herself speaking more formally, echoing his own speech patterns. "Could you arrange for someone to drive me to Mexico City? My flight home leaves at one."

He delicately cut into his poached egg, then looked at her. "That won't be possible, Anna."

"Oh." She paused. "Uh, well, is there a bus I could catch?"

"No, Anna, you will be staying in Mexico. As my guest, of course."

"Sebastien, I can't possibly stay here. I can't organize the gun buys from here."

"Anyone can follow the system you set up. I spoke with Ojos and made it clear my continued partnership in this endeavor is contingent on you remaining in Mexico." He put his silverware on the edge of the plate and wiped his mouth with a white linen napkin. "Frankly, you are far too valuable an employee to waste with the Disciples." Sebastien's face showed the distaste he felt for his American relatives. "You will work for me expanding our arms shipments and markets."

"But, my family…"

"Yes," he said, leaning forward. "Your family." There was no trace of the passionate teacher in his look. She was talking to the head of the de Oro cartel.

"I understand. I'll cancel my ticket," she'd said.

A shuddering breath from the bedroom broke Anna's reverie. She squeezed the excess water out of the cloth and walked back into the sitting area. Peel's head was on the back of the cushioned chair and her eyes were closed. "Here," she said, gently touching Peel's shoulder.

Peel opened her tear-swollen eyes and, seeing the tissues, pulled several from the box. "Thanks," she muttered, and blew her nose. "Now I have a crying headache."

"This will help," Anna said as she folded the washcloth. "Lay back and put this over your eyes." Peel did. "I'm going to get you some herbal tea."

"Screw that," said Peel. "I'm not giving up caffeine when I'm about to die. Would you bring me coffee? Oh, and a shit-lot of cream."

"Peel, you don't know that." She held up her hand at Peel's protest. "However, I can tell you are in desperate need of coffee. I'll be right back."

When she returned with the coffee, Peel was in the bathroom. Anna filled her own cup and thought about the conversation they needed to have. Before she'd figured out how to start, Peel was sitting in the chair across from her. Anna watched her fill half of the mug with cream before topping it off with coffee.

"Peel, listen to me. I haven't talked to Sebastien. I don't know anything more about why you're here or what's going to happen." She held Peel's gaze for a few seconds before continuing. "You're right. I was different this morning, but it's because I'm trying to keep you alive." She leaned forward in her chair, willing Peel to understand. "The less you know about me, this place, Sebastien, the more likely you are to go home. If he believes you are a threat to him, he'll have you killed." She steeled her voice. "You have to stop asking questions. Do you understand?"

Peel took another shuddering breath. "Do you honestly believe he's not going to kill me, regardless of what I do?"

Anna looked down at her hands. "I don't know." She looked back to Peel's face. "But please don't give him a reason. I don't believe he'd go to all of this trouble just to get rid of you. He could have done that in Denver. Instead, he sent me to buy you clothes and told me to take care of you." She shook her head. "No, there's something he needs from you. He's not going to kill you."

"And if you're wrong?" Peel asked.

"I'm not wrong," Anna said firmly.

"But if you are." Peel leaned forward and looked at Anna. "If you are," she repeated. "Will you help me?"

"I'm not wrong," Anna said again. She stood, ending the conversation. "Eat. In the meantime, I'll bring up the clothes I bought for you."

Peel didn't answer for a long moment. "I'm not sure I want to take anything from him, but I guess maybe I shouldn't antagonize him."

"True, and wouldn't you feel better in your own clothes?" When Peel opened her mouth, Anna amended, "Well, clothes that are at least your size."

"Yeah, I guess I would. I suppose you'd like to have your own clothes back, too."

"I don't mind sharing." Strangely, Anna found she meant it.

While Peel ate, Anna brought the bags up and started to unpack them, stacking shorts, jeans, and tops on the bed. She left the undergarments in the bags. Peel got up and joined her. She ran her fingers over the piles, stopping when she came to the T-shirts. "They're cute, but some of them are a little low cut."

Anna did her best to look apologetic. "Yeah, I know, but that was the only style they had."

"Really?" Peel looked surprised. "I guess I haven't been shopping in a while. You didn't happen to get me underwear, did you?"

"That bag." Anna pointed.

Peel reached in and pulled out a lacy black bra. She looked up at Anna. "Um, this is a little, um…"

Anna feigned contrition. "I know, but I bought all of this in the same neighborhood. Latina women like to look sexy, so that's the style. There are a couple of other colors and styles in there. Oh, and I got you boy shorts."

"Uh, yeah. Thanks." Peel pulled out two other bras in equally revealing styles. Anna hid her grin. When she got to the bottom of the bag, she pulled out the boy shorts, which matched the bras in colors and styles. Peel looked at Anna. "Would it have helped if I'd mentioned I'm gay?"

Anna laughed out loud. "Nope. I already knew."

"Oh God, did I come out during the bath?" Peel turned a deep red.

Anna laughed even harder. "No, no, I have excellent 'dar."

"Realllly." Peel stretched out the word. "Are you gay, too?"

"So, you're telling me you have no 'dar at all?" Anna teased.

Peel blushed again. "I'll take that as a yes." Then she stopped. "Why are you telling me this? Isn't that revealing too much?"

Anna shrugged. "It's not a secret. Everyone here knows I date women."

"Even Sebastien?"

"He used to be a university professor. He's surprisingly open-minded for a Mexican man."

"And a drug lord," Peel added.

"That, too." She paused, then despite her reservations said, "I'll be down in the kitchen if you want to come downstairs today. We can walk around the grounds if you like. There are sunglasses in one of the bags. Oh, and sunscreen."

"Anna." Peel put a hand on Anna's forearm, stopping her from leaving. "Please don't be cold to me. I promise I won't ask any more questions."

Anna nodded and looked away. The guilt resurfaced. "Okay."

* * *

An hour later, Peel walked into the kitchen wearing shorts, one of the low-cut T-shirts, and sunglasses. Anna thought she looked amazing. "*Buenas tardes*," she said to Rosita. "Lunch was wonderful." She looked at Anna, who translated her words to the housekeeper. Rosita smiled and patted Peel's arm.

"Are the sunglasses helping?"

"So far. Do you have a baseball cap? I think that would help when we go outside."

"Sure. Have another cup of coffee with Rosita while I get it."

"I could just go with you?" Peel made the statement sound like a question.

"No, have some more coffee," Anna said as she walked out. Within minutes she was back with a blue Cubs hat. Peel snorted at the logo and put the cap on. "Does anyone in that town cheer for the White Sox?"

"Yes, but we don't speak to them." Anna gestured to the doors. "Come on. The grounds are beautiful."

Anna opened a pair of French doors and motioned for Peel to step out onto a stone patio that ran the length of the back of the house. Dining and café tables were interspersed with cushioned chaises and benches. Potted plants broke up the hardscape with lush greenery. Three matching fountains were spaced along the length providing calming background sounds. A long bar top with stools facing an oversized TV filled one corner.

"Wow, I'd be out here all of the time," Peel said. "Does anyone ever use this?"

"Sebastien does. He likes to have parties. Sometimes if there is a big *fútbol*—you know, soccer—game, he lets the men sit at the bar and watch. Do you want to sit here, or do you want to see the pool area?"

"Let's go to the pool, but then can we come and sit up here for a while?" Peel asked.

"Sure. C'mon."

They followed a wide stone pathway over an expanse of grass. "Who takes care of all of this?"

"Gardeners come from Tierra. They're here every morning. I'm surprised you haven't heard them."

"I haven't heard anything. But I think I've been pretty drugged up." Peel looked around. "Where's the pool?"

Anna walked several feet ahead of her, then pointed below them. "Right there." The estate was landscaped in terraces. The upper terrace held the main house, the patio, and an expanse of lawn. As they continued down the path, the lower terrace opened up before them.

Peel stopped and turned a slow circle. "All of this is Sebastien's?" she asked.

"Yes. Rosita said it has been the family home for generations. You can see that all of this is relatively new, probably added by Sebastien." They continued walking, taking the stairs to the lower terrace. Sunlight sparkled off the deep blue mosaic tiles, giving the edges a jewel-like quality. The pool deck was wide and made of the same stone as the upper patio. Lounge chairs protected by large umbrellas surrounded the pool on three sides. On the fourth was a pool house and another covered patio, underneath which was another bar and kitchen area. TVs were mounted along the wall. "This is my favorite spot to be, even though the men are close by," Anna told her.

"The men?"

"They live in barracks behind that line of trees."

"Do you live in barracks?"

"No, thankfully I stay in a little casita right over there." She pointed to the small structure barely visible through a stand of trees. A stone walkway connected the building to the pool deck.

Peel grabbed her forearm. "Can we see it?"

Anna ground her teeth. "No."

Peel must have seen the set of her jaw, because she dropped it. "Do you use the pool much?"

"I swim laps every morning. Rosita thinks I'm crazy, but it's a form of meditation for me."

"Well, that explains why your arms are so defined."

"Oh?" Anna cocked her head. "Have you been checking out my arms?"

"You've been lifting me in and out of bed for days now. It's hard not to notice." Peel bumped up against Anna.

After they'd walked all the way around the pool deck, Anna asked, "Back up to the patio, or do you want to stay down here?"

"Let's stay here. I want to put my feet in the pool. Is it warm?"

"You'll love it. I'll get some towels and set up the loungers." When Anna came out of the pool house, she saw Peel had removed her new sandals and was dipping the toes of one foot into the water. She lowered herself onto the deck and stretched her feet in front of her. Anna watched as Peel stared at the water, moving her feet in circles.

Anna walked up behind her. "Do you want to sit on one of these towels?"

Peel startled, then turned, taking the towel. "Thanks. I was lost in thought." Anna sat down beside her and dropped her own feet into the water.

Peel took off her sunglasses and looked at Anna. Very quietly, she said, "Anna, could you just answer one thing for me? I promise this is it."

Anna looked straight ahead into the blue of the pool. Finally, she said, "If I can."

"Don't answer me if you aren't going to tell me the truth, okay?"

Now Anna turned to her, puzzled. "Okay."

"Is there a reason other than loyalty to Sebastien that you won't help me?" At Anna's grimace, she rushed on. "I guess, I really need to know if you are unwilling or unable."

Anna continued to stare into the pool. She found she wanted to tell this woman the truth and ignore potential consequences. "My family."

Peel nodded. "I understand. I promise, I won't bother you again." Peel paused. "Are they safe?"

"One question only? I should have known better." She shook her head and then stood up. "I'm going to get us bottles of water, then I'm going to sit in the shade."

* * *

Anna was awakened by a ringing phone. She fumbled around until Peel picked it up and placed it in her hand. She was in the chair next to Anna, smiling at her confusion. Anna rubbed her eyes and answered. "*Hola*, Rosita." After listening for a few moments, she said, "*Un momento*," then pulled the phone away from her ear. "Rosita wants to know where we want to have our snack."

"McDonald's," Peel answered.

"Ha ha, very funny. Do you want to eat down here?"

"That's too much bother. Let's go up to the house. Maybe we can get our plates and sit on the patio. The reflection of the sun off the water is beginning to get to me anyway."

Anna talked to Rosita, then put her phone away. "You should have said something sooner. I don't want you to have another setback."

Peel shook her head. "It's nothing like that. Plus, I'm being really careful. I'll probably take a nap just to be sure."

"Good." Anna stood and held out her hand to help Peel up. Peel stood but didn't release Anna's hand. They looked at each other for a long moment, then Anna stepped closer, starting to speak. The ringing of her phone stopped her. She pulled it out of her pocket and started to swipe across the bottom when her hand stopped in midair. Sebastien. She straightened, turned her back, and walked away from Peel. For several minutes, she had a quiet conversation. When the call ended, she took a deep breath and turned to face Peel.

"He's here," Peel said, her face ashen.

"Tonight. He'll be here after dinner. I'm supposed to bring you to his study at eight."

Peel nodded. "Please tell Rosita I'm sorry, but I'm not feeling well. I'm going to lie down."

"Peel…" Anna reached for her.

"It's okay. I'll see you tonight."

CHAPTER THIRTEEN

Peel paced from the bathroom to the sitting room. After nearly a week, she would finally find out why she was here. But as much as she wanted answers, she was terrified to meet Sebastien Gutierrez. There was a knock at her door, then Anna called, "Peel, it's Anna."

She pulled it open. "Anna," she began, but stopped abruptly when she saw her.

Anna was dressed in a black T-shirt tucked into black military-style pants. Her hair was pulled back into a severe ponytail. The grim line of her mouth and distant eyes warned Peel. Still, she tried to connect with her. "Anna?" she asked tentatively.

Anna's expression didn't change. "This way," she said, her voice flat. They walked down the staircase to a set of double doors Peel hadn't noticed before. Anna opened one side to reveal a long hallway that Peel guessed ran parallel with the back of the house. Anna led her past three closed doors, only stopping when they reached a massive wooden door at the end of the hallway. Anna knocked, opened the door, and gestured for her to enter. Peel stepped in and heard the door quietly close behind her. She looked back, but Anna was gone.

"Miss Primm, it is so nice to finally meet you." The man who spoke stood in front of a wall of floor-to-ceiling windows. He walked toward her, his hand extended. "I'm Sebastien Gutierrez." Without thinking, she clasped his hand.

Sebastien was taller than she, but not by much. He was dressed in dark pants, boots, and a white button-down shirt, the sleeves rolled up to reveal tanned forearms. His watch was military style, the band an army-green canvas strap. He wore rimless glasses, and his salt-and-pepper hair was trimmed close to his head.

Without asking, Sebastien went to a cart of liquor bottles, selected two balloon glasses, and poured two inches of liquor in each. "Cognac," he said as he handed the glass to her. Since it wasn't a question, she took the glass and murmured her thanks. The glass vibrated in her hand. Peel was sure he noticed.

Sebastien directed her to a chair in front of the window. "This is one of my favorite rooms in the house." His tone was conversational, friendly. Peel looked away from him and took in her surroundings. One side of the room was lined with glass cabinets lit from within. They were filled with a variety of objects Peel couldn't identify. Sebastien followed her gaze. "Are you interested in archaeology?" Without waiting for a reply, he continued. "I spent many years unearthing the treasures of my country for museums and universities. All that hard work only for the most valuable and unique artifacts to be stolen from the people and sold on the black market." He stood and walked over to the cabinets. "When I left the university, I decided that I would no longer participate in the misappropriation of the Mexican culture. Now I, too, buy off the black market." He took a sip of his drink. "Please try the cognac." Mechanically, she complied. The alcohol was smooth on her tongue, then burned pleasantly as she swallowed. She took another, larger sip.

Sebastien stood and beckoned for her to join him in front of the cases. She walked to the glass and looked at shelves of pottery, figurines, disks, and even a couple of masks. The condition of the artifacts surprised her. These weren't the shards or reassembled objects like she'd seen on her visits to the museums around Denver. Each piece was pristine. For the first time, she spoke. "Did you find all of these pieces?"

"Some," he said. "But many of my discoveries have been lost to private collections all over the world." His accent was lyrical, his English formal. "I have contacts who keep me informed when an artifact shows up. I make sure I am the highest bidder. Someday, when I am convinced the museums in Mexico are no longer corrupted by politicians, I will give this collection to the people. For now, I am merely a guardian." He walked over to the tray of bottles, refilled his glass, and then lifted the bottle to Peel. "Another?"

Other than the two swallows she had taken on command, Peel hadn't touched her drink. "No, thank you." Her voice was steadier.

He returned to his chair, crossed his legs, and straightened the pressed seam of his pants. "From the time I was a child, I was fascinated with Mesoamerica and our indigenous civilizations." She followed him and sat. "I wanted to unearth our ancient history and preserve it so generations of Mexicans could learn of the powerful people we once were. I wanted schoolchildren to go to museums and see all that was accomplished before the invaders destroyed Mexico. This is what is left of my dreams." There was a passion in Sebastien's voice and an intensity in his eyes that mesmerized Peel.

"Gabriel Devin killed my dreams."

Peel started in her chair. She sat up and placed the glass on a side table. "Who's Gabriel Devin? My great-grandfather's name was Charles Devin."

"So I've been told. Gabriel Devin is his grandson. For a while, I thought Gabriel Devin might be your father, but"— Sebastien gestured to Peel—"once I saw your picture, I knew that was unlikely."

"My picture? Where did you see my picture?"

In answer, he walked around his desk and picked up a piece of paper. He held it up so she could see. It was a printout from the Plains Public Library homepage. Peel's picture was there along with the other librarians and staff members. "You looked me up? Was this because I called the library in Tierra de Oro?"

"Yes. That was fortunate. It was also fortunate that you spoke to the wife of one of my longtime employees. She recognized the name right away."

"You kidnapped me because my great-grandfather is Charles Devin?" Even though Peel had suggested the connection to Detective Bellamy, the reality was hard to believe.

"No." Sebastien took a sip of his cognac, clearly enjoying the moment. "I brought you here to find Gabriel Devin."

"I have no idea who he is. I didn't even know the name Devin until a few weeks ago," Peel protested.

"Tell me how that is possible." The command was polite, but she heard the doubt in his voice.

Peel explained her family history and the discovery of the birth certificate. Sebastien tapped his middle finger on his crossed leg as she spoke. When she finished, he looked at her as if he were judging her honesty. After a long moment of silence, he said, "Gabriel Devin was in charge of the police force in the Tierra de Oro region. He was an angry and bitter man who despised my family and did everything in his power to destroy us. He and his brothers very nearly succeeded."

"Brothers?"

"Yes, he had three brothers, Pedro, Hector, and Cesar."

"Had? What happened to them?"

"Gabriel Devin's blind hatred of my family killed them." He looked at the glass on the table. "May I replenish your drink?"

"No, thank you," she replied.

"In Mexico, marijuana and heroin are big business. They are an essential part of our economy providing a guaranteed income to farmers and jobs for those who don't own land. In Tierra de Oro, the people depend on it, and they depend on my family to take care of them. We are an industry, just like any other. Gabriel Devin sought to destroy that industry."

Peel blinked and shook her head in confusion, "But isn't your business illegal in Mexico? If he was a policeman, wasn't it his job to stop you?"

He waved aside her question. "Yes, in the same way smoking marijuana is illegal in much of the United States. Does your police force waste time finding people who smoke marijuana?" He paused, but the question was rhetorical. "No, because it is not a crime they care about. That is how it is in Mexico. The drug trade benefits the people. It puts food on their tables."

Peel stared at him. Was that really how it was in Mexico?

"You've never heard this side of the story before, have you? Tell me, what does your government do about tobacco? They know it is harmful. What have they done to stop it?" Against her better judgment, Peel found herself nodding.

"It is easy for the United States to interfere in Mexico. No American farmers have to lose their farms, no husbands are out of work. The Mexican government has to appease Washington by making our industry illegal, but they don't have to enforce these laws."

"I don't understand," Peel said. "I've heard of the Mexican police arresting cartel leaders. What about El Chapo?"

Sebastien laughed. "And where is El Chapo now? The United States. Another form of appeasement." He looked at his watch, frowned, and set his glass down. "I'm sorry, I must cut our conversation short. There is business I must attend to." He stood and gestured for her to precede him. When they reached the door, he opened it for her. "We will talk more tomorrow." He looked at a man just outside the door. "Please escort Miss Primm back to her room."

The door closed softly behind her. That was it? She was no closer to understanding why she was here or when she could go home. With a heavy sigh, she followed the man back to her room.

She got ready for bed but was too agitated to lie down. Again, she paced, her mind whirling with the information she had learned. Gabriel Devin had been a policeman in Tierra de Oro who tried to bring down the Gutierrez family. What happened to his brothers? What happened to him? She wished she could talk to Anna. Maybe Anna couldn't help her escape, but maybe she could help her find out what happened. But then she remembered how Anna behaved when she escorted Peel downstairs. There would be no help there.

There was a light knock on the door, and she felt a surge of excitement at the sound. She hurried over and opened it. Rosita stood in front of her with a tray of tea and chocolates. When Peel didn't immediately respond, Rosita said, "From Anna."

Relief washed over Peel. Anna wasn't indifferent. Fervently, she said, "*Gracias*, Rosita. *Por favor*, tell Anna, *gracias*."

CHAPTER FOURTEEN

The next morning, Rosita appeared at Peel's door bearing her breakfast tray and a note: "Please join me for coffee in the solarium at 9:00. Sebastien."

Promptly at nine, Peel crossed the threshold to the beautiful garden room. Sebastien was seated at an iron table shaded by a canopy of citrus trees. Ceiling fans provided a gentle breeze while a three-tiered fountain splashed into one end of a pond. She caught glimpses of orange fish darting around the edges and near blooming lilies. Terra-cotta tiles interspersed with bright Mexican hand-painted ones covered the floor. In a different world, Peel would have been enchanted by the sights and sounds of the room.

"Miss Primm, please join me." Sebastien stood as she approached the table.

"Thank you," Peel murmured.

"I've asked Anna to join us this morning. She had to finish a phone call, so she may still be a few minutes. May I pour you some coffee?"

Peel found herself both charmed and disturbed by his manners. "Please." She reached for the cream, added it to the dark brew, and took a small sip. Now what? Should she make small talk? "This room is lovely."

"Ah, thank you. I love it in here. So peaceful. No matter how crazy the world is, I can always relax with the smell of the fruit and the sound of the fountain." Sebastien stood as he finished the sentence, and Peel looked up to see Anna approaching the table.

Anna was dressed exactly as she had been the night before. She wore the same aloof expression, too. Her eyes darted to Peel, then quickly looked away. Sebastien went through the same ritual of offering and pouring Anna coffee, then topping off his and Peel's.

After they each fixed their coffee and sat in silence for a moment, Sebastien said, "I know you are wondering why I brought you here. I want to thank you for your patience as I completed some business out of town." He paused as if waiting for a response from Peel. She nodded.

"I want to tell you both the story of my family." He turned to Peel. "I never wanted to run the family business. It was supposed to go to my brothers. From the time they were little, my father groomed them to take over. He was a good teacher, and they were both very smart. Before the arrests, my father was already moving more and more of the daily control over to them." He paused and sipped his coffee, looking to the fountain as he did.

"It was a happy time for the family and for Tierra de Oro. I remember going to mass on Sundays watching people pay their respect to my father or thanking him for some kindness he'd shown their family. He was like that. He felt responsible for the town, and he took care of its people." Sebastien looked directly at Peel, the wistfulness gone. "Little did we know there was, as they say, a snake in the garden." His direct look became a piercing stare. She couldn't look away. "Gabriel Devin." He spit the name out.

"Everything changed in 1987. One night, the Tierra Police and the Mexican Army broke into our home. They ordered my father and brothers to the floor and held guns to their heads while they handcuffed them. My mother and my brother's wife Yolanda cried and begged the soldiers not to hurt them. Even though he lay facedown on the floor in handcuffs, my father tried to calm them. The animals clubbed him in the back of the head for talking. Then they left him, left all of them, lying on the floor while they destroyed our home. Everything was torn apart. They ripped open cushions and mattresses, sliced paintings, our family portraits. They broke anything they could get their hands on." Sebastien's face was flushed as if he still felt the humiliation of that night. "The leader of those men." He paused for effect. "The man who hit my father." Another pause. "Was Gabriel Devin."

Neither Peel nor Anna spoke. Peel gritted her teeth, her jaw aching.

"My father and brothers were sent to prison. The estate and all of our assets were seized. My mother had to come and live with me in Mexico City. Yolanda took my nephew Eduardo and returned to her family. No one would tell me where they had been taken, just that they were in 'protective custody' for their own good. Of course, it was all a lie.

"After two years in prison, the Mexican government came to my father and told him the truth. They never cared about our family business. They wanted to rid Mexico of the American mafia. In return for telling them what he knew about the Vizcano family, Papa would be released from prison, our home would be returned, and my brothers' sentences would be commuted. Of course, he accepted. He, too, saw the American mafia as a blight on Mexico and regretted that his family had ever formed an alliance with the Vizcanos." Sebastien took a delicate sip of his coffee.

"My father's homecoming was a celebration in Tierra de Oro. For days people came to the estate with food and drink to honor Papa and welcome him home. While he had been in prison, our people struggled. The army and police offered little protection when other, more violent cartels tried to take over de Oro. My father's return ensured the people would once again be safe and the town prosperous."

Rosita walked in carrying a fresh carafe of coffee. Sebastien paused his story and spoke to Rosita. She patted his hand and bustled out. "Do you speak Spanish, Miss Primm?" he asked. When she shook her head, he translated. "I asked Rosita to bring us more pasties. Have you tried them yet? They're famous in the area."

Peel answered in the same polite tone. "I have. They are delicious."

They busied themselves refreshing their coffees until Rosita returned with the hot pasties. After she left and he had helped himself, Sebastien continued. "The celebration was short-lived. Within two months, both of my brothers had been murdered in prison. We were told it was retaliation from the Vizcanos, but my brothers should have been out of prison before then. Later, our lawyers told us Gabriel Devin was responsible for delaying their release.

"I never believed the Vizcanos were responsible for their deaths. They were already weak in Mexico and wouldn't have had enough allies in the prisons to arrange my brothers' murders." Sebastien leaned forward. "That left only two options: another cartel, or Devin."

Peel looked down, unable to hold Sebastien's intense gaze. She was beginning to understand why she was here. No matter how distantly related to Gabriel Devin she was, she would pay for his sins. She steadied herself and looked back up. "Is that why I'm here? Are you going to kill me like he killed your brothers?"

There was a long silence. Neither Peel nor Anna moved. Finally, he answered. "Not quite." Gutierrez sat back again, appraising Peel. "But, you are here because you are a Devin." Peel glanced at Anna. Had she known this all along?

"I was still in Mexico City when my brothers died. Papa called in the middle of the night to tell me what happened. I'll never forget the sound of his sobbing. I left the university the next day and never returned. My father was a broken man, so it fell on me to rebuild the family business. The first thing I did was collect on the debt owed to my family.

"For the two years my father and brothers were in prison, your cousin did his best to destroy Tierra de Oro. He didn't care that there were children without fathers or food. All he cared about was ruining my family and shutting down our business. He was arrogant." Sebastien's mouth tightened. "So very arrogant. He thought the people were grateful for what he had done. They didn't feel gratitude, they feared him. They despised him."

Peel could see the anger building behind Sebastien's polite façade. His eyes were pinpoint and focused on a tree in the distance. "Gabriel Devin owed my family a debt, and I made sure he paid." He looked back at Peel. "He knew the people were angry, so he tried to gain favor by building a *fútbol* field." Sebastien snorted in disgust. "Like the people could be bought with grass. When the field was completed, Devin planned a celebration where he and his brothers would make speeches about how they were the heroes of Tierra de Oro."

Sebastien leaned forward, fixing his gaze on Peel, making sure she heard his every word. "First, I had his wife killed. Then, while he rushed to her side, I killed all of his brothers, just as he killed mine." He paused before adding, "I left him a present, though. I spared the life of his daughter." She stared at him in horror, and his smile broadened. "But I promised I would be back for her."

Peel felt the bile in her throat. She covered her mouth, stood, and ran from the room.

* * *

Anna watched her go. Slowly, she turned to look at the man sitting across from her. Sebastien was still smiling. "Perhaps you should check on her," he said.

Anna stood and found herself a little unsteady. She was used to the violence of the cartel, but this was different. Sebastien's brief flash of anger was the only emotion he had shown during his story. That is, until the smile.

She reached the bathroom and knocked on the door. "Peel, it's Anna. Are you okay?"

Peel threw open the door. Her eyes were red and she could barely get the words out through her sobs. "Am I okay? Did you hear him? He murdered the entire family."

It was instinct, and she did it as much for herself as for the woman in front of her. Anna pulled Peel into a tight embrace while Peel sobbed in her arms. After a few minutes she lifted her head and looked into Anna's eyes. "Did you hear what he said when I asked if he was going to kill me?" She took a shuddering breath and repeated the words: "'Not quite.'"

Anna's response was to pull Peel back into her embrace. She, too, was stunned by Sebastien's response to the question. She thought about it while she held Peel. Did he want Peel dead? She didn't think so. No, he wanted Peel to play a part in a long-held revenge fantasy. The question was, what would happen to the woman in her arms when the fantasy was over? Anna loosened her hold on Peel but still held on to her upper arms. "Come on," she said quietly. "I'll take you up to your room."

Peel stepped out of Anna's arms. The two made their way up the stairs to the closed door of Peel's room. "Do you want me to have something sent up?" Anna asked.

Peel just shook her head, opened the door, and disappeared inside. When the door clicked shut, Anna let out a long breath she hadn't realized she was holding. She needed to go back to the solarium and tell Sebastien that Peel wouldn't be back.

When she returned to the solarium, Rosita was clearing the dishes. There was no sign of Sebastien. Rosita looked up. "He took a phone call. He wanted me to tell you that he will meet with you after lunch." Anna nodded, touched Rosita's arm, and left without another word.

CHAPTER FIFTEEN

Anna knocked on the open door to Sebastien's study. He was sitting behind his large desk working on a laptop. When he heard her knock, he stood and beckoned her inside. "Please sit, Anna." Warily, she complied.

"Where are we with the latest shipment?"

Anna straightened, surprised by the question. Earlier in the week when he'd ordered her to take care of Peel, they'd talked about the delay from Chicago. "Uh, I haven't contacted them since our last renegotiation. I assume they are still delayed."

"Assume?" He lifted his eyebrows at her.

He had her off-balance, and she needed to regain her confidence. It wasn't good for her to act unsure of herself, or worse, frightened of him. "Yes, assume. As you asked, I have spent the week nursing Miss Primm back to health. You told me to prioritize that above all else."

Sebastien inclined his head. "You are right. I did tell you that, but a few things have changed. Contact Ojos again. Tell him he has two weeks. If he can't make his deadlines, I will work with organizations who can."

Anna hesitated. "I haven't spoken to Ojos since he called about Miss Primm."

"I know. I've been keeping him busy, but now I need him to understand that any more delay will cause us to change our allegiances."

Anna stayed in her chair. "I don't usually speak directly with Ojos. He's more receptive if he doesn't feel like he's getting orders from me."

"Ah, yes. Ojos does have an ego. It is time for him to realize that he and his friends work for de Oro, not the other way around. The heart of the family is in Mexico, not Chicago. He also needs to learn that you speak for me. Make the call." Anna acquiesced with a nod. She stood.

"Let me know as soon as it is done," Sebastien added as she reached the door. "Make very sure he understands I have other options."

"Of course."

"We will continue our conversation with Miss Primm this evening. See that you are available."

Anna closed the door behind her. She walked through the house and across the grounds, noticing the number of guards patrolling the estate. Now that Sebastien was home, there were far more men around. Several traveled with him, but others were called into service when he was home.

She unlocked the door to the casita and checked each of the small rooms. Even though the men on the estate seemed to understand she was off-limits, Anna wouldn't leave her safety to chance ever again. Sighing, she sat on the love seat and looked out the French doors. Through the trees, she could just make out the blue of the pool.

She let the reflection on the water soothe her as she picked up the phone and dialed Ojos's number. He would refuse to answer. When it went to voice mail, she left a short message telling him she was calling on Sebastien's behalf and needed to talk with him right away.

Within minutes, her phone rang. It wasn't Ojos. It was one of his lieutenants, Mute. Like many other gang members who tried to create their own nicknames, Mute's had failed. He wanted to be called Mutant, but the extra syllable proved to be too much trouble for Ojos. Thus, the shortened version of his name.

"Mute?" Anna answered.

"Ojos is pissed. He wants to know why you haven't called before now."

"Mute, Sebastien knows he called me about the woman. He hasn't said anything about why she's here."

"You called to tell him that?"

"I have a message for him from Sebastien. I was told to give to him directly."

"Hold on." The phone was silent, then Mute was back. "He said you should tell me."

Anna knew this was how the conversation would go. She had to be both strong and deferential at the same time. "Look, tell him I don't like it either, but Sebastien has concerns about our deal. I'm like you guys, I just follow the orders I'm given." The phone was silent again. Then it disconnected. Anna sighed. She'd wait an hour or so and then try again.

Within ten minutes, her phone rang again. This time it was Ojos. "What the fuck is this?"

"Look, Ojos, I don't like being in the middle of this, but I don't have a choice. As long as I'm here, I do what he says when he says it."

"You fucking work for me. You do what I say when I say it." He was screaming. "Why did you tell Sebastien I called?"

Anna cursed. This was the problem with having her attention focused on Peel. She hadn't even considered how Sebastien knew about the call. Someone in the Disciples was leaking information to Sebastien. "No. I didn't tell him anything. Look, all I know is that I don't call the shots. Who I work for is between you and Sebastien, but if he tells me the deal is in trouble, you know I'm going to warn you."

Ojos wasn't appeased. "What's this bullshit, 'the deal is in trouble'? You're the one that made this fucking deal. You're fucking pissing me off, Anna."

"He says you have two weeks to fill the order or he's going to find someone else."

She could feel Ojos's rage through the phone. "Fuck you and fuck Sebastien. Tell him I'm done talking to a *puta*. This is between family." The phone went dead.

She threw her head back on the love seat cushion. She'd told Sebastien this is how it would go. He was insulting Ojos by having Anna call and make the threat. For what reason? Despite Sebastien's directive, she should have started with Mute.

She picked up her phone and dialed her brother. He answered with his usual greeting. "Hey, sis."

"Hey, Miguel," she replied. "What're you up to? You busy?"

"Just hanging out in the break room drinking a Coke. You called at a perfect time."

"Mama and Papa get moved?"

"Yep."

"Like we planned?"

"Yep. Why don't you call them?"

Anna ignored his question. "Any chance you can make a parts run, or do something to get out of town for a day or so?"

Miguel's voice was wary. "Why? What happened?"

Anna kept her brother in the dark about her work, but she was worried about Ojos's unpredictability. "Nothing too much. I just made Ojos even angrier, and I don't want it to blow back on you."

"He threaten you?" She could hear the tension in her brother's voice.

"No, just the usual. He was pissed, called me a whore, you know how it goes." Anna needed to downplay the interaction before Miguel overreacted and got hurt.

"He fucking called you a whore? Fuck that guy—"

Before he could go any further, Anna interrupted him. "Shut up, Miguel. You know better than to say shit like that. He's pissed at Sebastien, and for some reason, I'm in the middle of the fight. Just leave town, okay?"

She heard her brother's heavy sigh. "Okay, I guess I can make a run to St. Louis."

"Leave now, okay?"

"That bad?" he asked.

"Yes."

"Okay, I'll change and take off."

"Thanks, Miguel. I'll call you when it's okay to come back." She paused. "But don't change your clothes. Just go. Love you." She hung up, not wanting to delay him any longer.

Tapping her fingers on the armrest of the love seat, she contemplated her options. She had done exactly what Sebastien had ordered. She'd told Ojos. There was nothing else she needed to do other than share Ojos's response.

Sebastien was waiting for her. "What took you so long? Ojos called me ten minutes ago."

Anna didn't hesitate. "I called my brother."

"Wise. Ojos is very angry with you."

"Just me?" Anna wasn't surprised Ojos would blame her.

Sebastien chuckled at her reaction. "You thought he would be angry with me? He knows he is just a cog."

"Why did you want me to call him? You knew how he would react."

"That is precisely the reason. He needs to understand how little he means to our organization. If a *'puta'* can put him in his place, he is very small, indeed." Anna glared at him. "Ah, now I've made you angry. I was merely motivating him. I have a potential new buyer for the guns, but I can't wait for him to get organized. We have three weeks to get everything ready to deliver."

"A new buyer?" she asked. "Does that mean I need to get two shipments ready?"

"No, this is a special buyer. He takes priority. You have a different project for now. I need to demonstrate my loyalty to this buyer before he will agree to the sale. To do that, Miss Primm has a very important task to complete. You will continue to be my eyes on her at all times."

"Come through with what?"

"I'll explain everything tonight. This could be very big for us, Anna."

* * *

Peel spent the afternoon in bed. Her headache had returned, and she could hardly move. When Rosita brought her lunch, she took one look at Peel's pale face and handed her two pills. Peel took them gratefully and fell into a drugged sleep.

Rosita was back in the early evening with more chicken soup. She touched Peel's shoulder to wake her, then once again handed her a note. "Please join me at 8:00 in my study. Sebastien." Peel dropped her head back on the pillow and turned away from Rosita's eyes. A weight settled on the bed beside her. When Peel turned her head, Rosita placed a gentle hand on her shoulder. She gestured to the bowl. "*Sopa de pollo?*"

Peel raised herself up on the pillows. She was touched by the kindness of the motherly woman. "*Gracias.*" Rosita beamed and placed the tray on Peel's lap. With a soft pat on her leg, she left.

Although Peel wasn't hungry, she ate all of the soup hoping it would help her feel better. Once finished, she rested her head against the headboard. It didn't take long for the panic of this morning to return. Sebastien's story played over and over in her head, as did his answer to her question about whether he was planning to kill her: "*Not quite.*"

She got up and moved the tray to the dresser near the door, then headed into the bathroom to shower away the remaining medication hangover. She needed a clear head. He wanted something, and she was afraid he would exchange her life for it.

At 7:55 there was a light knock on her door. Peel was overwhelmed with relief when she opened it and found Anna standing in front of her.

"How are you?" Anna lifted Peel's chin and looked in her eyes.

"Not well," Peel admitted.

"Rosita said your headache was back. Is it still bad?"

"No, she brought me the prescription Tylenol and I slept." Peel was afraid to ask the next question but decided she'd rather hear it from Anna. "Did he tell you anything else?"

Anna paused. "A little, but nothing that made sense," she said. "I'll be with you again tonight. He wants us to find out together."

"Together?"

"Yes."

Peel's relief was palpable. "You'll help?" she whispered.

Anna shoved her hands in the pockets of her pants and looked away. "I don't know."

Peel didn't bother to hide her disappointment. "Oh."

"We should go." Anna held the door open for her and they made their way down to the study. Anna repeated her light knock and turned the handle when Sebastien bade them to enter.

Once again, he was holding the bottle of cognac. He added more to his glass, poured a second, then lifted the bottle to Anna. "Please," she said. He poured a third glass for her.

He handed Anna the tumbler and then picked up the other two, leading the women to the chairs. "I trust you are feeling better," he said to Peel. She nodded, and he continued. "I understand you may have felt a little overwhelmed this morning. It is a tragic story. Two families killing each other." He shook his head with what Peel saw as feigned regret. "It should have ended there, but Devin wouldn't let the scale remain balanced.

"I told you I left him his daughter. Don't mistake me for a sentimental man. It was pragmatism. I needed him to understand that there was more I could do if he continued to harm my family. When I told him I would be back for his daughter, my hope was it would motivate him to leave Tierra de Oro and abandon his obsession with my family." He sipped the amber liquid. "I believed I had been successful. He didn't even attend his wife's funeral. He took the girl and disappeared."

Sebastien had a faraway look in his eyes. Peel watched him, fascinated. If she didn't know better, she would think he was recalling a happy memory, not the murders of an entire family.

He took another sip and continued. "I should have known better. I should have killed them both when I had the opportunity."

Peel's gasp caused him to break his reverie. "You're shocked. Don't be. We live in a violent world and there is no room for sentiment. I made a costly error in judgment that I need to rectify." He waited, looking at Peel for a response. When she said nothing, he continued.

"As I told you this morning, my older brothers were the future of the cartel. While my father was teaching them the business, he was also working on a better future for the family. We're a small cartel. The mountains surrounding Tierra protect us from takeover attempts, but eventually that won't be enough. Papa knew we could only survive by building alliances with other families. He arranged a marriage between my oldest brother, Francisco, and the daughter of Dante Casalas." He watched Peel's face, maybe looking for a sign of recognition. At her non-reaction, he took an exaggerated breath before launching into his explanation. "Dante Casalas is one of the most powerful men in Mexico City. He is responsible for many of the large government construction projects. My father's dream was that one day Francisco's children would lead both families under the Gutierrez name. It seemed that dream would be realized when Francisco and Yolanda had a son and named him Eduardo after my father.

"When my brothers were imprisoned, Yolanda took their child back to Mexico City to live with the Casalas family. I made sure to visit them regularly. Eduardo needed to know what it means to be a Gutierrez." He looked down at his cognac. "I came to love that boy as if he were my own son. After Francisco's death it was my responsibility to raise him. After a suitable mourning period, I planned to propose to Yolanda and reunite the families." He stood, walked to the cognac bottle, and refilled his glass. Peel was surprised to see hers was nearly empty. He filled it without asking. Only Anna's drink lay untouched on a side table. Like Peel, she seemed entranced with the unfolding story.

"Do you know virtually no one went to their funerals?" When he saw her confused look, he clarified. "The Devins. The people had no respect for what they did to my family."

Peel doubted that was the reason no one attended the funerals. Sebastien could delude himself into believing his family was beloved, but she suspected the reasons had more to do with fear. "Later I found out that the day of his brothers' funerals, he left Tierra de Oro and went to Mexico City. When he should have been honoring his family, he was hiding outside the Casalas house. That day, Yolanda took Eduardo to play in the park, and Devin attacked her. He took Eduardo from his mother's arms and disappeared.

"Yolanda called me that morning. I could only understand that something had happened to Eduardo. It took me hours to reach her. When I arrived, Dante Casalas met me at the door. He invited me in but said she couldn't see me. He showed me the note Devin dropped when he took Eduardo. It said, 'As long as she is safe, he will be.' Dante asked what I knew about it, and I told him everything, including the fact that I used some of his men to carry out the hits against the Devins at the *fútbol* field. When I was done, he looked at me with sadness and anger. 'You are a child,' he said to me. 'You had no business playing a man's game. Because of your carelessness, I have lost the most precious thing in my life.'

"I protested angrily, but I knew in my heart he was right. I wanted Devin to live with the same grief I do. It was arrogant of me to think I was that important. If I had killed him, Eduardo would be with me now and know me as his father. Yolanda would be my wife and there would be many other children to carry on the Gutierrez name.

"I returned home and spent nearly twenty years learning by my father's side. I don't think Papa ever forgave me for Eduardo. I know Casalas hasn't. He killed the men I used at the *fútbol* field. Out of respect for my father, he let me live."

Once again, Sebastien stood and refilled his glass. Anna still hadn't touched hers. Peel reached her glass toward him. Maybe getting drunk would make this easier.

For the first time that night, Anna spoke. "No more." She said it in English to Peel, then turned to Sebastien and spoke in Spanish. He turned to Peel.

"She's right. I need you to be able to function, not be incapacitated with a headache." Peel glared at Anna but kept her mouth shut. For her part, Anna never changed the impassive expression she maintained around Sebastien. Sebastien watched their interaction. "That brings me to why I brought you here. Find Gabriel Devin and get him to reveal the whereabouts of Eduardo. You have two weeks."

Peel finally spoke. "What? You're kidding. How am I going to do that? I have no idea where he is."

"Anna will give you whatever support you need. I suggest you use your family connection to bring him out."

She looked helplessly at Anna, then turned back to him with upturned palms. "I don't have any idea how to do that. I don't know anything about Mexico. I don't even speak Spanish."

"Miss Primm, my ultimate goal is to reconnect with Dante Casalas. Returning Eduardo to the family would be the best but not the only way to accomplish that." He looked at her, making sure she understood his meaning. "I could offer him the life of a Devin. It doesn't have to be Gabriel." He paused again. "You will begin tomorrow. Ask Anna for anything you need." He turned to Anna. "She is your responsibility. Do what you feel is necessary. I'll be leaving tomorrow morning and expect daily updates." He stood and Anna did too. Peel sat, looking at the two of them in shock.

"I'll walk you to your room," Anna said. Peel stumbled a little as she got to her feet. Anna reached out a hand to steady her but stopped before she made contact. Without a word, she led them from the room. Peel was surprised when she walked past the stairs and instead went into the kitchen. Still not speaking, Anna opened a cupboard, pulled out the Tylenol, and shook two blue pills into her hand. She grabbed a bottle of water, opened it, and handed it to Peel. "Drink," she ordered. Peel obeyed. When the bottle was half empty, Anna handed her the pills and said, "Finish it." She did.

The silence continued during the walk to Peel's room. At the door, Peel turned around, her mouth open to speak, but Anna silenced her with an uplifted palm. "We'll speak tomorrow. You need rest. Drink another glass of water tonight," she said flatly and walked away. Halfway down the hall she stopped and turned back, her face reddening as she spoke. "While you're in Mexico, you need to think about your safety. The men around here, especially Sebastien, don't need consent to fuck you. Getting drunk with a man is an invitation you don't want to give." She spun on her heel and walked off.

Peel was stunned. She hurried to catch up to Anna before she reached the stairs. "Anna! Anna, wait, please." Anna stopped and turned around. Peel could see a cold fury in her eyes. "I wasn't thinking. I'm sorry. Thank you." She took a couple more steps toward Anna. "Thank you for keeping me safe."

Anna seemed about to speak but then thought better of it. She looked up to the ceiling, nodded, and then said, "Just be smarter, okay?"

Peel felt small and even more vulnerable. "I will."

CHAPTER SIXTEEN

Peel awoke with a surprising amount of energy and determination. She paced her usual path between the sitting room and the bathroom, ideas running through her mind. On the sitting room table, she found the pen and notepad Anna gave her when she made the clothing list. With pen poised over the paper, she took a few moments to organize her thoughts before starting a list.

1. Need a timeline. When did all of this happen? Start with the arrests of EG and his sons up until the kidnapping of Eduardo.

2. Who knew Gabriel Devin? Did he have friends? Are his parents still alive? Were they alive when this happened?

3. What about Devin's wife? SG mentioned family at the funeral. Could they have taken the children? Where are they now?

4. What information does SG already have? Has he tried to find Devin before now?

She chewed on her pen for a couple of minutes, letting her mind wander. When no new ideas came, she headed for the shower. Under the hot water, she thought about Anna and her anger the night before. Peel thought about Anna's changing emotions. When Peel pushed too much, Anna became cold and distant to keep her from asking more. Last night, Anna got angry when Peel was reckless. All along Peel had known Anna was the key to her survival. Getting her to care, to want to help, was essential. It was a delicate dance, but Peel had to keep pushing because she was making progress with the other woman.

Peel wrapped the towel around her hair and padded naked into the bedroom to get dressed. She screamed when she turned the corner and found Anna standing with the pad of paper in her hand. Anna jumped and started to speak. "Sorry, I knock—" She stopped midsentence when she saw Peel's naked form. A grin spread over her face as she watched Peel bolt back into the bathroom. "Sorry about that," she called out. "I knocked."

Peel poked her head out of the door, this time with the towel draped around her. "Well, where did you think I was when I didn't answer?"

"In the shower," Anna deadpanned.

"And you thought you'd just come in anyway?" Peel's voice rose a little at the end.

"You told me I didn't need to knock."

Peel swore. "Could you give me a little privacy, so I can get dressed?"

"How 'bout I turn my back?" Anna offered.

"How 'bout you go get coffee?" Peel retorted.

Anna grinned and pointed to the dresser. "Already done. Let me pour you a cup." With that she went to the dresser and poured two cups of coffee, adding cream to one of them. She walked toward the bathroom door with the cup in her hand and extended it to Peel. "Here you go."

Without thinking, Peel reached for the cup while still tightly gripping the towel to her body. It slipped a little and Peel had to clutch the coffee cup to her chest to keep it from falling farther. "What's gotten into you this morning?"

Anna's eyes dropped before answering. "I'm not sure what you mean. You're the one who walked into the room naked." She stepped closer to Peel and whispered, "Were you trying to proposition me?"

"Get out of here." Peel was exasperated. "Go. Give me ten minutes and come back. And knock this time. In fact, knock every time."

"If you say so." Anna gave her an obvious once-over and sauntered out the door.

* * *

When Anna closed the door behind her, she couldn't wipe the smile off her face. That had been fun. She wasn't sure what she liked best: seeing Peel naked or seeing Peel blush from head to toe. Exactly ten minutes later, she knocked on the door and called out, "Peel, are you decent?"

Peel threw the door open. "Oh for the love of God. What is with you?"

"Well, you practically threw yourself at me. How did you want me to react?"

"I did no such thing!"

Anna sniffed. "You're entitled to your version of events."

Peel threw up her arms and laughed. "Oh my, you are quite the flirt when you want to be. Does this routine usually work for you?"

Anna's smug grin grew broad. "Always." She walked over to the tray and took her cup, draining half before topping it off with hot coffee from the carafe. "Okay, in all seriousness. I saw you started a list. How can I help?"

Peel nodded and picked up the pad of paper. "Yeah, I'm trying to get some background. I don't know how to start, so I decided I'd do it like a research paper and just get every piece of information I can. What am I missing on that list?"

"I don't know. It seems comprehensive. What next?"

"Normally, I'd start on the Internet, but I've already done a cursory search of the family. Some of what Sebastien told us is on Wikipedia."

Anna frowned. "When did you do that?"

"I did it before I was taken. The guy who tried to grab me the first time had this tattoo." Peel pointed to a spot on her neck. "The police told me it was a symbol of the de Oro cartel, so I researched it."

"And you found information on Wikipedia? That's kind of a surprise." Anna crossed her arms and leaned against the wall.

"Not necessarily. Wikipedia is written by regular people who take it upon themselves to create an entry."

"Wait, I need to go back to something you said. They tried to get you once and failed?" Anna asked.

"Yeah, they attacked me when I was leaving work last week. I got away when my Anime kids scared them off."

Anna shook her head, trying to make sense of Peel's words. "What kind of kids scared them off? Anime?"

"It's a group I sponsor at the library. They were still there when I walked out. They saw the guy grab me and came running to the rescue. I don't think he saw them, but they did a great job sounding scary and chased the guy away. It was amazing." Peel's face was beaming. "They took a video of the whole thing." Her smile suddenly faded. "I wonder if I'll ever see them again."

Anna had been enjoying the bright smile on Peel's face and was sorry to see the worry return. "You will," she said. "Focus. How do we get this information if it's not on the Internet?"

"Newspapers." Peel froze. She looked at Anna. "That's where I was. It didn't happen at Linda's. I was going to the Denver library to check their international databases. That's what we need—a library with access to a newspaper database."

"There's a library in Tierra de Oro," Anna offered.

"No, not there. I called them when I was looking for information on my great-grandfather. That's how Sebastien found out about me. I don't want to go there."

"Okay. I'll go to one of the big libraries in Mexico City. Tell me what to do." Anna reached for the pad of paper and sat down.

"It would be a lot easier if I went with you."

Anna didn't hesitate. "No."

Peel blew out a breath. "I had to try." She moved to sit next to Anna. "Don't bother with the Internet. Go to a subscription database of newspaper and magazine articles. Most databases search just like the Internet, the only difference being your results will be newspaper or magazine articles. The newspaper articles will give us the immediate aftermath. Magazines can't be as current, so they often give a good overview of the events and more in-depth analysis. That could be really helpful. I'll make a list of search terms. Print everything you find."

Anna rolled her eyes. "I went to college. I know how to search a database." As soon as the words left her mouth, Anna realized the error. Out of the corner of her eye, she saw the words register with Peel. The other woman turned her head to look at Anna, but Anna refused to meet her gaze.

"Too many questions are dangerous," Peel whispered.

Anna closed her eyes briefly. "Thank you."

As if she hadn't heard, Peel asked, "Do you read Spanish as well as you speak it?" Anna nodded. "Then you're going to have to translate for me. It's a lot of tedious work, but I don't know what else to do." She took the pen and pad from Anna and started writing.

Anna watched for a moment, then said, "If you don't need me, I'll go pack a bag so I can leave as soon as you're done."

Peel was just finishing her list when Anna returned. "Ready?" she asked.

"Yes. Here's the list, but don't feel limited by it. You may uncover something else as you start looking through the articles." Peel sighed. "I wish I could go."

Anna looked at Peel, her eyes twinkling. "You actually get excited about research, don't you? You're mad you can't play in the library."

"Shut up." Peel gave Anna's arm a backhanded slap. "Go find something we can use."

* * *

As promised, Anna left immediately. She didn't bother with a book or the radio for her drive. The lighthearted flirting she and Peel shared this morning reminded her of happier times in college. She didn't often allow herself the memories, but today she wanted the distraction.

The day after Dr. Reynolds talked to her in the copy room of the business department, Anna knocked on the door to a tiny office tucked under the eaves of the renovated dormitory. Dr. Patricia Reynolds was in her mid-thirties, no more than five foot three with large, bright blue eyes and medium-length blond hair.

Anna was mesmerized by the charismatic professor. She wasn't alone. The men in the department openly flirted with her regardless of their marital status. Reynolds easily batted away their innuendos and suggestions with a laugh or a quick comeback. They loved it.

When Dr. Reynolds looked up at Anna's knock, a genuine smile crossed her features. "Anna!" she exclaimed. "I'm so glad you've come. Are you ready to be a business major?"

Anna didn't know how to respond. She didn't think she wanted to change majors, but she really liked being around this woman. "Um," she stuttered. "Uh, I really don't know anything about business."

"Well, let's find out what you do know." The professor gestured for Anna to sit in a chair in front of the desk. "How are you with numbers?"

"Pretty good." Anna shrugged.

"What math class are you currently taking?"

"Linear Algebra."

"You're a first-semester sophomore taking linear algebra and you're majoring in criminal justice? That's a waste of a good brain. Tell me more about you." The professor leaned forward, resting her chin on a closed fist.

Anna was lost in the intensity of the older woman's interest. She told her about her neighborhood and family, and that she didn't want to be a teacher or a nurse. Dr. Reynolds hung on her every word, making Anna feel like what she said mattered. After talking nonstop for thirty minutes, she caught sight of the clock on the credenza behind the professor. She was mortified and could feel her face heat as she stumbled through an apology.

Before she could finish, Dr. Reynolds interrupted. "Nonsense. I've enjoyed talking with you." She looked down at her calendar. "I assume you're free at this same time Thursday?" It wasn't really a question, but Anna nodded. "Good. I'll expect you a half hour earlier." She stood and reached a hand out to Anna, who took it. "I look forward to seeing more of you, Anna. Enjoy the rest of your day."

Anna's whole body tingled as she stumbled down the stairs and out of the building. Back in her dorm room she threw herself on the bed and replayed every second of their interaction. When her roommate walked in, Anna couldn't help herself. She wanted to talk about Dr. Reynolds, so she told her about the meeting. The shock on her roommate's face threw her. "What?" she asked.

"You have never voluntarily shared anything about yourself. What's wrong with you?" her friend teased.

It took a few more meetings before Anna figured out what was wrong with her. She had a crush on Dr. Reynolds. A full-on, lust-filled crush. When the professor continued to schedule appointments with Anna, she started to hope Dr. Reynolds felt the same way. One day she suggested they continue their conversation over lunch. When Anna hesitated, she stood up, grabbed Anna's hand and said, "Don't be shy. No one will call you teacher's pet." She squeezed Anna's hand. "At least not yet."

Anna was completely overwhelmed. At night she fantasized scenarios where the older woman would confess to being in love with her. The confession would lead to Anna's first kiss, but the fantasy would get fuzzy from there. Thinking back now, Anna laughed at her naïveté. She wondered how she could have missed the careful seduction that was taking place.

The kiss Anna had been longing for came when Dr. Reynolds hired her to bartend a party. Anna arrived at the house two hours before the start of the party and was stunned by the woman who answered the door. It was the first time she'd seen the professor in anything other than professional attire. She was wearing low-rise skinny jeans and a tight tank top. Long earrings dangled from her ears, and she wore a light dusting of makeup. Anna thought she would die on the spot.

"Anna, you're right on time," the professor said as she opened the door wide. "Did you have trouble finding it?"

"No, your directions were perfect." Anna stood awkwardly in the doorway.

"Come in. I'll show you where the bar will be, and you can set up the glassware. We'll open a few bottles of red wine in a bit. You do know how to work a corkscrew, don't you?" She winked at Anna.

The wink slammed into Anna. "I-I've done a bit of waitressing."

"Great, come in." After showing Anna around, she left her to set out the bottles and glasses. When Anna couldn't find a corkscrew, she called out in the direction the professor had disappeared. "Um, Dr. Reynolds?"

"I'm in here." Anna followed the voice into an open kitchen. "Would you pop the champagne and pour us each a glass? I think this will be a night to celebrate." Anna did as asked and handed one of the bubbling glasses to her.

"Before we toast, there are a couple of things to take care of. I think 'Dr. Reynolds' is too formal when we're not at school. When it's just us, or we're off campus, please call me Patricia. Can you do that?" Anna's heart was hammering. She could do that. She nodded.

"Second, this is a very special party, and I asked you to be here because I trust you completely." Patricia leaned back against the counter as she eyed Anna. "I'm a lesbian, and so are all of the women who will be here tonight. Many of them work on campus, so your discretion is a must."

Anna's glass trembled in her hand. "I don't have a problem with gay people."

Patricia laughed out loud. She stood on her tiptoes and kissed Anna's cheek. "Oh, honey, I know that." She lifted her glass to Anna. "Let's toast to new experiences."

As promised, the night was full of new experiences. Anna tried to focus on mixing the few basic drinks Patricia taught her, but she couldn't stop watching the women around her. Every time she saw a couple in an intimate embrace, she felt a flutter of arousal.

At Patricia's urging, she'd had a couple of beers to calm her nerves. That might have explained her response to the athletic-looking woman who approached the bar. "Hello," she said, sticking out her hand. "I'm Janine, and you're new here."

Anna shook her hand. "I am. I'm Anna. Can I make you a drink?"

"I'd love a gin and tonic if you have Bombay Sapphire." Janine leaned on the bar.

Anna leaned in, too. "I do. Would you like a double?" She never took her eyes from the other woman. She was flirting with someone. Not someone. A woman. And it felt awesome.

Janine touched her hand. "Just a regular. I've got to pace myself."

Anna turned to make the drink and heard Patricia's voice behind her. "Janine! I see you've met Anna."

"I have," Janine said. "Great party as always."

"Thank you. It's nice to be with everyone again. Speaking of, I invited someone I want you to meet." Anna placed a napkin on the bar and put the drink on it. "That looks lovely, Anna. Would you make me one of those while I take Janine to meet a friend?"

"Of course," Anna said.

When Patricia returned, she walked behind the bar and stood next to Anna. Taking a sip of her drink, she gave a murmur of pleasure. "How are you doing? Are you still okay with gay people?"

Anna blushed. "I'm sorry. That was a stupid thing to say."

"Nonsense." She stroked Anna's arm. "I've been watching you. You seem fascinated by the women dancing."

"Um, I've just, uh, have never seen it before."

"And now that you have?"

Anna didn't know where her courage came from, but she made eye contact with Patricia and said, "I think it's hot."

Patricia gave a throaty chuckle and put her drink on the bar. Taking Anna's hand, she led her onto the patio where couples were dancing to soft music. At the far edge, Patricia pulled Anna to her. "I don't know how to dance," Anna whispered, her voice shaking.

"Oh, honey," Patricia whispered back. "Dancing is just an excuse to get close to someone you're attracted to. Just move with me and you'll be fine."

The word "attracted" made Anna's stomach flip. Was Patricia attracted to her? Then a worry crossed her mind. Was she being nice to the awkward girl who obviously had a crush on her? She stumbled. Patricia pulled her tighter. Anna had to know. "Are you attracted to me?"

Instead of answering, Patricia reached her hand around Anna's neck and whispered, "Kiss me." She did. Patricia's lips were soft on hers and so very gentle. "All right?" she asked Anna.

Anna could hardly speak. "Yes," and Patricia was kissing her. This time she parted her lips and put her hand on Anna's cheek. "I've wanted to do this for such a long time," she murmured. Anna gasped, and Patricia took advantage of the moment to caress Anna with her tongue. Anna responded, opening her mouth and inviting Patricia deeper. At one point, Patricia pulled back and looked up into her eyes. "Who taught you to kiss?" she teased.

"You did." Patricia caressed Anna's cheek, then tucked her head under Anna's chin.

Even though there were several people still dancing and drinking, Patricia walked Anna to the door at midnight. "You are so enticing," she whispered as she ran her fingertips down Anna's forearms. "I need to send you home before I take this too far." She gave her one more kiss and pushed her out the door. "Call me when you're alone tomorrow."

Patricia continued her slow seduction over the next few weeks. She whispered to Anna as they kissed, telling her what she liked about her body and how she wanted Anna's touch. By the time she caressed Anna's breast, Anna thought she would die. A month after the party, Patricia met her at the door in a robe, kissed her ear, and said, "I'm going to make love to you."

In the bedroom, Patricia removed her robe and lay back on her bed. Anna moved to follow but was stopped by the other woman's upraised palm. "No. Get undressed. I want to see you." Anna hastily toed off her shoes at the same time she pulled her T-shirt over her head. She stumbled a little as she tossed the shirt to the floor. "Slow down, honey," Patricia said. Anna blushed, and Patricia, seeming to read her mind, laughed. "No, silly, not a striptease. I want to enjoy the reveal. Take off your bra." Anna reached behind her and unhooked the black lace bra. She reached up for the straps and pulled the material down her body. "Beautiful," Patricia said.

Anna doubted her breasts were beautiful, and she fought her shyness as she unbuttoned her pants. She pushed the tight jeans over her hips, being careful not to pull her matching lace briefs down, too. Patricia murmured her approval. "Very nice. You dressed for tonight. Did you know?"

"I hoped," Anna admitted. She stood in front of Patricia, trying not to cover herself. She was so afraid she'd do something that would cause Patricia to change her mind. That problem was solved when she finally looked from the other woman's eyes to her breasts. Every thought disappeared as she took them in. They were soft, the skin creamier than her own, the nipples rosy. Anna stared.

"Come here," Patricia said. Anna stepped forward, and Patricia pulled her onto the bed. "I love your skin," she murmured as she ran her hands up Anna's arms and down the center of her chest. "Look at this delicious color—you glow." She pulled Anna on top of her and kissed her deeply. Anna was lost. All she could think about was where her skin touched Patricia's. It was silk beneath her. Patricia pulled away, gasping for breath. "Roll over." Anna complied. Patricia lay on her side, one hand tracing the line from Anna's throat to her belly button. Anna watched her eyes and marveled at the desire she saw in them. She couldn't believe it was because of her. Patricia met her eyes, a slow smile forming. "I want you to put your arms above your head."

Anna blinked. "Do you want to tie me up?"

"Oh no, honey, I want to explore every inch of you, and I don't want to be distracted by what your hands are doing to my body." She reached across Anna to place a hand under her elbow. Gently, she slid Anna's arm above her head, and Anna lifted her other arm up to meet it. Patricia took her time looking at the woman stretched out next to her. "Your body is incredible," she said as she leaned down to kiss Anna. Her hand skimmed from Anna's arm down the side of her breast, to the edge of her lace underwear. She slipped her hand under the waistband to lay her palm on Anna's hip bone. The possessiveness of the move excited Anna even more than the kiss.

Patricia pulled away from the kiss and sat up. "Lift." Anna raised her hips, and Patricia peeled her underwear down her body. She cringed when she felt the trail of her own wetness. "So, so beautiful," Patricia murmured. This time she ran her hand up the inside of Anna's leg, skimming her moist center. Anna jumped at the touch. Patricia gathered the wetness and drew circles around Anna's nipple until the moisture was gone. Anna couldn't move. She barely breathed.

Then Patricia slid on top of Anna, pressing her own wetness into Anna's thigh, and slowly rotated her hips. She moaned. "Anna, open your eyes." Anna did. "Do you touch yourself?" Anna blushed and looked away. "Darling, it's okay." Patricia reached for her face and turned it back to her. "Everyone does. I'm sure when you touch yourself, you're very quiet, hmm?"

Anna nodded. Patricia stroked her face "I don't want quiet. You have to let your lover know what feels good. You have to tell me if you like something." Patricia rocked her hips into Anna, spreading her own wetness up and down Anna's thigh. She moaned again. "There are lots of ways to tell me." She kissed Anna deeply. "Can you do that for me?"

She nodded again. Patricia held her gaze, not moving. Anna finally understood. "Yes," she whispered.

"Good girl." Patricia bent down and took a nipple in her mouth. Anna caught her breath. When Patricia sucked, Anna moaned.

When Patricia bit, Anna raised her hips and whispered, "Yes."

"Yes?" Patricia teased as she bit her other nipple.

"Yes."

Patricia spent several minutes playing with Anna's nipples, eliciting more fervent responses. Then she brought her mouth up to Anna's ear, placed a hand on her wet center, and whispered, "Are you ready?"

"Yes."

"Open your legs for me. Let me see you, beautiful girl." Anna complied, but Patricia wasn't satisfied. "No, never be shy. Sex is so much more fun if you embrace your body and all that you're feeling." She knelt between Anna's legs, gently spreading them apart. "Hmm, you are very wet." She trailed a finger down from Anna's clit to her opening, slowly circling before she pulled away. "Bend your knees." Anna did and heard another appreciative hum from Patricia.

"I really wanted this to last much longer, but I can't help myself with you." She stretched herself out on her stomach and pulled Anna open. Anna gasped at the contact when Patricia blew on her clit. "I wonder what you will like best…" Patricia seemed to be talking to herself. She reached out her tongue and slowly ran it up from Anna's opening to her clit. "Do you like that?"

Anna gasped. "Yes."

Patricia flattened her tongue and made languorous circles over and around Anna's clit. "Oh, oh that. I like that." Anna moaned. Patricia sucked Anna into her mouth, providing pressure as she tongued her. Anna pushed her hips into Patricia. Her body was roaring toward an orgasm. Her muscles tightened and burned as she got closer. This was so much more intense than anything she'd felt before. Her body quaked against Patricia's mouth, and she screamed as the orgasm tore through her.

Patricia slid up Anna, who moaned as the pressure triggered a series of tiny aftershocks. At Anna's lips, she said, "Taste yourself on me," and kissed her hard, pushing her tongue into her mouth. The sheer eroticism of the woman was overwhelming.

Anna reached for her face. "Teach me how to do that to you."

"You have me so turned on, I'm going to have to give you a crash course." She straddled Anna and lowered herself onto her mouth. Anna was a fast study.

Their affair lasted through the rest of Anna's college years. During the summer, Anna worked downtown in her internships while Patricia traveled and, Anna assumed, slept with other women. As desperately in love with Patricia as she was, Anna knew it wasn't a long-term relationship. She convinced herself to enjoy it while she could.

Her heart was broken when Patricia finally ended things, but Anna would always be grateful to the older woman. She had taught Anna to become her own woman. "You get to decide now, Anna," she'd told her. "You're not trapped by the person you were before. Take this beautiful woman"—she ran her hands down Anna's body—"and let her find her new place. She's strong and oh, so very adaptable. I can't wait to see who you become."

She hadn't been in love since. She'd had several short-lived affairs and many one-night stands, but no relationships. Despite being open to her family and in every aspect of her life, she had no time for love. It was enough for her to constantly risk the lives of her family members with her job. She couldn't do that to a woman.

It only took three hours to reach the main branch of the Mexico City library system. She found a computer next to a printer station and started her search. Anna had to admit she was curious to read the results. There was much she didn't know about the de Oro cartel and the Gutierrez family. Every piece of information was important to her life.

She worked for over two hours amassing a stack of articles, mostly from Mexico City newspapers. The articles about the soccer field massacre and the murder of Sonja Devin were thorough. The reporters had put together the connection to the de Oro cartel and, surprisingly, also identified the gunmen as Casalas associates. No wonder Casalas killed his own men, she thought. They were sloppy. Sebastien was fortunate he was still alive.

She continued searching the years just after the murders and Devin's disappearance. A pattern began to form. The more she looked and printed, the more convinced she was. It couldn't be this easy, could it? How had Sebastien missed it? She printed the last of the articles and quickly gathered her pages and stuffed them in the bag.

As tempting as it was to drive back, her eyes hurt and she was tired. A beer and a quiet night in a hotel appealed to her. She backed out and turned toward Zona Rosa and Juanita's bar. Her phone rang beside her. "Hello, Sebastien." He talked for several minutes before she said, "Let me pull over. I need to write the address down." She forced her way across two lanes of traffic and pulled onto the gravel shoulder. "Could you say it again?" Her hands shook as she wrote. "Are you sure this is necessary?" After another lengthy silence in which she listened to Sebastien's urgent tones, she said, "All right. I'll go now."

She typed the address into the navigation system, and a route appeared. She was pleased to see it wouldn't take her too much longer to get to her new destination. Fifteen minutes later, she pulled up to a security gate blocking the entrance to a long drive shrouded by thick foliage. When she told the guard who she was, he reached inside the guardhouse and handed her a package. "Pull in and turn your car around. There will be someone inside the gate to help you."

It took less than ten minutes for her to complete the errand and return to the road leading to Zona Rosa. Her stomach was in knots. She wanted to turn the car and drive back to Tierra de Oro, but she couldn't. Sebastien had been explicit in his instructions, and she knew better than to challenge him.

It was dark by the time she parked her car in the hotel's garage and checked in. She took her bag upstairs to the room and sat down heavily on the bed. All she wanted to do was get undressed and climb under the covers. Instead, she took a deep breath, pushed herself up, and made her way into the night. She walked two blocks in the opposite direction of the bar. The wait was nerve-racking, and she thought she might be sick.

It didn't take long. She heard a voice, but not the one she expected. "Turn around, Anna." She did, and looked into the eyes and the gun of Mute.

"Mute," she said her voice just above a whisper. "I never thought it would be you."

"Yeah," he said. "It's nothing personal, Anna. You know I've always liked you. This is business. Just business."

She nodded. "Could you do me a favor? For my family? *Mi madre*? Not the head?"

"It will take longer to die," he said.

"I know. I'd like to spare them the pain."

"Okay. It's your funeral." He laughed at his joke, then raised the gun and fired two shots.

CHAPTER SEVENTEEN

"So, now you're back to knocking?" Peel asked as she threw open the door. She didn't recognize the woman who stood in front of her with a note. "I've returned to the estate to attend to an unexpected issue. Please join me in my study at 9:30 as this impacts you as well. Sebastien." She looked at the clock. It was late, already nine o'clock. Peel hoped Anna was back from Mexico City and would be with her when she met with Sebastien.

Peel waited until 9:35 before she decided to leave her room without the usual escort. The door to his study was open and she could hear his voice. He sounded tense, angry. "Ojos, I have been trying to reach you for hours." He paused, then lowered his voice. "I don't want to hear excuses. This is a billion-dollar business. When something comes up, I need to know you are responsive."

Peel stepped away from the door, conscious of Anna's warnings. She debated whether she should go back to her room and wait. Deciding that was the best course of action, she turned to walk down the hall, but his next words destroyed her. "I need you to fly here immediately. Anna was shot in Mexico City two hours ago." A pause. "I don't know. A mugging or an angry lover. They found her near her hotel, dead."

Peel had been holding her breath, but when she heard that last word, she couldn't help herself. She cried out and sank to the floor, burying her head in her arms. Her ally, her only hope to escape Mexico, was gone.

Gentle hands rubbed her back and a soothing voice spoke to her in Spanish. She looked up at the woman kneeling beside her. It was the same woman who brought her the note earlier. Sebastien stood in front of them, hands behind his back, his face stony. "I'm sorry you heard that," he said. "I think it would be best if you go to your room now." He spoke in Spanish to the woman, who nodded repeatedly. Then, with a gentle tug, she pulled Peel to her feet.

She didn't know how she made it to her room. Grief overwhelmed her. Anna was the only hope she had to find Devin. Without her, there would be no newspaper searches, no translator. She couldn't do it on her own. When she thought of the enormity of the task she was facing, she collapsed on the bed. She would not survive this ordeal.

Gradually, her thoughts changed. She realized the depth of her grief was not only about her situation, but also the loss of the beautiful woman who had been kind to her. She thought of Anna's smile and her expressive dark eyes trying to convey distance but never quite succeeding. She thought about the family Anna left behind and if they would ever know what happened to her. She thought about all her attempts to get Anna to care about her. Peel thought she might have been successful, but what she knew for sure was she was the one who had gotten attached. She was the one who cared.

* * *

Anna's body ached where the bullets slammed into the Kevlar. Huge bruises blossomed over her torso, and it hurt to breathe. Hearing a knock, she took a deep breath to call out but groaned instead. She shouldn't have bothered. The door opened, and she heard Rosita's familiar footsteps followed by the sound of the refrigerator and a few cabinets opening.

"You feeling better?" Rosita asked her when she finally appeared next to Anna's bed.

"No."

"Let me see how it looks this morning," Rosita pulled back the sheet and went to lift Anna's top.

"Rosita." Anna protested, trying to squirm away. She groaned in pain.

"See," Rosita scolded. "Stay still. I've seen your boobs before."

"You have not!"

"I might as well. Every other woman in Mexico has."

"Very funny," Anna said, but relented and allowed Rosita to lift her shirt.

"Ay, that bruise is bad." She tsked. "I brought more ice down. I'll make some packs to put on your chest. That should help a little."

"But it gets so cold."

"Ah, it's good to see you feel well enough to whine. That means it helped last night."

"It did. Thank you. So did the pain pills I got in the emergency room. Do you know if someone drove the car back?"

"Juan did, and he got your bag from the hotel, too."

Anna's eyes went wide and she tried to sit up. "Rosita! I need to talk to Peel. I forgot all about what I found yesterday. Can you bring her down here?"

Rosita gently pushed Anna back. "No. Sebastien wants her to stay in her room today. She overheard him on the phone last night. He was not happy with her."

Anna grabbed Rosita's wrist. "What was she doing? Was she wandering around the house? I warned her."

Rosita shrugged and patted Anna's hand. "I was here with you last night."

"Rosita, there are papers in my bag. Could you take them to her?" Anna tried to sit up again, then stopped herself in frustration and pain. "Ugh, never mind. She can't read Spanish." She dropped her head back on the pillow. "Will you take her a note? I think I found something that will help us find Gabriel Devin." Anna wasn't surprised when Rosita didn't react to the name. Rosita knew everything that happened in the house.

In reply, Rosita walked out of the bedroom. Anna heard her rustling around in the kitchen, dropping ice cubes into bags. When she returned, she said, "I will take her your note after you have these on you for twenty minutes. Without whining," she added.

* * *

After a long, emotional night, Peel didn't want to face the person at the door. She didn't want another command request from Sebastien to appear in his study. What was the point? A second, more insistent knock reminded her she had no options here. Peel pulled open the door and threw herself into Rosita's arms. "I'm so very sorry about Anna. I know you loved her." Rosita rubbed Peel's back and made soothing sounds as she sobbed.

After a few minutes, Rosita pulled back and reached for Peel's face. "¿Qué pasa?"

Peel shook her head as fresh tears rose. "Anna," was all she could get out. Rosita tsked and reached in her pocket. Peel looked at the folded paper and shuddered. She was going to need to pull herself together to face Sebastien. Gesturing for Rosita to come in, she walked into the bathroom and rinsed her face. Once her eyes and her hands were dry, she opened the note and read.

"Peel, I think I may have found something in the newspapers. I'm going to read over them today. I don't know what happened with Sebastien last night, but please stay out of his way. I will bring everything to you in the morning. Anna."

Peel read the note again. And then a third time. Finally, she stuttered, "Is-is Anna alive?" Rosita looked confused, so Peel tried again. "Where is Anna?" She shook her head in frustration.

Finally, she came up with a rudimentary phrase. "*¿Dónde está Anna?*"

Rosita frowned slightly. "Casita." Peel dropped the note and ran.

When Peel reached the casita, she pounded on the door. "Anna! Anna, it's me! Are you in there?" Her heart slammed against her chest. "Please, God, please, let it be true," she prayed. She pounded again, then rested her head against the door. "Anna, please. If you're there, please open the door."

Then she heard it. The deadbolt turned and Anna stood in front of her, furious. "Peel, what the fuck are you doing? Sebastien—"

Peel lunged for Anna, wrapping her in a tight hug. "I thought you were dead. He said you'd been shot and that you were dead."

* * *

At once, Anna understood the tears. Rosita had said Sebastien was angry because Peel overheard a call. It must have been when he was talking to Ojos. Despite the pain, she held Peel close. "Shh, shh, it's okay. I'm fine. I was shot, but I'm not dead."

Peel gasped, quickly pulling back from the embrace. She kept her hands on Anna's biceps, but stepped back to look her over. "Where were you shot?"

"In the chest. Twice." Anna grimaced. Peel's eyes widened in shock, but before she could speak, Anna lifted the bottom of her loose T-shirt. "I was wearing a vest."

Peel reached a hand toward Anna's stomach when she saw the dark bruise. "My God, Anna, shouldn't you be in the hospital?"

"I went to the emergency room last night. It's fine, just a little sore." She grinned. "Especially when someone tackles me."

Peel dropped her hands and stepped back. "Why didn't you say something? Should you be lying down?"

"Why didn't I say something? When? When you were flying at me? When you were clutching at me crying uncontrollably?"

"I was not crying uncontrollably!"

"Oh, you were. You couldn't stand the thought that something had happened to me."

"Nooo." Peel drew out the word. "I was worried about your replacement."

"Come on. I've got to lie down. We'll discuss how devastated you were once I'm in bed." She couldn't help it. She made her way into the little room and sat on the edge of the bed. Peel's reaction touched her.

"Do you need help?" Peel was right on her heels.

"Could you prop up the pillows?" Peel leaned over her, stacking the pillows against each other and then fluffing them. While she did, Anna made a show of looking down the front of Peel's T-shirt.

"Okay, lean back and I'll lift your legs," Peel said. Anna tried not to smile as the vee of the shirt opened even more. Peel lifted her legs up and then looked up. When she saw where Anna was staring, she slapped her hand over the opening of her shirt. She glanced down at herself and then back up. "Have you been looking at my boobs this whole time?"

Anna scooted back against the pillows and gave Peel her most innocent look. "I thought you wanted me to. You burst into my house wearing only that tight T-shirt. It seems like an invitation to me."

Peel threw her arms in the air. "Unbelievable! Do women actually fall for you?"

"Only the ones who invite me into their rooms wearing nothing but a towel." Anna was teasing, but then her grin faded. She reached for Peel's hand and pulled her down on the bed. "I'm sorry you were scared," she said and placed Peel's hand between both of hers.

Peel's eyes welled, and she looked out the window on the other side of the bed. The tears started to fall, and she wiped her cheeks with her free hand. "It wasn't just about who would replace you," she whispered.

"I know," Anna answered. "Thank you for caring."

Peel's eyes went wide. "Anna," she whispered. "Why were you wearing a bulletproof vest?" She dropped her voice even lower. "Are you a cop?"

Anna grabbed her arm. "Don't ever say that. Even the accusation is dangerous." She looked hard at Peel. "Why can't I get you to understand? You have to be smarter."

Peel looked chagrined. "I'm sorry. It just came out."

"Sebastien called me last night and told me there was rumor of a hit. He sent me to get a vest."

Peel started to say more when they heard the front door of the casita opening. Anna held a finger to her own lips and then pointed to the bathroom door. Peel stood and Anna called out to cover any sound as she moved. "Hello?"

Both women breathed an audible sigh of relief when Rosita called out, "*Hola!*" She came in the room and started speaking. Relief washed over Anna. She translated for Peel. "Sebastien was in the fields when you came running down here. He doesn't know you disobeyed him."

Anna spoke to Rosita and the older woman shook her head. They talked for a little longer, then Rosita returned to the kitchen. "He's back now, so you're going to have to stay for a while." Anna said. "Rosita's making us lunch because she's afraid you'll starve down here."

Peel whispered, "Anna, are you sure she won't tell him I'm here?"

"I'm sure. You don't need to worry about her."

"Why? She's been with him for years. I've seen how she is with him."

"No, Peel, you've seen what she wants him to see. Rosita knows a lot of Sebastien's secrets. She knows if she ever tried to leave, he would have her killed." At Peel's shocked expression, she said, "Yes, even Rosita. Sebastien talks of family loyalty, but he really is only loyal to himself. Don't forget that. Rosita doesn't. Her loyalty is to her church and her God. She would never do anything to cause harm to another person." Anna grimaced as she tried to get comfortable. "She's protected me many times. She'll protect you, too."

* * *

The three women ate in Anna's bedroom, Rosita at the foot of the bed and Peel leaning on the headboard next to Anna. Anna did her best to talk with both of them, but Peel and Rosita could see she was tiring. Finally, Peel stood and said, "I'm going to clean up the dishes, and then rest on your couch for a while. I didn't sleep very well last night." Anna translated for Rosita, who jumped up protesting in Spanish. Peel looked at Anna. "Tell her I've got this. She needs to get some rest, too. We all need a *siesta*."

Anna translated and Rosita seemed to give a halfhearted argument, but she followed Peel out of the bedroom. At the door to the casita, Peel pulled Rosita into a tight hug. "*Gracias*," she whispered. "For everything."

After finishing the dishes, she dried her hands and collapsed on the love seat. "Peel?" Anna called.

She peeked her head around the doorframe. "Okay?" she asked.

"You can't sleep out there. It's not big enough."

"It's fine. I can sleep in the fetal position."

Anna patted the spot Peel had occupied during lunch. "There's plenty of room in here. This is a queen bed."

Peel rolled her eyes. "You are unreal. I am not getting in bed with you."

"Look, I'm not strong enough to fight you off right now, but I trust you to keep your hands to yourself."

Peel raised her eyebrows. "To fight me off?"

"Well, clearly I'm incapacitated, so the only reason you wouldn't lay down in here is because you can't resist me. Why else would you argue that the love seat is more comfortable?"

Anna's false innocence was adorable. "I see what you're doing here. Frankly, I'm too tired to argue with you." Peel walked around the bed and got in. "But if you try to touch me, I'll give you a love slap on that bruise."

"Deal." Anna grinned and closed her eyes.

Peel woke to the sounds of running water and muffled groans. She sat up and wiped at her eyes. They were scratchy and probably red from all of the crying she'd done the previous night. Another groan from the bathroom got her out of bed. She knocked on the door. "Anna? Are you okay?"

"No, I've been shot." Anna grunted.

Peel laughed and pushed the door open. "Why are you taking a shower? You should still be in bed."

"I have a meeting tonight."

"Is there anything I can do?"

"Yes." Anna groaned again. "You can wash my hair. It hurts to lift my arms."

"Oh no. Nice try. I am not washing your hair." Peel started to turn away.

"Really?" Anna poked her head around the shower curtain, a look of disbelief on her face. "Uh, I believe you owe me. I washed puke out of your hair."

Peel rubbed her face. "Okay, okay, you're right. How do you want to do this?"

"Why don't you just come in here with me? It will be easier." Anna gave her a sweet smile.

"Forget it. Hand me the shampoo and turn around."

"I can't. The spray hurts when it hits my chest."

"Turn it off."

"It will be too cold."

Peel wanted to be exasperated, but she found she really liked this side of Anna. Plus, catching a glimpse of that body wouldn't be all bad. "All right. Angle the nozzle toward the wall and move to the back of the tub."

Anna did as instructed, and Peel pulled back the curtain a little. While she rubbed the shampoo into Anna's hair, she entertained herself by watching the rivulets of water run down Anna's flawless brown skin. It was all she could do to keep from tracing a finger along the path the water took over Anna's butt and down her muscular thighs. She was in incredible shape, Peel mused. She patted Anna's shoulder, said, "Rinse," and turned her back.

"Don't go far," Anna called after her. "We still need to do the conditioner." Peel groaned.

Twenty minutes later, Anna padded into the living area wrapped in a long towel. "Could you comb out my hair and put it up?" She held out a wide-toothed comb and an elastic band.

"Could you put some clothes on?"

Anna lowered her voice in a fake seductive tone. "See? I knew you couldn't keep your hands off me."

Anna was more right than she knew, thought Peel. Aloud, she said, "Is it getting old yet?"

"What?" Anna was all innocence.

"This fake player routine you started yesterday."

"Oh, Peel," Anna said with a little shake of her head. "There is nothing fake about me. Do you want to see for yourself?"

"I don't know if I've ever rolled my eyes this much in my life," Peel said to her. "Sit down." She patted the cushion. Anna started to lower herself but stopped with a quiet groan.

Peel reached for her and eased her down. "It really hurts, huh? Can you tell Sebastien you can't make the meeting? You should be in bed."

"It's not an option." All teasing was gone from Anna's voice. "Look, we need to figure out how to get you back to your room." Peel ran the comb through the long strands of Anna's hair, reveling in the thickness.

"I've been thinking about that, too. Where is your meeting?"

"That's the bad part. It's at the pool bar. Sebastien didn't want me to have to go very far."

"How thoughtful," Peel said dryly.

Anna ignored her sarcasm. "When I leave, I want you to go into my closet and close the door."

"What? Why? Do you think they're going to come in here?"

"No." Anna turned and faced Peel. "Could you just trust me? It's really important that you stay in there and that you don't make a sound." She took Peel's hands. "You may hear some things tonight, but you cannot react. Don't scream or call out. No matter what you hear, you stay in that closet." Anna looked intently in Peel's eyes. When Peel nodded her agreement, Anna continued. "At some point, they'll all leave, and I'll have to go with them. Rosita will take you back to your room. No matter what, go to your room. There shouldn't be anyone around to see you, but you still have to be careful. Sebastien can never know you were down here."

"Anna." Peel's voice was shaking now. "Are you in danger? Is he going to hurt you?"

"No. I'll be fine." She released Peel's hands and turned back around. "If you're done making love to my hair, could you put it up for me?"

CHAPTER EIGHTEEN

Ojos and Mute stepped out of the black Escalade and walked toward Sebastien. "Cousin," Sebastien said to him. "Welcome to Mexico." They clasped hands, then embraced, Ojos pounding Sebastien's back a bit harder than necessary.

"It's good to finally be here," he said. Gesturing over his shoulder, he added, "That's Mute." Sebastien nodded at the other man, then turned back to Ojos.

"It's a beautiful evening. I asked Rosita to put refreshments down by the pool for us. Come." He looked over his shoulder at the driver. "Put the bags inside the door for now. We will sort out rooms later." He gestured for the other men to follow him through the house but spoke only to Ojos. "Would you like to see some of the family estate?"

Ojos had been seething since they pulled onto the Gutierrez estate. He finally understood his grandfather's bitterness at being banished to Chicago. When Carlos Gutierrez used to rail against Eduardo, then Sebastien, Ojos thought they were the ramblings of a homesick old man. After all, who would want

to live in Mexico when he could be in the United States with
unlimited opportunities to expand? Now it was obvious what
his family was missing. The wealth was here. He looked around
at the sprawling Spanish-style home with its lavish gardens. He
was going to take it all away from Sebastien. Shit, if he had a
gun, he'd kill the prick right now.

Ojos stared at his cousin as he rambled on about architecture
and furniture, pointing out examples of local craftmanship. He
looked at Sebastien's creased jeans, shined boots, and matching
Mexican-style belt, and snorted. Fag, he thought.

Sebastien turned when he heard the snort, a question in his
eyes. "Something wrong?"

Ojos didn't bother to hide his contempt for his Mexican
cousin. This man was soft. "Yeah, can we get a fucking drink?"

Unfazed, Sebastien smiled graciously. "Of course. The tour
can wait." He turned and strode out of the house. Mute shot him
a concerned look. Ojos stared him down, daring his lieutenant
to comment. Mute looked away, and Ojos smirked. Mute knew
better than to challenge him.

Outside of the house, they walked across an expanse of lawn
and down stone steps to a pool deck. On the other side of the
pool Ojos could see a bar lined with liquor bottles. He looked
at the pool and pictured the parties he would have. Bikinis.
Everywhere. Fuck, why bother? He'd pay for the women and
they wouldn't wear anything. Sebastien was talking again. Ojos
couldn't believe he'd ever taken orders from such a man. "Give
me an *añejo*," he interrupted. "And a dark beer. I don't want any
of that Mexican piss." He stared at Sebastien, daring him to say
something.

"Of course." Sebastien poured the amber tequila in three
shot glasses, then reached under the bar for the bottles of dark
Mexican beer. He handed a glass to each man. "A toast," he said.
"To family."

Ojos drank his down without a word and then slid the glass
back to Sebastien. "Another." With a slight nod, Sebastien
poured another shot for each of them. Ojos drank his without a
word. Mute downed his as well.

When Ojos slammed his shot glass on the table for a third pour, Sebastien put the bottle in front of him. "No need to stand on formality. Help yourself." Ojos poured two more shots in rapid succession. Then he picked up the bottle and wandered over to an umbrella-shaded table He took his time looking at the pool and surrounding gardens.

"This is quite the life you have here, Sebastien."

"Yes, it is. And what about you, Ojos? Do you have quite the life in Chicago?" Sebastien asked.

"Not like this place."

"Why is that? What have you done with the money you have made from Gutierrez product? I choose to invest my money into the family." Sebastien gestured around him. "I take care of the family home. What is it you do with the money, Cousin?" Sebastien emphasized the last word.

The tequila was hitting Ojos. "Fuck you. Francisco built this place." Not Eduardo, and definitely not this *maricón*. "Don't act like you did any of it."

"I assure you, the estate is much changed from my grandfather's time." Sebastien looked over his shoulder. "Could you get our friend to join us, please?" he said to one of the men standing behind him.

"What friend?" Ojos watched the man walk down a stone path.

"What does the family estate look like in Chicago? What did Uncle Carlos build when he was in Chicago?"

Ojos took a swallow of tequila from the bottle. "You want to talk about our fathers? Let's talk about how Uncle Eduardo and the two cunt aunts forced my father out."

Sebastien didn't flinch. "Do you need another beer?"

Ojos felt powerful in that moment. His cousin was weak. He would kill anyone who talked to him the way he was talking to Sebastien. "Yeah, why don't you get me another fucking beer."

"Ah, there she is," Sebastien said. "Join us, Anna."

Ojos stumbled as he spun around. Anna stood next to Sebastien. "Hello, Ojos," she said.

He turned to Mute and said, "You said she was dead."

Mute looked Ojos in the eye, contempt showing on his face. "No, I said I shot her."

Anna rubbed her chest. "Yeah, thanks for that, by the way."

"What are you crying about? It was such a small gun, I thought it was going to shoot BBs."

"Is that why you shot me twice?"

"Nah," he said. "That was for effect."

"What the fuck is going on here?" Ojos pointed at Sebastien. "You told me she was dead." He looked between Sebastien and Mute. "What the fuck, Mute?"

"As you can see, Anna is very much alive. Your colleague was wise enough to call me when you first began to question my business. I might have forgiven you, but then you put a hit on Anna."

"You fucking dyke cunt," he spat at Anna. "I'll have your family wiped out."

Sebastien shook his head. "That's why we're in this situation. Just like your father, you are ignorant and greedy. You couldn't see that Anna will increase our profits tenfold. She is far more valuable than you ever were."

Now Ojos was enraged. "You fucking fag. I'm going to fucking feed your tiny dick to you." He lunged for Sebastien but was caught by two men.

"I would have played with you a little longer, Ojos, but you are tiresome. I can't stand your presence." To the men, he said, "We will be there in an hour. Make sure he is awake."

They picked him up and dragged him across the deck and up the stairs. He hurled insults at the group until finally Sebastien called out, "Silence him." They heard the sound of two rapid punches, and then silence.

"Have you eaten?" Sebastien asked Mute and Anna.

"No, and I'm starving," Mute answered.

"Help yourself. Rosita is an excellent cook. Anna, something to drink? Seltzer water?"

"Thank you." She helped herself at the bar. Her hands were shaking, but she knew the importance of looking unfazed.

When they were seated again, Sebastien asked Mute, "Do you anticipate any problems with the transition?"

"No," Mute said. "Ojos has been losing it over the last year. He ordered some questionable killings. The men will fall in line."

Sebastien turned in his chair. "Anna? What is your opinion?"

She answered carefully. "Mute knows the men best." She stood, knowing she wasn't welcome while they talked business. "If you'll excuse me, I'm going to make my way to the house. I'm a bit slow today."

"Will you be in the kitchen?"

"Yes, with Rosita."

"You will ride with me. Make sure you are ready."

She knew what he meant by that. "Of course."

Less than an hour later they drove along a dirt track up a hillside. "I debated burying him in the family cemetery," Sebastien said conversationally. "But you know how I feel about loyalty to the family. His father betrayed my father, and now he has betrayed me. I owe him nothing."

Anna let out a quiet groan when they hit a bump. He touched her arm gently. "I'm sorry he hurt you."

"Sebastien, I'm thankful you saved my life. The bruises are nothing." The SUV pulled next to a pickup truck and was joined by a second SUV containing Mute and two other men. They were laughing as they got out.

Sebastien spoke to the two men leaning on shovels against the front of the pickup. They nodded, and Sebastien beckoned Anna and Mute forward to the edge of a hole. It was deep, maybe five feet, and at least six feet long. Even though the headlights of the cars illuminated the area, it was dark in the hole. One of the men shined a flashlight into the darkness. Ojos was at the bottom, his arms and legs buried in sandy soil. His face was bloody and swollen. He screamed obscenities when the light hit his face.

Sebastien reached for a shovel, scooped up some of the loose soil, and tossed it onto Ojos's face. He spluttered, shaking his head to clear his mouth and nose of the dirt. Then Sebastien squatted down at the edge of the grave and looked down at Ojos. "Our family fortunes started in the mines. It was dangerous, hard work."

"You fucking pansy-ass fag. You're not a Gutierrez," Ojos screamed.

Sebastien stood, shoveled more dirt on him, and continued to speak. "The greatest fear of the miners was being buried alive." He tossed another small shovelful into the hole. Ojos spit and coughed. "Not everyone I kill dies this way." He threw a little more down in the hole. "Only those who betray the family. You, Ojos, and your grandfather betrayed the Gutierrez family and sullied our name."

"My men will kill you!"

"You mean Mute's men? He runs the Disciples now, and they will do whatever I say." He handed the shovel to Anna. "Cover his face." He squatted down. "It is fitting, don't you think, Cousin? Anna will be the one to bury you. Thank you for bringing her to me."

She groaned in pain as she lifted a shovelful of dirt from the pile and threw it onto Ojos. She watched for a moment as the soil slid off his face and piled on either side of his head. He tried to spit but coughed as he inhaled. She threw a second scoop over him. And then a third. And a fourth. He was silent after six. She stopped counting at ten.

Back in the Escalade, Sebastien handed her a towel. "Was that your first?"

"Yes." She prayed he wouldn't ask more.

"You did well." He paused. "I hope you do as well with Miss Primm."

Her stomach dropped, but outwardly she showed no emotion. She stared at the dark landscape as they drove.

CHAPTER NINETEEN

Fields Destroyed

August 20, 1991

TIERRA DE ORO, HIDALGO—US DEA agents reportedly fumigated nearly 100 acres of poppy and marijuana fields surrounding Tierra de Oro, Hidalgo. The fields are reportedly owned by the de Oro drug cartel.

Midnight Raid Destroys Drug Trafficking Planes

September 26, 1991

TIERRA DE ORO, HIDALGO—Mexican forces and United States Drug Enforcement agents burned a warehouse containing ten small airplanes. A spokesman for the DEA said the planes were used to carry drugs across the border to the US.

Disciples of Gold Targeted

January 20, 1992

CHICAGO, IL, US—The Disciples of Gold, a Chicago gang reputed to be the United States arm of the de Oro cartel, was targeted in a series of coordinated raids. Carlos Gutierrez, brother of Mexican drug lord Eduardo Gutierrez, was arrested along with other reported gang members. Drugs with a street value of $1.5 million were also seized in raids.

Dante Casalas Arrested
February 19, 1992

MEXICO CITY—Alleged Mexico City crime boss Dante Casalas was taken into custody by United States Drug Enforcement agents during raids on homes and businesses owned by members of the Casalas family. Working with the Mexican police and army, the DEA seized $100 million in drugs and US currency.

"There's more like this, but I think you get the idea," Anna said to Peel the next morning. They were sitting on the long patio at the back of the house, Peel listening as Anna translated the first paragraph of the articles she found. "It can't be a coincidence that Devin disappears and within three years, the two families responsible for his family's deaths are targeted by the DEA. He had to be working with them."

Peel couldn't contain her excitement. She jumped up and hugged Anna. "I can't believe it! You found him in one day."

Anna moaned. "Still shot," she said as she pushed Peel away from her.

"Oops, sorry." Peel paced. "What do we do now? Do you think he would still be working for them? How do we figure out where he is?"

"What we do now is call Sebastien. He might have people inside the DEA. But this is a long shot, Peel. Devin would have joined them over thirty years ago, but maybe there are records."

Peel's elation disappeared, and she sank back into her chair. "You're right. Chances are he retired a long time ago. He's probably sitting on a beach in Miami."

"I don't think he was ever in the US," Anna said. "He had accurate information three years after he disappeared. When I was in Chicago, we moved warehouses all the time to avoid alerting the DEA. For them to get that much from the Disciples, someone must have been on the inside."

Peel stared at Anna. "You're in a gang?" She pointed to an article on the table. "You're in the Disciples of Gold?"

"Peel," Anna said in a warning tone. "Don't. Ask. Questions."

Peel's shock kept her from registering Anna's tone. "How is that even possible? You're nothing like these people." Peel gestured around her.

"I'm not like these people?" Anna's voice raised. "Really? I killed a man last night. I shoveled dirt on his face until he suffocated. Still think I'm not like that?"

Peel grew pale at Anna's words. "You-you killed someone? No. I don't believe you."

"I don't really care if you do. But don't fool yourself. I belong here."

Peel stood. She felt sick. "Would you mind if I took a break?"

"That's a good idea. You should return to your room." There was no inflection in Anna's voice. "I'll come to you after I've talked with Sebastien."

Peel rushed into the house.

* * *

Anna watched Peel leave. All her talk of no questions, and in one reckless moment she'd confessed to murdering a man. If Sebastien knew what Anna had just told Peel, nothing could save her.

Anna picked up her phone and pressed Sebastien's number. When it went to voice mail, she left a short message. "Sebastien, this is Anna. Miss Primm may have found something, but she needs your resources. Please call me when you can."

Five minutes later, it rang. "What has she found?"

Anna outlined the information from the articles. She didn't share her conclusions but instead waited for Sebastien to draw his own.

"I should have seen it." Sebastien's voice was so quiet, Anna wasn't sure he was talking to her. "I blamed my father. I thought he was too distracted after my brothers were killed, making mistakes, not strong enough to lead." She listened without comment. After a short silence, he asked, "What resources do you need?"

"Do you have any contacts in the DEA? Anyone who could search their files?"

"I might know someone," he said. "What is Miss Primm looking for?"

"Anything connected to those raids."

"That's broad, and the files would be old. They probably aren't computerized."

"I know. I don't know how to narrow it. Maybe if they just get the Casalas files. They weren't targeted when your father and brothers were arrested. The newest information would be there."

"Do you think Devin worked for them?" Sebastien asked.

"Americans think all Mexican officials are corrupt. They wouldn't trust that he was legitimate. I think he's an informant."

"That will make him harder to find in the files."

"Yes," she admitted. "But it's a start."

"How are you feeling?"

Anna was surprised by the question, but she was careful not to show it. "I'm fine."

"Really? I'm not just asking about the bruises."

"I'm fine," she repeated. "Thank you."

"Good. I'll make a couple phone calls."

Anna put her phone down and sighed. She was tired and sore. Sleep had been difficult. Although her mind had replayed the muffled curses, gasps, and ultimately the silence, that wasn't what kept her awake. She was at peace with what she'd done. Ojos threatened her family and ordered Mute to kill her. He was a brutal man who deserved the death he got. No, killing Ojos didn't keep her awake.

Sebastien's words to her on the drive back were what haunted her sleep. *Was that your first? I hope you do as well with Miss Primm.* She had considered asking him what he meant, but in truth she already knew. Sebastien expected her to help Peel find Devin and the children. And, he expected her to kill Peel when it was all over.

* * *

In her room, Peel paced. Anna was a murderer. That was why she made Peel hide in her closet until Rosita came. She didn't want Peel to hear. The panic that was never far below the surface rose in her chest. Could she trust anything Anna said? She was a killer. Peel rubbed her eyes. Just yesterday, she admitted to herself that she was attracted to Anna. She balled her hands into fists and yelled, "Fuuuuck!" She froze, hoping no one would come. The hallway remained silent. "Fuck, fuck, fuck, fuck, fuuuck," she screamed, pounding her fists on her thighs.

Finally, she threw herself on the bed and stared at the ceiling. A few minutes later, she sat up and blinked several times, a new thought hitting her. Anna made it all up. "She's trying to push me away. I got too close. She's trying to keep me safe," Peel said aloud. There was no way the Anna she knew would kill someone.

Peel decided not to wait for Anna to come to her. She opened the door and stepped into the corridor. It was a little nerve-racking to be out of her room, but Anna had said she was going to call Sebastien. That meant he wasn't here and probably wouldn't be today. She made her way down to the kitchen, hoping to find Anna there.

When she reached the closed door, she knocked softly and pushed it open. Anna was sitting at the weathered kitchen table staring out the window. She turned when she heard the knock. Seeing Peel, she turned back toward the window and said, "I thought I told you to wait upstairs."

Her words and tone irritated Peel. "Really? Because I have so much time to figure out where this guy is? I don't have the luxury of waiting until you're ready."

Anna looked out the window for a few more seconds before turning back to Peel. "Have you eaten?"

"No."

Anna returned her gaze to the garden. "Rosita went into town. She left you a salad in the refrigerator."

Peel wanted to say she wasn't hungry, but that wasn't true. She pulled the salad out and joined Anna at the table. "Did you eat?" she asked.

"Yes."

"Did you talk to Sebastien?"

"Yes."

Peel's irritation was growing. "Aaand?"

"He's going to make some calls."

"That's it? That's all he said?"

"No, he agrees with us. He thinks Devin worked with the DEA in the early nineties. I asked him to see if he could get the files of the Casalas raid. He's not hopeful, but he said he'll try."

"Why the Casalas raid?"

Anna shrugged. "It's a gut feeling. It's also the biggest, and it was the first major inroad the police made into the Casalas organization."

Peel nodded. "So, we wait?'

"Yes." Anna returned to her short replies.

"Okay. I've been thinking, too. So far we've taken Sebastien's word for how the people of Tierra de Oro reacted to the Devin murders. What if there were people who were supportive of Devin? He disappeared with two babies. No one knew where he went? How did he take care of two infants? I bet someone knows something."

Anna nodded. "Let's look at the articles about the soccer field." She stood. "Eat your salad. I'll go get everything."

Anna returned, shuffling through printouts. "Here's one," she said. "It looks like it's the day after the shooting." She read silently for several minutes. "It was a bloodbath," she said under her breath. "They killed their wives and children, too. No, that's not right. None of them had children. Three kids who weren't related to the Devins died. Nine people were killed." She handed the article to Peel. There were pictures of the soccer field and what looked to be official photos of the three policemen.

Peel didn't think she could still be shocked. "Three innocent children? Three grieving families? People may not have said anything, but there must have been anger."

Anna started reading another article. "This newspaper sent a couple of reporters here. They tried to talk to the parents but couldn't get near them." She scanned down the article. "'Gabriel Devin is in seclusion following the deaths of his wife and brothers,'" she read. "Oh wait, this might be something. 'Padre Benito Alvarez condemned the violence and is praying for the families.'" Anna looked up. "I wonder if Padre Benito is still in the area."

"Would Rosita know? You said she's religious, right?"

"Yes, but she's not here."

"Anna, what about what Sebastien knows? He must have tried to find Devin after the kidnapping. Can you ask him?"

"Yeah, I'll do that. I'm sure Dante Casalas tried, too. I wonder if Sebastien knows what he discovered," Anna mused.

"Okay, so what's next? Do you think there's anything else in these?" Peel pointed at the copies of articles.

"I don't know. Let's look through them while we wait for Rosita to come home."

They spent the next two hours reading and making notes. There wasn't any new information, but they used the articles to create a timeline of events. "Okay, so here's what I have so far." Peel shoved the paper over to Anna. "Does this look accurate?"

February 12, 1989—Francisco Gutierrez killed in prison.

February 13, 1989—Alejandro Gutierrez killed in prison.

August 5, 1989—Nine people including Pedro, Hector, and Cesar Devin are killed at the soccer field dedication.

August 5, 1989—Sonja Rosales Devin's throat is slit in their home.

August 9, 1989—Funeral for the Devin family members.

August 11, 1989—Funeral for Sonja Devin

Anna nodded, pushing the paper back to Peel. "Think so."

"There was nothing about little Eduardo's kidnapping in any of those articles?" Peel asked.

"We've read through them twice. There's nothing here."

"Do you think you missed it?"

Anna smirked. "Look at all the articles about the Casalas family. Do you really think I would have missed something as big as that? No. They didn't report it to the police. Or, they were able to keep it quiet. Probably both. A man as powerful as Dante Casalas wouldn't want his rivals to know it was that easy to get to his family."

"It doesn't make sense." Peel shook her head. "Why wasn't he more cautious?"

"Why would he be? Remember what Sebastien said? Casalas didn't know his men carried out the hits at the soccer field."

"Right, but still, shouldn't his family have been better protected? Look at this place." Peel gestured out the window. "There are armed guards everywhere."

"Yeah. I guess that's another thing to ask Sebastien." Anna leaned back and stretched. "Do you want something to drink?"

"Sure," Peel answered as she stood. "Maybe we could go for a walk? My butt is tired of sitting."

Just then the kitchen door opened and Rosita walked in carrying a large straw purse. She stopped when she saw the two women in her kitchen. Anna started what seemed to Peel to be a teasing conversation. The affection between the two women was obvious. Once Rosita even reached up and ran Anna's braid through her fingers, all the while speaking rapidly. Anna's eyes were soft as she batted Rosita's hand away and laughed. Finally, Anna looked over at Peel, her face and voice becoming serious. Rosita looked puzzled at first, then nodded when Anna said, "Padre Benito."

"Sí, sí."

Anna continued in Spanish. After a short conversation, Rosita patted Anna's arm again and left the room. "She knows him. He's in his eighties, retired now. She's going to call and ask if he'll see me."

"Did you tell her why?"

"Yes, but she's not going to tell him. She's just going to say I need spiritual guidance." Anna grinned.

"Do you think you can see him today?"

"She's asking."

"I should go with you."

"You should, but you're not going to. If I take you, Sebastien will expect me to take a couple of the men, too. I don't want to scare the padre."

Peel inhaled deeply and blew out a frustrated breath. "I guess you're right. Do you want me to make a list of questions?"

"I think I can handle it," Anna said dryly.

Rosita returned to the kitchen and handed a piece of paper to Anna. Anna gave her a big hug and Rosita laughed. When they pulled apart, Anna said to Peel, "He'll see me as soon as I get there. Rosita says he's lonely and likes to have visitors."

Peel followed Anna to the door. "Take notes. You don't know what might be important. Write everything down."

"Peel. I'm not going to do that. He may be taking a risk by talking to me. Trust me."

Peel thought back to their earlier conversation. No matter what, she did trust Anna. "I have to. You're all I have."

CHAPTER TWENTY

Padre Benito Alvarez had confused hair. Other than a small monk's fringe surrounding his head, he was completely bald. The rest of his head and face made up for it. An explosion of white, curly hair burst from each ear and joined random patches on his lobes. Each nostril was accented by a curtain of white trailing onto his upper lip where it was absorbed by a scraggly mustache. When he answered the door, his face lit up. "You must be Anna," he said in greeting. "Come in." He led her inside the small cinder block home. "Do you want coffee?"

Although Anna was dying for coffee, she was afraid of what she'd find in her cup, so she declined. "No thank you, I'm fine."

"Are you sure?" he asked. "Señora Martinez from the church made some fresh when she brought my lunch. She also brought cookies."

"Well, you can't eat cookies without coffee," Anna conceded. "I'd love some. Let me get it." She jumped up before he could argue.

"Thank you. It's hard for me to get up and down." He grunted as he sank into a chair.

When Anna poured the coffee and found the container of cookies, she returned to the living area and sat on the couch across from the padre's chair. He slurped his coffee, dipping his white mustache into the brown liquid with every sip. "Tell me what I can do for you."

She'd used the drive to think through her approach, starting with a broad question to see what she could get from him without having to reveal why she was asking. "I was hoping you could tell me about Gabriel Devin."

The old man's massive eyebrows shot up. "Gabriel Devin? I haven't heard that name in years. Why do you want to know about Gabriel?"

The use of Devin's first name and the shrewd look in the man's eyes caught her attention. She abandoned subtlety and leaned toward him. "Padre, there is a woman whose life is in danger if I don't find him within the next week."

He shook his head and looked out the window. "Tragedy follows that man. Who is this woman and why is she in danger?"

"She's an American. She recently discovered that her great-grandfather is Gabriel Devin's grandfather. The man was married in the US before he came to Mexico."

"Her life is in danger because she is related to Gabriel?" The confused look on the old man's face concerned her.

She decided to push him. "In a way. Sebastien has given her two weeks to find Devin and the baby he kidnapped."

The priest started. "What? He kidnapped a baby? Gabriel?"

"Yes. The child is the grandson of Eduardo Gutierrez and Dante Casalas," Anna explained.

He clutched the earthenware mug to his chest. "Oh dear. I had no idea. When did this happen?"

"Right after his wife and brothers were killed."

"Are you sure about this? Because I have to tell you, that does not sound like Gabriel. He was a policeman, dedicated to the law and the people." The padre was shaking his head as he spoke. "I can't believe he would hurt a child."

"Padre Benito, it happened after Sebastien Gutierrez threatened his child. I think, maybe, Devin took the boy as insurance."

The old man chewed on his mustache. Anna waited, knowing he was trying to make her story fit the man he knew. "He was so broken those last days. Everything he loved and cared about was destroyed. Only the little girl was left. That would explain why I never saw her with him. He must have been hiding her from Sebastien."

"Was he your friend?" Anna's tone was gentle.

"I thought of him as a friend, but I don't know if he felt the same. He was hard to know. We used to have long theological debates. I think if his life had been different, he may have gone into the priesthood. He loved to argue the nature of man and whether the Holy Spirit could be present in man."

"What does that mean?"

"For him it meant that God empowers men to do his work on earth. He believed God had chosen him to fight evil. He felt the Holy Spirit lived in him."

"Did he see the Gutierrez family as the evil he was chosen to fight?"

"Yes. He believed they brought suffering to mankind through drugs and violence. I tried to make him see that God's spirit was healing, not avenging."

"Avenging? That's different from a policeman seeking justice."

The old man sat back in his chair, took another slurp of coffee, then clasped his hands over his stomach. "Yes, it is, but I believe he was seeking vengeance. You see, when Gabriel was just a boy, he had a best friend, Tomás Flores. They were inseparable, Tomás and Gabriel.

"Tomás's dad, Juan Flores, was a blackberry farmer. Each year it got harder and harder to find workers. Juan couldn't compete with the wages pickers earned in America, and the men who stayed in Mexico worked for Gutierrez. Gabriel told me that one day a man approached Juan and told him he could get him all the workers he needed to pick his blackberries. But after that, he would have to plant marijuana for the cartel. Juan explained that his family had always grown blackberries. It was what they knew. According to Gabriel, they parted peacefully.

The man asked him if he was sure, and Juan thanked him and shook his hand."

The older man continued. "That night there was an explosion at the Flores house. The entire family was killed. I came to Tierra de Oro a couple of years later. By that time, no one was growing blackberries."

"Do you know when that was?" Anna asked.

Padre Benito looked up in the air, searching his memory. "Maybe 1968?"

They ate their cookies in silence as the padre stared into space. Finally, he continued, "That's why they built the *fútbol* field."

"For Tomás."

"Yes. Everything Gabriel did from that day on was for Tomás. He and his brothers all became policeman because of what Don Eduardo did to Tomás's family." Padre Benito stared out the window. "All of the bloodshed was because one man wanted to grow blackberries on his family farm."

"But then Don Eduardo made a deal with the government and got out of prison," Anna prompted.

"Yes, and Gabriel was furious. It was Eduardo who killed Tomás's family, so he was the one Gabriel most wanted to see in jail."

Anna hesitated. "Sebastien thinks Gabriel had his brothers killed. Was he capable of that?"

Padre Benito looked up at the ceiling. Finally, he looked at her again. "I don't think so. I know you say he kidnapped this child, but before his brothers and Sonja, he believed in the law. He wanted vengeance, but he wanted it delivered through public arrests and trials. He wasn't a murderer."

"What about his parents? Are they still alive?"

"I don't know. After the boys were killed, they left town. Who could blame them? There was nothing here for them. People said they moved to the United States because, as you know, Gabriel's father was American. Others thought they moved to South America. All I know is, like Gabriel, one day they were gone."

"Did you know he was going to disappear? Did he tell you?"

"He did. He came to me one night with an envelope. It was the deed to his house."

Anna blinked in surprise. "The deed to his house? Why?"

The priest looked up again and seemed to be fighting tears. "It was just before Sonja's funeral. He needed money to have her interred in a mausoleum in Mexico City. He said Sonja was terrified of being buried alive." He looked at Anna. "That's how Gutierrez would have his enemies killed. I think she was always afraid they would come after her for marrying him."

Anna closed her eyes, trying to block out the memory of Ojos gasping for breath. "Yes, I can understand," she said softly. "So the house was to pay for the internment?"

"Yes. We had to borrow money from the church and from people in the town. Eventually, I was able to repay all the money." The old man reached for another cookie. "Do you want one?"

"No, thank you," Anna said. "They are very good." She waited a beat, then asked, "Did he have any other friends? Is there anyone else he would have seen that night or given the children to?"

"No. He wasn't close to anyone but family. If I had to guess, I would say the children are with his parents. That's who he would trust."

The old man seemed to be tiring. The cookie remained untouched in his hand. Anna tried one last question. "Can you think of anything else that can help me find him?"

"As I said, I haven't spoken to him since the night he gave me the deed to his house."

"What happened to the house?"

Padre Benito looked at her in surprise. "You're sitting in it," he said. "No one wanted to buy it after the murder, so rather than let it rot, the church sold the rectory. Now Padre Pablo and I live here."

"Does it bother you?" Anna asked, looking around the small home. The old man stood slowly, and Anna scrambled to her feet, afraid she'd offended him. "I'm sorry."

"No." He waved a hand at her. "I want to show you where she died." He pointed to a two-foot-high statue of the Virgin Mary. "We remember her every day."

When she turned back to the priest, she saw his eyes were filled with tears. She touched his arm. "I'm sure she is honored." She took his hand in hers. "Thank you for your help."

He wiped the tears from his eyes. "I don't know if I hope you find him, but I do hope you can keep that young girl safe."

"Me too."

CHAPTER TWENTY-ONE

When Anna arrived back at the estate, she went directly to Peel's room and knocked on the door. "Peel, it's me. I'm back."

Peel threw open the door. "Well? Anything?"

"Let's go get some dinner from Rosita and eat at the casita."

"Really?" Peel's voice rose up a notch. "You're inviting me to your place?"

"Don't get your hopes up. I'm too tired to put out tonight." Anna smirked.

Peel rolled her eyes. "Somehow I doubt you've ever been too tired."

Anna put her thumb and her forefinger on her chin and looked up, feigning careful thought. "You may be right."

They grabbed plates of sandwiches and fruit from Rosita and made their way through the gardens to the lower terrace. At the pool deck, Peel nodded toward one of the umbrella tables near the bar area. "Do you want to eat out here?"

Anna looked to where she'd been when Ojos was dragged away. She averted her gaze. "Not tonight. We need more privacy."

"You got something from him?" Peel turned to her.

"No. I don't know. I just want to make sure we're careful about who's listening."

Peel followed Anna down the path to the casita. When Anna handed Peel her plate and reached into her pocket for the key, Peel asked, "You keep it locked?"

"Long story."

"Did someone break in?" Peel persisted.

"Peel." Anna's voice had a warning tone.

"Right, right. No questions."

Anna ignored her comment and held the door open. "Do you want a beer? I can get a couple from the bar."

Peel set their plates on the counter and looked at Anna in surprise. "You would let me drink? How is this different from when you were so mad about the cognac?"

"Tonight is different. Sebastien is gone and so are most of the men."

"Is that why you lock your door? Because of all the men?"

"It's why you should," Anna replied. "Beer?"

Peel sighed. "That sounds really good."

Anna returned with two bottles. She put one beside Peel's spot at the counter and then slid into the stool beside her. They ate in relative silence with only short exchanges about the food. Finally, Peel looked like she was about to burst. "I'm dying here." She stopped herself. "I guess that's not hyperbole anymore." She waved off Anna's protest. "What did Padre Benito tell you?"

Anna told her about the priest and his friendship with Gabriel Devin. She shared the story of Tomás and the soccer field Gabriel built in his honor. Then she talked about the house and the statue memorializing Sonja Devin in the middle of the living area. When she finished, Peel said, "That is an incredibly sad story."

Anna nodded. "He said the most poignant thing. He said all of this happened because a man wanted to grow blackberries on his family farm." They were both silent.

"What a terrible waste," Peel finally said. After sitting for a few moments, she asked, "Do you think he went to the US with his parents?"

"If he's responsible for the DEA raids, there's no way he could have done it from the States." Anna took a sip of the beer, savoring its cold bite.

"Why?"

"The information for those raids had to come from someone that was here, close to where the families do business."

"Do you think his parents took the babies?" Peel asked.

"That's what the padre thinks. He doesn't believe Gabriel would trust anyone else."

"You don't sound like you believe it."

"It's just hard to imagine that three adults and two children disappeared, and no one knew anything."

"That they're saying." At Anna's questioning look, Peel continued, "No one knows anything that they are saying. There had to be other people who felt like the Devins did. If not when Tomás was killed, then certainly when the kids were killed on the soccer field. Did Padre Benito know if he had other friends? Someone in the police department, maybe?"

Anna shook her head. "He said he didn't make friends. Ever since Tomás, he was only close to his brothers."

"Okay, anything else?" Anna shook her head. "Then, what about Sebastien? Did you ask if he ever found anything?"

"Not yet. That's why I wanted you to come down here. I thought we could call him together. That way you can ask him whatever questions you want."

Peel hesitated. Anna knew she was afraid, but Peel straightened and said, "Okay, let's do it."

Anna picked up her phone and pressed Sebastien's number. He answered on the third ring. "What do you have for me, Anna?"

"Questions," Anna said simply. "I'm with Peel. You're on speaker. She has some questions for you about Devin."

"Miss Primm, Anna tells me my faith in you was warranted."

"Oh?" Peel cast a questioning look at Anna.

"You figured out the connection between Devin and the setbacks we experienced in the early nineties," he said.

Peel started to speak, but Anna waved her off. Peel took a breath. "Anna says you agree?"

"Yes. I should have seen it. Looking back, it was obvious. Over the years I wondered if he killed Casalas's men, but I don't think so. I think that was Dante."

Anna and Peel watched each other as he spoke. Anna saw Peel's expression. The deaths of the men were nothing to him.

"What can I help you with?" he asked.

Anna nodded at Peel to go ahead. "We..." At the shake of Anna's head, she said, "Um, I was wondering if you did anything to try to find Devin right after he disappeared."

"Of course, I did." His answer was clipped.

"Well, um, it might help us now to know what you found."

"I'm sure it would, if I found anything. Over the years, I've hired many people to search, mainly concentrating in the United States. They have found nothing." Irritation crept into his voice.

"The United States?" Peel asked.

"You must realize by now that your shared ancestor afforded Devin's parents American citizenship. They left Tierra right after the funerals and were rumored to have immigrated to the US. It seemed the likely place to take the children."

"You never found any trace of them?"

"No. The Mexican American community in the United States is large. Undocumented immigrants live among those with green cards and citizenship. No one talks for fear of deportation."

"Do you still think they are in America?" Peel asked.

"Yes." Another clipped answer.

"But you think Devin is here?"

Sebastien blew out an exasperated breath. "Miss Primm, I brought you here to get a fresh perspective. Where do you think he is?"

"I don't know," she said.

"Well, then it seems you are wasting time talking with me."

Before he could hang up, Anna said, "Sebastien, any luck on the reports?"

"I've made contact and people are looking." His tone was slightly less impatient with Anna.

"Do you know how long it will take?"

"I've impressed upon them the urgency of the situation."

Anna looked at the woman sitting next to her and took a risk. "Is there anyone else you could contact?"

After a few moments of silence, he said, "Perhaps." The phone went dead.

Anna looked at Peel. "What do you think?"

"Why did you tell him I found the connection to the raids? That was all you." Anna looked away, not willing to explain her motivation. She heard Peel's sharp intake of breath. "If you're the one figuring all of this out, there's no reason to keep me alive. Is that it?" When Anna didn't reply, Peel slid her hand into Anna's. "Thank you." They were quiet, both looking at their intertwined hands. Peel broke the silence between them. "You took a risk asking him to contact other people."

Anna shrugged. "Somewhat, but I think he has more resources than he's using."

"Really? What makes you say that?"

"He gave us a deadline that coincides with another deadline I'm working on. That means both are connected. The connection has to be Casalas. They are a larger organization that has existed longer than we have without any major problems. I'm sure they have their own contacts in the DEA."

Peel looked impressed. "You are wicked smart, aren't you?" She bumped Anna's shoulder with her own. "Come on, what did you study in college?"

"Really want to know?" At Peel's nod, she said, "Accounting." She stood and cleared their plates from the counter.

"Accounting?" Peel's voice jumped an octave. "You're an accountant?" She laughed. "You don't look like an accountant."

Before Anna could respond, her phone rang. She showed Peel the display before answering. "Hello, Sebastien."

"I've been promised information from the DEA by tomorrow night."

"That's good," Anna said.

"No, that is very good. Don't think I didn't notice your reticence to suggest I make that call. Never be afraid to offer suggestions. You've shown me a lot in the last few days. Good night, Anna."

"Good night, Sebastien."

Anna had pulled the phone away from her ear as soon as she realized the conversation was about Devin. Peel looked at her, impressed. "He thinks you're smart, too. If you're not careful, you're going to be running this thing."

Anna turned sharply and grabbed Peel's arm. She felt her face flush red as she glared at Peel. "Look, maybe I haven't made things clear enough for you," she said, anger causing her voice to shake a little. "You do not suggest I'm going to usurp Sebastien, you do not suggest I'm a cop, you do not ask questions. What is it going to take for you to get it?"

Peel jumped from her chair and yanked her arm from Anna's grasp. "What the fuck, Anna? I know that, but it's just you and me here. You picked the casita because you said no one could hear us. What is wrong with you?"

"What's wrong with me? What's wrong with me is you don't seem to get it. No matter how many times I tell you, you still don't get it."

"Really, Anna? I don't get it? I'm the one who was dragged to Mexico and is being held prisoner by a psychopath." Peel pointed at Anna. "But you're right, I don't get it. One minute you're flirting with me, the next you tell me you can't be trusted. Then you lie to Sebastien to keep me alive, now you're... you're...I don't know what you are."

Anna's face was flushed. She took two steps toward Peel, who retreated into the counter. Anna watched Peel's chest heave as she moved in closer. "You don't know what's wrong with me?" Her voice was low, almost threatening. She looked at Peel's mouth.

"Don't you dare," Peel whispered.

"You wanted to know what's wrong with me." Anna used one arm to pull Peel against her while the other threaded in her hair. She forced Peel's head back. "I think you know exactly what it is." She bent her head close to Peel's lips. When Peel didn't pull back, Anna kissed her.

* * *

It wasn't the kiss Peel expected. Their anger and Anna's tight hold on her should have led to a hard press of lips. That kiss she could have resisted. This kiss was soft. Anna moved her lips over Peel's, caressing her mouth. The hand in her hair slid forward until she cupped Peel's face. The gentle touch broke through any remaining reserve Peel had. She parted her lips and welcomed Anna's tongue. At her moan, Peel felt Anna smile. She pulled back slightly and whispered, "Don't get cocky," then closed the distance again. Anna responded by pulling her tighter. Peel's arms were around Anna's neck, her hands in Anna's hair. She tugged the elastic out and enjoyed the silky weight of it in her hands.

This time it was Anna who groaned. She broke the kiss for a second and looked into Peel's eyes. "You are infuriating."

"You have too many rules."

"You make me absolutely crazy. You don't listen."

"Maybe you talk too much." Peel pulled Anna hard against her.

Anna groaned. "I'm a little sore."

Peel pulled back, but Anna tightened her arms. "That doesn't mean I want you to stop." She bent her head again, but Peel leaned back and put her fingers on Anna's lips.

"Wait. I don't want to stop, either, but you did just get shot."

Anna ignored the second half of her comment. "You don't want to stop?" She raised an eyebrow.

Peel grinned. "Maybe all of your flirting has worn me down."

"I am really good at flirting."

Peel pointed to her eyes as she rolled them. "And now, I'm really good at rolling my eyes."

"Any chance you want to check out my bedroom, Miss Primm?"

"I saw your bedroom yesterday, Miss…" Peel paused, then held up a hand. "I'm not asking, I'm merely pointing out I don't know your last name."

"Well, that's an improvement. I think you should visit my bedroom, again. I've redecorated since yesterday."

"Then, of course I'd like to see your bedroom."

Anna took her hand and led her across the tiny living area into her room. When they reached the bed, Anna turned into Peel's arms. This time Peel didn't wait. She stood on her toes and pulled Anna to her. This kiss was more intense than the first. Peel couldn't get close enough to Anna, and she was having trouble remembering to be careful. She needed to feel connected to someone. Anna broke their kiss with another groan.

"I'm sorry," Peel whispered, trailing her hand down Anna's chest. She kissed her again, gently this time. "Take your shirt off," she said against Anna's mouth. Anna stepped back and slowly lifted the shirt over her head. Peel gasped when the full extent of the bruising appeared. "Oh, Anna," she said and ran light fingers over the discolored areas. "Does it hurt?"

"Not at the moment," Anna murmured.

"Why are you wearing a bra?"

The cheeky grin was back. "Because you haven't taken it off yet."

"Not what I meant. But let's get it off. I'm sure you'll be more comfortable." Anna reached around her back and flipped open the clasp. Peel slid the straps off her shoulders, never taking her eyes off Anna's. When the bra dropped between them, she leaned in for another long kiss.

Anna pulled back from the kiss to look at her. "Have I mentioned that I really like your new clothes?"

"You didn't like me in your clothes?"

"I like these better." Anna grabbed the bottom of Peel's T-shirt and pulled it over her head. "I especially like this bra." She ran a finger along the edge of the cup.

"Tell me the truth. Were these the only bras you could find?"

"Wellll…"

Peel slapped her arm. "I knew it! Even then you were plotting."

"No plot. But if I have the opportunity to dress a beautiful woman, I am definitely going to take advantage of the situation."

That comment silenced Peel long enough for Anna to kiss her again. Then she reached for the straps of Peel's bra. "Can I take this off?" At Peel's nod, Anna undid the clasp and pulled the bra away.

"Wow," Peel said. "You've done that a few times."

"I'm quite good with my hands." Anna grinned.

"I hope so. This might be my last time." The words were out before Peel had a chance to think.

Anna cupped Peel's face in both hands. "It won't be, I promise." Then she kissed her. They stayed like that for a while, gradually pulling each other closer until their breasts were touching. "You feel so good." Anna breathed into her mouth. "I want you naked." She rubbed the back of her hand against Peel's stomach, sliding her fingers into the waistband of Peel's shorts. "Take these off."

Peel stepped back and undid her shorts, removing them and her black boy shorts in one motion. She reached for Anna. "Do you need help?" Without waiting for an answer, she unbuttoned Anna's pants and slid the zipper down. Then she stepped back and watched Anna pull them off.

Normally, Peel felt awkward standing naked in front of someone. Not with Anna. Maybe it was because she couldn't take her eyes off Anna's body. Glossy hair tumbled around her defined shoulders, ending just above the softness of her breasts. She was tall and lean, her hips rounded, her legs toned.

Anna reached one hand to her and used the other to pull back the covers. Peel slid onto the bed and pulled Anna on top of her. "I love that feeling," she whispered and ran her hands down Anna's back. Anna responded with a long, slow kiss. Peel could feel Anna's wetness on her thigh, and she pushed up into her. Anna responded by spreading her legs and sliding on the soft skin beneath her. Peel ran her hands over Anna's butt and pulled her tighter.

Anna continued to move as she slid her palm over Peel's breast. Moving in slow circles, she leaned down and kissed just under Peel's ear. "What do you want?"

Everything about this moment was out of character for Peel. "I want you to fuck me," she whispered.

She could tell her response excited Anna. She opened her legs wider and pressed herself into Peel. "You like to be fucked?" Anna took a nipple in her mouth, sucking gently. When Peel didn't answer right away, Anna lifted her head. "Hmm?"

"Yes."

"Do you want me to fuck you now?"

"No, I want you to suck my nipples." Peel couldn't believe how she was responding to Anna's raw sexuality. She was more excited than she'd ever been in her life.

Anna took a nipple in her mouth and rolled it against her teeth. She sucked gently at first, then added more pressure. Peel was on fire. "More." Anna responded, making Peel realize she'd spoken out loud. Anna moved to her other nipple, alternating between sucks and soft bites. Peel moaned.

Anna moved back to just below Peel's ear. "Are you wet enough for me?"

Her hand moved to Peel's inner thigh, staying away from her center. Anna groaned as she moved closer. "You're very wet." She moved her hand to just outside her opening, then dipped one finger inside. "What do you think?"

Peel gasped. "Yes."

Anna bit Peel's earlobe and slowly entered her with two fingers. Peel hissed in pleasure. Anna took her time moving in and out of Peel, her fingers straight and her thumb away from Peel's clit. The teasing was making Peel crazy. "More," she whispered.

Anna kissed her, pushing her tongue into Peel's mouth. "More what?"

Peel was on the brink of losing control. "Fill me." Anna groaned and added another finger. Peel hissed again. "Yes. Anna." Her hips took over the rhythm and Anna let her, moving her fingers in and out. Peel bucked against her hand, looking for more. Anna finally gave it to her, curling her fingers inward to the sensitive spot. Peel writhed beneath her, groaning. "Right there, yes."

Peel's thighs tightened and started to quake. Her movements against Anna's hand became erratic. She came hard. Anna's hand slowed but kept a steady movement inside Peel. Rather than push her away, Peel responded, "Yes, Anna." Just as Peel felt the tightening begin again, Anna leaned down and took a nipple in her mouth sucking gently. Peel came in an explosion of movement and sound.

When Peel fell back onto the mattress, Anna kissed her nipple and gently pulled her fingers out of her. "That was amazing," she whispered.

Peel reached a hand up to caress her cheek. "No one's ever made me feel like that." Even though she felt exposed and raw, she didn't look away from Anna. If this was her last time, she was going to feel everything.

Anna brushed Peel's hair back and kissed her gently. "Maybe you've never let yourself feel like that."

"Hmm, maybe. Your vast experience seemed to bring out my wild side," Peel teased in a low voice.

Anna kissed her again. "I think that's your vulnerable side. You should let it out more often."

"I hope I get a chance to." Peel turned her head and looked out the window. She didn't want Anna to see her tears.

It was as if Anna sensed exactly what she needed. Leaning on one arm, she turned Peel's face back to her. "Do you think we're done?" Her tone was playful, then she drew a finger over Peel's bottom lip. "I hope not because I really need your mouth on me."

The vulnerability faded. "I can't wait to taste you." With the slightest pressure she pushed Anna to her back. She ran her hand up the inside of Anna's leg, pausing when she felt the wetness on her inner thigh. She trailed her fingertips through it, leaning down for a long kiss. "You have a beautiful body."

It was Anna who broke the kiss, gasping for breath. "Are you going to tease me all night?"

"Would you like me to?" She trailed a finger from Anna's thigh into her center. She paused at her clit, making slow, featherlight circles. Anna lifted her hips, trying to force the contact. Peel laughed and pulled her finger away. She circled a nipple, then bent and sucked on it.

Anna grabbed the back of Peel's head and pushed her into her breast. "If you don't stop, I'm going to start without you."

Peel lifted her head, meeting Anna's eyes. "Do you always have to be in charge?" She flicked her tongue over an erect nipple. "I wonder what it would be like if you weren't in charge." A light nibble. "Would you be able to handle it?"

"Please, Peel. You can have anything you want next time, but I need you now."

"Next time, huh? Anything?" Peel moved between Anna's legs, spreading her open with her fingers. Then she ran her tongue from her opening to just above her clit. "It's a deal," she said and took Anna fully in her mouth, sucking hard on her clit.

"That's it. Yes. Just like that."

"Like that? How about this?" Peel swirled her tongue around Anna's opening.

"Please, Peel, just suck my clit. Don't tease me." Anna went silent for a few seconds as Peel sucked, her clit becoming larger and harder. Then, with a cry of, "Yes, oh Peel," she put her hand on the back Peel's head, pushed her hips into her mouth, and came. After the first wave eased, Peel replaced her mouth with a hand. She looked up. Anna's neck was arched and her nipples were taut. She rocked several times against the pressure and gave a long, "Ohhhh," as she rode out the aftershocks.

Careful not to touch Anna's bruised torso, Peel moved up her side and whispered, "You are even more beautiful when you come." It sounded like a line, but she didn't care.

Anna turned her head, dark eyes meeting hers. "I feel the same about you. I want to watch you again, but I can't move." She rolled onto her back and tugged at Peel. "Straddle me."

"I'll hurt you," she said, but the protest seemed feeble since she was already spreading herself over Anna's center.

Anna moved her hand between Peel's legs, not bothering to be gentle. "Do you like when I fuck you?" she asked as she entered Peel with three fingers.

"Yes." Peel's eyes held hers, the fire building rapidly between her legs.

"Then show me." Peel braced herself on Anna's hip bones and began riding her fingers. It didn't take long before she felt her breath leave her. The orgasm was on her in seconds. She gasped and moaned, riding Anna's fingers until she couldn't take the intensity anymore. When she was finally able to open her eyes, she saw tenderness in Anna's. "Thank you," Anna whispered.

To hide her tears, Peel teased, "I think I'm supposed to thank you." She leaned forward, now on her hands and knees, and kissed Anna. "You wore me out. I need a drink."

Anna ran her fingers through Peel's curly hair. "On it."

"Not a chance. Just lay there and look hot. I'll be right back with two waters."

When she returned, Anna was sitting up. Peel could tell the activities of the evening were taking a toll on her. She handed her the water and said, "I think you should take something for the pain."

"Yeah, I will." Anna's easy grin returned. "I'm starting to feel the effects of your wild side."

Peel slid off the sheets. "Tylenol in the bathroom?"

"Yes."

When Peel returned with the bottle, Anna shook out two pills and downed them with the water. While she was doing that, Peel started looking for her clothes. She sat back on the edge of the bed and pulled her underwear on. "Hey, what are you doing?" Anna asked.

"Um, getting dressed? I thought you were the genius in this pair."

"Why would you get dressed?"

"I'm going back to my room."

"You can't. It's really better if I walk you up there. I don't want the couple of guys on the wall to harass you. And, as you just pointed out, I'm in too much pain to get up." Anna gave her a pitiful look.

Peel chuckled. "Poor you. Well, I wouldn't want to cause you any further pain." She pulled off the recently donned underwear and climbed back on the bed. "But we are done for the night. You need to rest."

"Good news. I've recently had an incredible orgasm, which always makes me sleepy." She slid down on the bed, then rolled on her side. "Come. Be my little spoon."

Peel lay on her side, facing Anna. "Do you always get your way with women?"

"So far."

Peel laughed and kissed her gently. "Your ego." They were both asleep in minutes.

CHAPTER TWENTY-TWO

Where did I leave the damn phone? Anna wondered as she slapped at the nightstand.

"Make it stop," Peel mumbled beside her, burrowing deeper under the covers.

"Trying. Where did I leave it?" On cue, the phone stopped ringing. Anna draped her arm around Peel, ready to drift back to sleep. The phone started again. "Shit."

"I'll find it." Peel rolled out of bed and staggered toward the kitchen. Anna grinned, enjoying the view.

"It's Sebastien." She tossed the phone to Anna.

"Good morning, Sebastien." Anna made her voice sound raspy. "You called earlier? I must have slept through it." She paused briefly, listening. "Yes, we stayed up going over the newspaper articles again."

Anna was quiet for at least a minute. Finally, she said, "What time?" After getting an answer, she hung up and looked at Peel. "I've got to go to Mexico City to get the DEA report."

Peel nodded. "When do you need to go?"

"Right after I shower."

"That early?"

Anna climbed on the bed, sliding a hand up Peel's inner thigh. "I was planning on taking a long shower."

Ninety minutes later they walked up to the estate to have breakfast. As usual, Rosita was in the kitchen preparing the feast. Anna greeted her with a kiss on the cheek and reached for the coffeepot. She poured two mugs, filled one with cream, and carried both to the table where Peel waited. They drank their coffee in comfortable silence.

Rosita joined them with plates of hot pasties. Without waiting for the others, Peel grabbed one and took a large bite. "Oh, oh." She blew air out of her mouth and waved her hand in front of her face, causing both Rosita and Anna to giggle.

"What?" Peel mumbled through a mouthful of burning pastry.

"Hungry?" Anna raised an eyebrow.

"Shut up." Peel playfully backhanded her arm. Rosita watched the exchange in amusement. She spoke to Anna in Spanish and pointed to the women's wet hair. Then she nodded at Anna's response.

"I told her we'd been swimming," Anna explained to Peel.

"Good one, because I may eat a dozen of these." Her mouth was full again.

Anna turned back to Rosita and had a longer conversation. A couple of times, Rosita gestured toward Peel as she spoke, raising alarm on Peel's face. Before Anna could translate, Rosita tutted and left the kitchen. "I told her I have to go to Mexico City today," Anna said.

"What did she say?"

"She wondered if I was going to stay overnight."

"Are you?"

"Probably. Otherwise it's eight hours of driving in one day. I don't mind the drive to Mexico City, but the traffic through the city wears me out." Anna sighed.

Peel frowned. "Will you be safe there?"

"Are you worried about me?" Anna teased.

Peel reached her hand out to cover Anna's. "I am. Be careful."

Anna turned her hand over and interlaced their fingers. "I'm going to pick up the report and head to the motel. That's it. There's no threat anymore." Anna left the rest unspoken. She stood, kissed the top of Peel's head, and said, "I'll see you tomorrow."

Anna spent most of the drive to Mexico City reliving the night before. Peel had been incredibly responsive and surprisingly erotic. The memory of the sounds she made and the way her body moved as she came elicited a surprising response from Anna—tenderness. She was tempted to try to do the trip in one day so she could get back to Peel, but she knew it was a bad idea. There was too much she needed to do on too little sleep.

A little after noon, she pulled up to the same security gates she'd gone to Wednesday night. This time when she entered, she was escorted up the long drive to a walled complex. She parked next to the security vehicle and followed the guard as he led her through another gate, this one into the garden. The gray cinder block visible on the outside of the walls was completely hidden by vines on the inside. A low hedge created a second boundary around the outside of the garden. The large lawn was interspersed with trees and flowering plants, giving the entire area a park-like feel. She marveled at how successfully the landscape hid the sights and sounds of the large city.

When she finally turned to the house, she was surprised to see a modern home with large expanses of glass and stone. Her escort led her into the house and pointed to a low couch facing a wall of windows looking out to the garden she'd just come through. "Please wait here. Señor Casalas will be with you in a moment." Anna sat on the edge of the couch trying to get comfortable as her hips sunk below her knees.

Within minutes, a young woman entered rolling a modern industrial cart. On it was a carafe of coffee, silver containers that Anna assumed were cream and sugar, as well as a selection of fruit and sweets. She left without a word.

Anna was about to help herself when she heard footsteps behind her. She stood and turned toward the sound. The man entering the room looked to be in his mid to late seventies. His silver hair was cut close to his head on the sides, longer on top. The slight downturn at the corners of his eyes gave him a sleepy appearance, but the eyes themselves were alert. He offered his hand. "I'm Dante Casalas. You are Sebastien's Anna?"

"Yes." She shook his hand.

He walked to a chair and sat. "Would you mind pouring? I'm not as steady as I once was."

"Of course. Cream and sugar?" Anna placed a delicate china cup on a saucer and poured.

"Black is fine, thank you. Please help yourself."

When Anna settled back onto the couch carefully balancing the saucer on her knee, Casalas said, "Thank you for coming here today. I've been looking forward to meeting you." At Anna's surprised expression, he continued. "Sebastien speaks very highly of you."

She'd been right. Casalas was Sebastien's "special buyer" for the guns. She considered the timing. Had Sebastien approached him before he knew of Peel's existence? From Sebastien's story, it was obvious he had long sought a way back into the older man's good graces. Peel's existence was most likely his way in.

Looking at Casalas, Anna could see similarities between the two. They both spoke formally and were unfailingly polite. Just as Sebastien was always neatly dressed, Casalas was wearing suit pants and a starched white shirt. When he crossed his legs, Anna caught sight of what she was sure were expensive shoes polished to a high shine. She wondered if Sebastien deliberately emulated Casalas.

"I'm impressed with the work you've done for him thus far. I am considering partnering with him, but we have a few details to work out."

Unsure of how to respond, Anna remained quiet. She sipped her coffee, hoping to look confident. Dante Casalas was far more powerful than Sebastien. While the cartels fought for a piece of drug production and trafficking, Casalas ran a lucrative construction business in Mexico City, winning major contracts through a combination of bribery and intimidation. After years of success, Casalas had branched out into other enterprises including gambling and prostitution. He was said to be the most powerful man in Mexico City.

As if reading her mind, he said, "Many years ago, I decided to diversify my construction business. We had always done well, but I knew I was an economic downturn away from being vulnerable to other entrepreneurs. That's when I met Eduardo Gutierrez. He was looking to increase his production but didn't have the capital to do so. Eduardo was a smart man, and I liked him and Rosa. In our business there aren't many people with class, but they had it. We became like family, so when my daughter Yolanda came of age, a marriage was arranged. Soon little Eduardo was born." The old man reached into his shirt pocket and pulled out a photograph and offered it to Anna. The picture was of a dark-haired boy crawling toward the camera with a big smile. A string of drool trailed to the floor.

"He's adorable. Look at those dimples."

It was the right thing to say. "Yes, those are his mother's dimples. He was a happy boy." He took the photograph back from Anna and looked at it fondly before returning it to his pocket. "What do you think of Sebastien's plan to find him?"

Anna was taken aback. She wasn't sure there was a plan, and if kidnapping Peel was it, she thought the chances of success were slim. She hesitated. Finally, she decided to be honest. "I'm not sure what you mean."

"This information about the raids. Do you believe it will lead to anything?"

Again, Anna opted for honesty. "I don't know. All we can do is look at the reports and see if there are any clues to who tipped off the DEA. If it was Devin, we will at least have a way to start looking."

"You know that information is nearly thirty years old." He lifted the delicate cup to his lips.

"I do."

The china clattered as he returned the cup to its saucer. They both ignored the sound. "And you still think it is worth it?"

"I think we'll have to see."

"Yes. We will." He placed his coffee on a side table and struggled to his feet. She quickly put her cup and saucer down and rose. He extended his hand again. "I can see what Sebastien sees in you. You're careful not to promise what you can't deliver." He walked to a desk behind the couch and pulled a thick manila envelope out of the drawer, which he handed to her. "Good luck." Before he'd taken more than five steps out of the room, he turned back. "There is nothing I won't do to see my grandson again. If you find him, I will make you a very wealthy woman. Whatever you want is yours." He left without another word.

The woman who delivered the coffee returned. "This way," she said, gesturing to the door Anna had come in. Anna followed her through the garden and back out the gate. At her car, she was met by the same guard who escorted her in. Casalas was cautious, she thought. She wondered if he had other children and grandchildren and if they lived behind the walls.

Anna drove straight to Zona Rosa and checked in to a hotel several blocks from where she'd been shot. That was only Wednesday, she thought. She'd been nervous when Sebastien called her about the hit. But walking down the street, waiting for someone to approach her, had been terrifying. Too much was left to chance. She was fortunate it was Mute holding the gun, and that there was only one other man with him. If it had been Ojos, he'd have laughed when she begged him not to shoot her in the head.

Anger burned in her chest. She forced herself to relive the night she killed him. What if she'd had the option to spare his life? Would she have? It didn't take any thought. No. He had been a threat to her family for too long. It was the better of two bad choices. She had no regrets.

Now there was Peel to think about. Anna tried to pinpoint the moment she started to feel something other than pity for the woman. Was it the morning she held Peel following Sebastien's cold recounting of the murders? The night when she was so angry at Peel's reckless drinking? Or, could it have been when Peel's terror at Sebastien's return forced Anna out of her stoicism? If she were honest, it was before all of that. There had been something about Peel from the moment she opened that one blue eye.

Anna called Miguel. She hadn't wanted to call him until she knew Mute was back in Chicago and word about Ojos had spread. He answered on the first ring. "Anna?"

"Hi, little brother. Are you still in St. Louis?"

"You told me to stay until you called. Are you okay?"

"Yes, I'm fine. You can head back to Chicago now."

"Is Ojos still pissed at you?" So, he hadn't heard.

"You haven't talked to anyone?"

"No, I've kinda taken a vacation. This place is great for watching baseball. There's a bar down by the stadium with a screen bigger than a drive-in…"

Anna zoned out while he rambled about baseball and hot bartenders. Finally, he noticed her lack of response. "You didn't answer me. Is Ojos still pissed?"

"Sebastien removed Ojos from the Disciples." Her voce was flat, emotionless.

"Removed? Removed as in"—his voice dropped to a whisper—"had him killed?"

Anna didn't answer. She didn't need to. "Mute's in charge now. He knows to take good care of the family."

"Anna, what happened?" For all of Miguel's bravado, he was still her little brother looking for reassurance.

"Miguel, all I know is he's gone," she lied.

"Well, there won't be too much crying. He's gotten kind of crazy going off on people for nothing at all. Everyone was scared to say the wrong thing to him."

"Mute's a good guy," Anna reassured him. "You won't have that kind of problem with him."

"Yeah, I like him. He talks a lot, but at least you know what he's thinking. Okay, so I should go back?"

Anna rubbed an eye. Was this a good time to get him out? Probably not, but Peel's presence had accelerated a lot of things for her. "Anna?" Miguel interrupted her thoughts.

"Sorry, I was thinking about something else. You know what? Don't go back. Head to Miami."

"What about you?"

"I'll be okay as long as you're safe." She meant it too. She had more options if her family was out of danger.

Although Miguel seemed surprised, Anna thought she detected relief in his tone. "Are you sure about this?"

"Yes. It's time. Go take care of the parents."

"I will. I love you."

"Love you, too." She tossed the phone onto the bedside table and pulled back the covers on the bed. One way or another, it would be over soon. She wanted to start reading the file but could barely keep her eyes open. Maybe just a short nap.

It was 6:30 when she awoke. After thinking it over for a few minutes, she decided to wait to read the report until she was with Peel. She needed an evening to get lost in the atmosphere of Juanita's bar. After a quick shower, she strode out into the night.

The usual smell of smoke and beer greeted her when she walked through the door. Immediately, she relaxed. This bar was the only place in Mexico where she felt safe and at home. "Anna! Oh my God, Anna. I was so worried about you." Juanita came running from behind the bar and wrapped her in a tight embrace. "Are you okay? One of the girls said you got shot."

Anna let herself be hugged even though she was still tender. "No, no," she said. "I was shot at, not shot. Somebody mugged me. He shot in the air a couple of times when I wouldn't give him my wallet."

Juanita looked at her. "They said an *ambulancia* came for you."

Anna waved away her concern. "He knocked me out, so the police made me go. Look at me. I'm fine, but I missed you. I was on my way here when it happened."

Juanita made a sound of disgust. "The *policía* need to do a better job of protecting Zona Rosa. We can't have *turistas* scared to visit."

"Don't worry, they got him, and I got my wallet back." Anna threw an arm around her friend's shoulders. "And my wallet has money that I want to spend drinking. Come on, get my beer."

"So bossy."

"You love me."

"I do." Juanita's smile dimmed. "Be more careful."

"That's what my brother said. I will." Then, to distract Juanita, Anna made a show of looking around the bar. "Anyone fun tonight?"

"Not for you, but the night is young."

"That's okay. I might be too tired tonight," she admitted.

Anna pulled up a barstool and talked to Juanita while she served customers. She enjoyed watching the other woman's efficient movements as she lined up glasses and poured drink after drink. After a few minutes of working the other end of the bar, Juanita dropped a napkin and a new beer in front of her. "I gotta stay down here. That girl is making eyes at me."

Anna laughed. "Does she know your girlfriend is scary? Want me to tell her?"

"Nah, what she don't know won't hurt her." Juanita winked at her.

"Juanita! What's gotten into you?"

"I'm just playing. You been staring into space so long I had to see if you were paying attention."

"I was just admiring your work."

"I'm good, huh?"

"Yep, you're good."

A woman came up beside Anna. "Can I get a margarita?"

"Sure, what size?"

She looked down at Anna with a flirtatious smile. "What do you recommend?"

"You should always go big." Juanita nodded and started mixing the drink.

"I'm Lisa." The woman reached out her hand.

Anna sighed inwardly before clasping her hand. This was not who she wanted to be tonight. Lisa gave her a meaningful look, and Anna responded with a slight nod and pulled out the stool next to hers. "I'm Anna. Wanna sit?"

"Sure, just let me tell my friends where I'll be."

Juanita put the drink in front of the empty stool. "I thought you were too tired."

Anna shrugged. "She's hot." Juanita laughed and walked down the bar to take another order.

They finished their drinks and ordered another. Anna allowed herself to enjoy the flirtation. "I'm really glad I came out tonight," Lisa said.

"Yeah. Me too." And she was. Lisa was a good distraction from her thoughts of Peel.

"Another drink, or would you like to walk me to my hotel?" Lisa asked.

"I've had plenty. A walk would be nice."

Lisa leaned down and gave Anna a long, wet kiss. "You'll come in, won't you?"

The kiss did nothing for Anna, but she stood and wrapped an arm around Lisa's waist. "Of course."

CHAPTER TWENTY-THREE

Peel was chopping vegetables when Anna entered the kitchen. "Sunday dinner?"

"Anna!" Rosita answered. "*¿Encontraste el amor?*"

Anna felt the flush. "No, no." She waved her hands in front of her.

"What did she ask you? I know it was something about love."

"She asked me if I found love. I did not," Anna said to both women.

Peel waved her knife at Anna. "And why would she ask you that?"

"I may, occasionally, go out when I'm in Mexico City."

"Hmm." Peel tapped her lip and tilted her head to the side. "In your dictionary, is 'occasionally' defined as every time?"

"It is not. I met a very nice girl last night, and all I did was share a drink with her and walk her to her hotel." Anna gave Peel her most pious look.

"Is that what they call it in Mexico? 'Sharing a drink?' Did you and I share a drink Friday night?"

Anna took a step into Peel's personal space. "Oh, Miss Primm, you and I shared much more than a drink." She checked that Rosita wasn't watching, then ran a fingernail over Peel's nipple. "Interested in doing it again?"

Peel took a step back and shook her knife at Anna. "Did you forget there is a two-week deadline here? I can't spend time sharing drinks with you."

"I thought we established we weren't sharing drinks."

"There will be no sharing of anything right now." Peel set the knife down, grabbed Anna by the shoulders, and shook her. "Focus. Did you get the report?"

"I did." Anna grinned. "Want me to share it with you?"

Peel laughed out loud. "Meet you at your casita?"

Anna's eyes widened. "That was actually easier than I expected."

"No!" Peel gave her an exasperated look. "Do you want to read the report at your casita?"

"That's disappointing. I have it with me. Shall we go to the patio?"

"Ask Rosita if she'll be okay if I don't finish." Peel pointed to the vegetables she was chopping.

"She'll be fine, but I'll tell her I need you." Once out on the patio, Anna opened the large envelope and spread the papers out in front of them. "How would you like to do this?"

"At least it's in English. Is there more than one document?"

"Yeah, I think so. Here, I'll take the first section." Anna slid papers to the side until she found a break. "Do you want to take the next one, or look through the stack?"

"I'll take the next one. Aren't we looking for whatever evidence they found to get the warrants? Is that how it works in Mexico?" Peel asked as she pulled off a section to read.

"I don't know, but let's assume it is. Here, mark anything you think is relevant." She handed Peel a pen.

They read in silence for a while, both marking sections. After nearly a half an hour of reading, Peel looked up. "Anything?"

"I'm not sure. I've marked a few spots, but I don't know what they mean." Anna turned the papers to face Peel.

Peel looked at Anna's stack and turned hers around, too. "Same here. I'm not sure if what I've highlighted is important."

"Let me see." Anna pointed to a paper. "You wrote all over this page. What's on it?"

"It's about who carried out the raids. The DEA was definitely there, but they were observers. The raids were done by the military. Is that normal in Mexico?"

"It is, but I think they usually provide support to the Federales." Noting Peel's confusion, she clarified. "Like the FBI. They're the national police force."

Peel raised her eyebrows. "These are DEA files, right?"

"Yes."

"They should be pretty thorough, right?"

"I would think so."

Peel spread the pages out. "I don't know if it matters, but see if you can find any mention of the police." Silently they scanned the pages of documents. Again, they marked sections.

"I see what you mean," Anna said.

"Yeah, maybe we're completely off track, but Devin was a police officer. He would be working for the Federales, not the military." Peel rubbed her forehead.

"It's just too much of a coincidence. The timing. The fact that it was both de Oro and Casalas. It has to be him." Anna tried to keep any trace of excitement out of her voice, but for the first time, she felt hope.

Peel rested her chin in her palm. "Maybe he didn't trust the police after what happened."

Anna nodded. "Who led the raids? I mean, who was in charge? Is there a name?"

"Yeah, someplace. This isn't who was in charge, but it's a name." Peel shuffled through the pages. When she found the one she was looking for, she pointed to the name and pushed the paper to Anna. "Subteniente L. Martinez."

"I wonder if that's his real name. Martinez is like Smith in the US. It's a very common name."

"Is *subteniente* his rank?" Anna nodded, and Peel looked back at the documents. "It does seem like a lot of the identifying information is left out. You know, when you see pictures of raids, the police cover their faces. It's probably the same thing, but I'd think the DEA reports would have had more information."

"Why? The DEA has to be careful, too. We're holding a classified report that it took only a day to get."

"You're right. How did Devin ever trust anyone?"

Anna nodded. "Yeah, and why did he trust the DEA?"

Peel sat forward. "Maybe we have this wrong. Maybe he trusted the army, and they brought in the DEA."

"Padre Benito said he didn't have any other friends, but maybe he knew someone in the military." Anna stood. "Let's go find Rosita." When they didn't find her in the kitchen, Peel knocked on the door to Rosita's private rooms.

Anna looked at her sideways and Peel shrugged. "We watched TV yesterday."

"The two of you?" Anna was surprised and somehow vindicated by the news. Peel had charmed Rosita, too.

"Yeah. She invited me in. I'm now a big fan of telenovelas."

"But you don't speak Spanish."

"I took Spanish in high school and in college. Some of it's coming back. Plus, you don't need to understand the language to watch heaving breasts." She winked at Anna. "I don't think she's here."

"Let's see if she's in the solarium."

* * *

They found the older woman sitting at the iron table reading her newspaper and drinking coffee. "Good for her," Peel whispered.

"I know. She should relax like this more often."

They made their way through the French doors and into the heart of the room. Peel looked around. It should have been relaxing, but the beauty was poisoned for her by the memory of Sebastien's dispassionate recounting of the murders. Anna was speaking when Peel caught up to her. Rosita moved aside sections of the paper and pulled out her phone. She scrolled for a few seconds before pressing the priest's name. When he answered, Rosita chatted with him before handing the phone to Anna.

While Anna spoke, Peel used the opportunity to look at her. Anna wasn't in the black-on-black uniform today. She was dressed in tight jeans and a tank top that showed off her defined arms and shoulders. The tight jeans gave Peel a nice view of her ass. After their night in bed, Peel was a big fan of Anna's ass. She was staring at it when she heard Anna say, "*Gracias*," and disconnect the call. She looked at Peel. "You were staring at my ass." Peel was surprised to hear a snort from Rosita. Anna said something to Rosita and they laughed together. Then Rosita shook her finger at the two of them, making a tsking sound. "It seems Rosita is learning English," Anna said.

Peel smiled at Rosita, then followed Anna out of the solarium. As they walked, Anna relayed the gist of the call. "All of the Devin brothers served in the army before becoming policemen. He said from the time they were kids, Gabriel planned for them to join the army. I guess they were in some kind of special forces."

Peel stopped short. "Really? He planned that when he was a kid?"

"Yeah. The other day, Padre Benito said Tomás's death changed Gabriel."

"Okay, so how does that help us?"

"I don't know. I asked him if Gabriel had any friends left in the army or if he ever mentioned anyone. He couldn't think of anything, but he said he'd get back to me if he did."

"Did you ask Padre Benito about Subteniente L. Martinez?"

"Why, yes I did. Weren't you listening?"

Peel ignored the gibe. "So, nothing?"

"Right. Now what?"

"I'm not sure. Any ideas?"

"Let's read the report again. There has to be more in it."

Peel touched Anna's arm. "Anna, truthfully, what will he do when we don't find these children? Please don't lie to me."

"We're going to find them. We've already gotten more than Sebastien found."

"Everything we have is nearly thirty years old." Peel turned to face Anna fully. "Anna, just tell me so I can be ready."

Anna caressed her cheek, and Peel's stomach flipped again. "I'm not going to let anything happen to you. I promise."

Peel reached for her hand and held it in both of hers. "Anna, I need you to promise me—"

"That is a promise, Peel."

"No. I need you to promise me you will do nothing when the time comes." Anna's eyes widened in shock, and she started to speak. Peel let go of her hand and held hers up to stop her. "I'm alone in this world. Other than a couple of good friends, there is no one. If you help me, you and your family will pay the price. I can't live with that. I won't allow you to exchange my life for someone else's." Peel wiped tears from her face. "Anna, please promise me to protect your family."

Anna looked away and Peel thought she saw a shimmer of tears in her eyes. Finally, she said, "That's not fair."

Peel nodded. "None of this is fair." She started walking again. "Let's get back to work."

"I need to swim." Anna dropped the papers on the table with a long exhale. "My brain isn't working. Come with me?"

"I guess it wouldn't hurt."

Peel turned to go into the house but Anna tugged her back. "Borrow one of my suits."

"I should. Yours are likely less revealing than whatever you bought me." Peel poked her.

Anna slapped her forehead. "Ugh, I forgot all about that. Mine are going to be too long for you."

"Too late. Lead the way."

After splashing in the shallow end by herself, Peel decided to lie in the sun and watch Anna do her laps. She found the graceful way Anna's body cut through the water mesmerizing. And hot. It was definitely hot. This had been a good idea. For a while, all concerns of Devin and the future slipped away.

After an hour during which Peel had been in and out of the water three times and Anna had stopped only briefly to drink from a water bottle, Peel had enough. She hopped back in the pool and stood directly in Anna's path. When Anna reached her, she stood up and pulled her goggles over her cap. "Bored?" she asked.

"Horny. Shower?"

Peel loved the delighted grin Anna gave her. "Definitely."

* * *

Peel was snuggled into Anna's side, sleeping soundly. Anna stared at the ceiling. She was thankful she'd sent Miguel away from Chicago because one way or another, her time on the estate was coming to an end. Sebastien's plan to find the children had only one outcome for Peel. An image of Ojos flashed into her mind. Her heart pounded, haunted by the thought of Peel at the bottom of a grave, terrified eyes looking at Anna.

The sound of the deadbolt turning caused Anna to jump and reach for her gun. Peel sat up next to her, pulling the sheet to her chest. Rosita walked in the bedroom and spoke to Anna and gestured at Peel. Anna blew out an exasperated breath, shook her head, then at Rosita's insistent tone, translated. "She says she thought you had better taste."

Peel laughed out loud. "Tell her I thought I did, too."

Anna rolled her eyes but complied, causing Rosita to laugh with Peel. Then she turned back to Anna. They spoke softly for several minutes.

"Hey. What's going on?" Peel touched Anna's arm as she spoke.

"One second. It's good, though." She finished her conversation with Rosita, and the other woman hurried from the casita, locking the deadbolt behind her.

"Padre Benito called her this afternoon and asked her to go to confession. When she was in the confessional, he told her that he and Gabriel Devin have remained in touch all these years. He talked to Devin after my visit and told him about you.

He said they agreed that the safest course of action was to do nothing. After I talked to him on the phone today, he called Devin and told him that we were getting close to finding him."

Peel pulled back, looking at Anna in surprise. "We were? How?"

"I don't know. But he wants to see us tomorrow."

"Padre Benito?"

"No." Anna grabbed her hand and squeezed. "Gabriel Devin."

Peel's eyes widened and her voice went up an octave. "He talked to Gabriel, and he'll see us? He's willing to meet me?" She collapsed back on the bed. "I can't believe it. I never thought it was possible. I may start crying."

"We don't have time." Anna got out of bed and walked to her closet. She handed Peel a backpack. "Go pack overnight clothes. He wants to meet us tomorrow morning in Mexico City."

Peel took the backpack and started getting dressed. "I get to leave the estate?" she asked in disbelief. "Do you need to ask Sebastien if it's okay?"

"No."

Peel reached for Anna. "Anna, promise me you will protect your family."

"I'm going to protect all of you." She pulled Peel in for a kiss. "Now, go get packed."

CHAPTER TWENTY-FOUR

On the drive to Mexico City, Anna filled Peel in on the rest of what the old priest told Rosita. "He said they were worried that we were going to lead Sebastien to Gabriel. He's agreed to meet with us as long as no one else knows."

Peel was still struggling to take in the sudden turn of events. "Why does he trust us?"

"I don't know, but Padre Benito trusts Rosita, so that's probably part of it. That, and you're Devin's family. Family is very important in Mexican culture, especially in small towns like Tierra."

Peel turned in her seat, leaning against the door so she could watch Anna. "He believes I won't betray him."

"I think so."

"Am I going to betray him?" Peel said it loud enough for Anna to hear, but she didn't expect an answer.

Anna reached a hand to her. "What is betrayal in this situation? Whatever happened is between Sebastien and Devin. You shouldn't be a part of it."

Rather than replying, Peel asked, "Where are we meeting him?"

"I don't know. Rosita asked where we were staying tonight. I think he's going to contact us somehow."

Peel settled back into her seat and stared out the window. It wasn't often her mind was completely devoid of thought. The landscape passed before her eyes but she failed to take it in. Anna, too, was silent. Peel finally spoke. "What will you do if Sebastien finds out?"

Anna shrugged. "I'll tell him the truth. We can't find the children if we can't talk to Devin. And Devin won't talk to us if Sebastien or his men are there. How could he argue against that logic?"

Peel nodded and looked back out the window. "Are you tired? You've made this drive a lot lately."

"I don't mind the drive. I like to get off the estate, too."

"Are we close?"

Anna leered at her. "I thought we were pretty close last night. Why? Picturing me naked again?"

Peel looked at her in disbelief, then started laughing, "I honestly don't know what to say to you anymore. Let me say this in simpler terms for you. Are we close to Mexico City?"

"Yes, to the city. We still have a way to go to get to the hotel." Anna paused, then turned to Peel with a big grin. "Hey, let's go to my friend Juanita's bar tonight."

"You want to go to a bar?" Peel was struggling to keep up with Anna.

"Yeah. It's a lesbian bar. Let's have a couple of beers and make out on the dance floor."

"Ah, so it's foreplay."

"We could skip the fore and go right to play, but I thought since you haven't been out of the house, you may like to see the area."

"Anna…" Peel started.

"Look, I know this is strange. We can go to the hotel, but I think you're going to be jumping at every sound. You'll like Juanita, and I think it will be a good distraction."

Peel reached across the console and put her hand on Anna's thigh. "That's sweet. It sounds fun. Let's do it."

Anna picked up the hand on her lap. She kissed it, then interlaced their fingers. They rode like that until Anna looked at her a little sheepishly. "Sorry, I need two hands to drive through the city."

Peel pulled her hand away and put it in her own lap. "Then I won't distract you. I don't want to go through all of this only to die in a car accident. Although," she said, tapping her finger to her chin, "it may be a better way to go."

Anna played along. "Really? A fiery death? That's what you'd choose?"

"No, I guess not. What would you choose?"

"A heart attack in my sleep," Anna answered immediately.

"Good choice. I'll pick that too." She pointed out the window. "Be my tour guide. Tell me what I'm looking at."

For the rest of the drive to Zona Rosa, Anna told Peel about Mexico City. She pointed out landmarks and explained what she knew of the history of the area. Peel enjoyed the feeling of normalcy Anna's chatter gave her.

At the hotel, the desk clerk asked Anna a couple of questions, glancing at Peel as he did. Anna nodded. Then she leaned down and whispered to Peel, "He wanted to know if we wanted a king bed. I think it's much more comfortable to 'play' in a large bed."

"Pretty sure of yourself, aren't you? Maybe all I want tonight is foreplay at the bar."

Anna bumped her with her shoulder. "You keep telling yourself that."

They got ready quickly and walked hand in hand through the streets of Zona Rosa. Anna stopped a couple of times, pointing out to Peel the shops where she'd bought her clothes. Peel shook her head in front of one store window, pointing to a mannequin. "Look, there is a perfectly respectable shirt right there. You must have been really impressed by my boobs that first night."

"They are impressive boobs."

"No, they are just regular, everyday boobs."

"Huh-uh, I know regular, everyday boobs when I see them. Yours are impressive."

"How many boobs have you seen?"

"Single or in pairs?"

"Some women only let you see one boob?" Peel loved their banter. She could almost believe she was a tourist on vacation.

"Women let me see whatever I want. I meant, do you want me to count your boobs as one or two boobs?" Anna pointed at the boobs in question.

"You're enjoying this too much. No more talk of boobs."

"I'd like to point out that you are the one who first brought up boobs, asked me to count them, and now that I think about it, you are also the one who watches telenovelas for the heaving breasts."

"Busted." Peel snickered.

Anna gave an exaggerated groan. "Puns are the lowest form of humor." She pointed to a door. "That's where we're going."

The large, dark room was loud and smelled of beer and cigarettes. Over the bar neon lights advertised beer companies' support of the gay community. She grabbed Anna. "This place is great!"

"Come on. I want you to meet Juanita." Anna pulled her through the crowd until they were standing two deep at the bar. Juanita and two other women were moving from customer to customer in a smooth dance.

"I love watching bartenders work," Peel said.

"I know what you mean. That's Juanita." She pointed, then called out, "Juanita!" over the noise.

"Anna! There are a couple of hot ones here tonight," Juanita called back, then caught sight of Peel by her side. "Oh, you've already found one."

Peel was standing in front of Anna. She looked over her shoulder. "Seriously? You have the bartender scout women for you?"

Anna shrugged. "She lives vicariously through me. Her girlfriend is very jealous."

"Yeah, I'm sure that's it," Peel said, but she was smiling. Nothing was going to spoil this night.

"Do you want a beer?" Anna asked in her ear.

"Sure."

Anna caught Juanita's attention and put up two fingers. Juanita nodded. When she handed the beers over the crowd, Anna said, "This is Peel."

"Peel?" Juanita asked.

"Long story," Peel shouted. "Nice to meet you, Juanita."

"We're going to try the patio," Anna told Juanita, who waved back at her.

Once outside, Anna led them to a spot on a low wall. "Why is it so busy? Isn't it a Sunday?"

"Yeah, I don't know. It's good people watching, though."

Just then a blonde with an American accent called from across the patio. "Anna!"

Anna looked up, her face wary, but then it brightened into a smile. "Jamie? What are you still doing here?"

"We were having such a great time, we decided to stay longer. Sadly, we're going back tomorrow." She pointed to the table where two other women waved. "Come sit with us. We have a table over there."

"We'll be there in just a second." Anna held her smile until the blonde bounced off.

"Peel, listen. They're from Denver. You can't use your real name and you can't say you're from there."

"Why not?"

"Because I don't know how public your disappearance has been. What if your face and name are all over the news?"

"You're afraid they'll try to help me."

"That, or they'll think you've faked your disappearance so you can party in Mexico City."

"That's crazy."

"But here you are. Partying in Mexico City."

Anna was right. "Okay, I'll be Emma."

"Emma?"

"That's Mrs. Peel's first name. Mrs. Emma Peel."

"Of course." Anna walked across the patio to a table of three women. "Hey! Good to see you guys. Jamie, Deb, Carla, this is Emma." The women scooted chairs together, making room at the table. "You decided to stay longer," Anna said to Deb. "Did you see the archaeology stuff you wanted?"

"Yes. There are amazing museums and digs here. We're going to come back someday."

Jamie turned to Emma. "Are you from the US?"

"Yes," Peel answered.

Before she could say more, Anna stood. "Let's dance." She motioned to the table. "Come on. It's your last night in Mexico." They made their way back through the bar and onto the crowded dance floor.

Anna kept them dancing most of the night. They danced in pairs or in a group laughing with each other. Occasionally, one person would break away to get more drinks or go to the bathroom. When it was Peel's turn, Anna asked in her ear, "Do you want me to go with you?"

"I'm fine," Peel shouted back. "This way, right?" She pointed to the back of the bar.

Anna nodded and went back to dancing.

As always, the line to the bathroom was long and was made longer by couples who tried to use the stalls for more than they were intended. When she finally made it back to the bar, she looked around for Anna. Carla waved to her from the dance floor. "Outside," she mouthed, pointing over her shoulder. Peel waved back and made her way to the patio. It took a minute to spot Anna and Jamie. Anna's back was to Peel and she could see that Jamie's arms were wrapped around her. They were engrossed in each other.

The sight of Anna holding another woman caused a sharp pain. She'd accepted she had feelings for Anna, but the pain of disappointment surprised her. Even this morning when Anna admitted she'd been with another woman, it didn't hurt like this. Seeing Jamie in Anna's arms was more than she could bear. Peel rushed back inside.

Back on the dance floor, Deb looked at her with a question on her face. Peel gave an exaggerated shrug. "Didn't see them." Just then Anna and Jamie reappeared.

"Ready to go?" Anna asked Peel.

Peel wanted to play it cool, but the words were out before she could stop them. "If you walk me to the hotel, you can come back."

"Why would I want to do that?"

"I saw you and Jamie on the patio. It's okay if you want to stay with her tonight. Can you be back early just in case?" Peel was struggling to keep the tears at bay.

Anna looked at the other three women. "It's good to see you guys again. Travel safely home." Without waiting for an answer, she grabbed Peel's wrist and dragged her to the door.

Once outside, she transferred her grip from Peel's wrist to her hand. "I'm sure what you saw looked bad. I tried to pick Jamie up last time I saw them, but we ended up in her hotel room talking. That was before anything happened with us." Anna didn't break eye contact. "Jamie's not over her ex-girlfriend. Tonight, she was upset because the ex called asking for Jamie's enchilada recipe."

"Why is that a problem?"

"Because she wanted to make them for her new girlfriend. The one she claimed she wasn't sleeping with before they broke up. Jamie's upset by the affair and by the callousness of her ex."

"I would be, too." Peel looked away. "Now I'm embarrassed." How could she have gotten so clingy? "I'm sorry."

"Don't be. I liked it." Anna kissed the top of her head and pulled her close. "And I liked the foreplay." They talked and laughed as they walked the few blocks back to the hotel. Once in the room, Anna said, "I smell like smoke and sweat. I'm going to take a shower." She pointed to Peel. "You're invited."

Peel reached for the bottom of her T-shirt. "Try not to hog the hot water this time."

It turned out the shower was only big enough for showering. They had some soapy teasing, but after getting blasted in the face by the spray one too many times, Peel called it quits. "Take your time. I'm going to dry off."

Anna gave her a slippery kiss full of lots of tongue and even more promise. "Be out in a couple of minutes."

When Anna came out of the bathroom, Peel was propped up against the pillows wearing the hotel robe. She dropped the remote on the bedside table. "Looking for some fake lesbian porn?"

"Yuck." Peel pulled back the covers. "Come here."

"Are you wearing that to bed?" Anna plucked at the tie closing Peel's robe.

"Only if you're wearing that." Peel pointed, but she stood and shrugged off her robe. She reached for Anna, opened her robe, and pushed it down her body. "You are beautiful."

Anna answered by kissing her deeply and walking backward into the bed. "Sit on the edge," Anna whispered. "Sit on the edge and open your legs for me."

She looked at Anna and slowly spread her legs. Anna watched. "Wider," she whispered.

Only with Anna could one word arouse Peel so much. She opened her legs wide and leaned back on her elbows. Anna knelt in front of her. "I don't even have to touch you to know how wet you are."

"You do that to me every time." Peel sighed. Anna reached under and cupped her ass in both hands, pulling Peel to her.

"I like the way you taste when you come," she said as she bent down and took Peel's clit in her mouth. She swirled her tongue around it while she gently sucked. There was no teasing tonight.

Peel pushed herself into Anna, crying out with every flick of her tongue. Anna moved down to Peel's opening, pushing her tongue deep then swirling it around the entrance. When Peel moaned, Anna moved her tongue back to her clit and sucked hard. At the same time, she plunged two fingers in, thrusting deeply. Peel feverishly rocked against Anna's mouth and fingers, feeling the quivers start deep inside. Anna stroked and sucked her until she came hard, her body folding over Anna, one hand gripping Anna's shoulder.

Anna pushed Peel onto the bed and covered her body with her own, and started thrusting into her. "I'm sorry," she whispered. "I want you so much." Peel answered by reaching between their bodies and opening herself. Anna groaned. She bent Peel's knees and pushed herself up on her arms, thrusting wildly. Finally, she pushed into Peel's wetness and stayed there. Peel watched the orgasm overtake her. "Peel. God, Peel," Anna cried, her head thrown back, her body shaking. "Peel," she whispered and collapsed on top of her.

They lay like that for nearly a minute. "That was incredible," Peel said. "I've never felt so wanted."

Anna rolled beside her and gathered her against her body. "I've never wanted anyone like that."

* * *

The note was delivered by a bellman the next morning. Anna handed it to Peel. It was in English:

Victoria Army Base
9:00 a.m.
Park your car in the neighborhood and walk to the gate.
Give the soldiers your names. Bring nothing with you.

"We need to get ready," Anna said. They'd been up since six alternating between pacing and watching TV. Conversation had been infrequent, their usual playful banter absent this morning.

Peel looked up from the note. "Do you know where this is?"

"Yes. It will take forty-five minutes to get there. Let's talk on the way." Once Anna pulled into traffic, words exploded from each of them.

"He's been on a military base."

"He never left the army."

They looked at each other. "It's the perfect place to hide," Peel said. "If it's like the US, no one can get on a military base without going through a lot of security."

"Right. But there's corruption in the army, too. The cartels own people everywhere. How could he be in the army and no one knew about it?"

"That's true. Do you think he's L. Martinez?" Peel asked.

"He must be. He couldn't use the Devin name."

"Do you think he kept the children with him all this time? I mean, in the US families live on bases." Even as she asked, Peel knew it was unlikely.

"I don't know." Anna reached over for her. "What's your plan for getting him to tell you where little Eduardo is?"

"That's all I thought about last night." At Anna's grunt of disbelief, she blushed. "Okay, not all night, but after you fell asleep, I tried to think of ways to convince him. He has no reason to reveal the boy's location. All this time, Eduardo has been his safety net to protect his daughter. Why would he risk that for me?"

"Everything I've heard makes me think he is a good man. He may do it because he knows you're not part of this," Anna said.

"Maybe." Peel was skeptical. "Where do you think the kids are?"

Anna put her hand back on the steering wheel. "I need two hands to drive." She gripped the wheel tighter. "I've spent a lot of time thinking about what I'd do in his situation. I keep coming back to his parents immigrating to the US. That has to be what happened. Even if it was too dangerous for them to keep the kids, they could have taken them to Catholic Services to be adopted."

"That's kind of what I thought, too. If it were my child and I wanted to absolutely guarantee her safety, I'd make sure I didn't know where she was." They looked at each other. "This could all be for nothing." Peel looked down at her hands. They were shaking.

"Look, we've gotten this far. Farther than anyone else." She looked over at Peel. "Let's see what he says."

As instructed, they approached the gate on foot. At the guardhouse, the soldier asked for their names and had them sign in. Peel went first, signing, *Esther Peel Primm.*

Anna grinned next to her. "Esther." She snorted under her breath. Peel punched her arm and handed her the pen. She watched as Anna scrawled her name on the page: *Anna Sandoval.*

Peel started. "Sandoval, huh? Finally, I learn your name."

Anna looked at her out of the corner of her eye while she signed. "Yeah, well forget it now that you've heard it."

Before Peel could say more, another soldier appeared behind them. "This way," he said.

As they walked, Peel whispered to Anna, "They're all speaking English."

"I noticed that, too. He knows you're from the US. It seems he wants you to feel comfortable." They climbed into a jeep and were driven through the base to a long, low building.

"Follow me, please," their driver directed. Once inside, he knocked sharply on a closed door.

"Enter," came the sharp command.

Peel's knees were shaking. She held back, and Anna turned to see what was wrong. She must have seen Peel's growing panic because she reached for her arm and pulled her close. "I'm with you," she whispered. Peel nodded and allowed herself to be led forward.

The soldier saluted sharply. "Father Martinez, your visitors."

CHAPTER TWENTY-FIVE

"*Gracias, soldado,*" Father Martinez said. The private saluted again and left the room, closing the door behind him. Peel stood frozen, her mouth hanging open. She stared at the man who stood in front of them. Over a standard military uniform he wore a large cross on a heavy chain, but no clerical collar. Even though his hair was a youthful brown, his face was marked by heavy lines around his mouth and between his eyes. The years had been hard on him. He gestured to two chairs in front of the desk. "Please, sit."

They did, and he took the chair behind the desk. Without preamble, he asked, "Which one of you is my cousin?" Her mouth dropped open. She never believed they would actually find him. "Yes," he said in response to her shock. "In another life, I was known as Gabriel Devin."

Peel tried to get herself together. "I'm Peel…um…Peel Primm. From Denver," she added unnecessarily.

He reached his hand across the desk and took hers. "Peel. I am very sorry that you have been brought into this. Like so many victims of the Gutierrez family, you are an innocent."

Peel didn't know what to say. "Thank you," was all she could come up with.

He turned to Anna. The gentleness was gone. "You are Anna?" She nodded. "And you work for Sebastien."

"Yes." She held his gaze.

"Benito believes you are a good person. He says I can trust you."

"You can."

"I hope so." He stared at her, but Anna didn't look away.

Peel broke the deadlock. "Should we call you Father Martinez?"

"That's who I am now." He shrugged. "Tell me what happened. How did you come to be here?" She started with her parents' deaths, told of finding her grandfather's birth certificate, and her belief that her mother had never seen it. Father Martinez interrupted. "Charles Devin is your great-grandfather?"

She nodded. "Yes."

"He was my grandfather." There was no smile. "He wasn't an impressive man."

"Since he left my grandfather an orphan, I have to agree with you," she replied.

"Then what happened?" Peel explained about her search on the genealogy site and the ill-fated call to Tierra de Oro. Father Martinez frowned at that. She told him about the attempt at the library and then what she remembered of her eventual kidnapping. When it was clear she was finished, he turned to Anna. "What part did you play in this?"

"None. I knew nothing of Ms. Primm prior to her arrival at the estate."

He looked to Peel. "Do you believe that?"

"Yes. Anna has taken care of me. She's helped me find you."

He made a noncommittal sound, then looked at Anna. "Who do they have?"

Anna sat still for a long moment. "My brother."

Peel gasped. "Are they holding him prisoner, too?"

"He's fine. I'm working on it." She turned away from Peel's gaze and back to Martinez, giving him a hard look. Peel recognized that look. No more questions.

"Tell me what he told to you." This question was directed back to Peel.

Peel recounted the three meetings with Sebastien. As she talked, she left out the vitriol and the pride Sebastien had taken in the murders. When she got to the day at the soccer field, she hesitated, afraid the story would make him relive the horrors of the day.

"It's okay," he assured her. "Your words can't be worse than my memories." After a pause to gather herself, she told him the rest.

"So, he gave you two weeks to find his nephew. Why two weeks? What's happening in two weeks?" This time he looked at Anna.

She looked back at him but didn't answer.

"I see," he said after a long moment. "I could have you arrested and kept on base."

Still, she held his gaze. "You could."

Peel jumped in. "Please don't put her in this position. She's here because she's helping me."

He looked at Peel. "Two weeks," he repeated. "And how long has it been?"

"Six days."

For the first time, he gave a wide smile. "Six days. I'm impressed. You say you are a librarian? Maybe you should have been in the police."

Peel shook her head and pointed to Anna. "She figured out you were behind the raids of de Oro, Casalas, and Disciples of Gold. But don't say anything about her being a cop," Peel added quickly.

"You give me too much credit. That was easy," Anna said. "You figured out the army connection." They grinned at each other.

Their smiles dropped when Martinez said, "He wants to know where the boy is?"

"Yes," Peel answered.

"I'm sorry." His voice was kind, regretful even, but his eyes were steel. "I won't give you that information." He leaned back in his chair and steepled his fingers. "He told you his story. Let me tell you mine, and then you will understand why I can't help you."

* * *

1989
Tierra de Oro, Mexico

The sun shone brightly on the fresh green turf of the *fútbol* field. A ribbon stretched across the entrance and a table with flowers and several pairs of scissors were near its center. It was perfect. He looked up, thinking of Tomás. After all these years he could barely remember his best friend's face. He looked at the families gathered for the dedication. Tomás would probably look like any number of the boys in the crowd.

Above him was the sign they had erected yesterday: *Tomás Flores Memorial Fútbol Field*. He looked up at it and felt peace. He'd made it his life's work to avenge the death of his boyhood friend. It had taken years, but finally the de Oro cartel was destroyed. Yes, Eduardo had been released, but his sons were dead, and the cartel's assets had been seized.

All around him families picnicked and kids kicked black-and-white balls on the new field. This is what the town of Tierra de Oro would be now. No more children killed by the cartel. A hand on his arm stopped his thoughts. "Señor?" The small boy held a folded piece of paper. "A man told me to give this to you. He said you should hurry."

Confused, he looked at the youth as he reached to take the note from his outstretched hand. "Are you ready to play on the new field?"

The boy pointed to the note. "Yes, sir. But the man told me to tell you it was an emergency. He said to hurry," the boy repeated.

He opened the note and read. He looked at the boy in confusion and then read it again: "If you hurry, you can see her before she dies."

He grabbed the boy and shook him. "Who gave this to you?"

The boy's eyes were wide and he backed away, trying to free himself from the man's grip. "I don't know. He told me you were very important and that you would know what to do."

He scanned the crowd. He recognized most of the people gathered for the celebration. No one seemed to be watching him. He let the boy go and ran over to his brothers. "I have to get home. Something is wrong with Sonja." He took off in a dead sprint.

He'd been cross with her that morning. He wanted her by his side on this special day, but the baby was sick and Sonja wouldn't let a crying baby distract from the moment. He insisted, but she knew how to handle him. She kissed him and made him promise to teach their daughter *fútbol* on Tomás's field.

As soon as he'd read the note, he knew he would be too late. Eduardo Gutierrez would make sure of that. He wanted Gabriel to live his life wondering if he had just listened to the boy the first time or driven a little faster—would he have saved her?

The front door was open a few inches. Crouching at the side, he listened for a moment. There were no sounds. With the flat of his hand, he pushed the door open the rest of the way but stayed off to the side. Nothing. He crouched low in a shooter's stance and entered the house.

His vision narrowed and a terrible pressure in his ears muffled all sound. His beautiful Sonja lay crumpled on her side in a pool of blood. So much blood. It obscured what little he could see of her face. He knelt and turned her toward him, careful to cradle her head. The horrible gash in her throat gaped open. In a daze, he tried to reposition her head so the deep wound would close. If he could get it closed, maybe she would breathe. It was no good. Sightless eyes met his. He wanted to close them, to stop the accusing gaze, but he couldn't. He deserved her blame. He laid her back down, careful to make sure her hair wasn't in the spreading pool of blood. She would hate that.

He got to his feet and stumbled into the kitchen. His hands were soaked in her blood. Everything he touched was marked. He pressed the buttons to dial the station. It rang, but there was no answer. He hung up and dialed again, his hands shaking, fingers slipping off the buttons. Again no one answered. A third time. Nothing. He yelled in frustration and pain, slamming the phone down on the receiver over and over until it broke off in his hand.

That's when he heard her. Absently, he thought, "Sonja is going to be mad you woke the baby." As the fleeting thought vanished, reality crashed back. He rushed to the bedroom and peered into the cradle. She was untouched. He reached for her with hands soaked in his wife's blood. He held her to him, blood from his shirt and hands staining the baby's blanket and face. He recoiled in horror when he saw what he'd done. He put her back in the cradle. While the baby wailed, he washed his hands, changed his shirt, and wet a washcloth to clean her face. Only then did he pick her up again, but she continued to cry. He looked at her helplessly. How could he comfort her when his whole world had been destroyed? Finally, she worked a fist into her mouth and started to suck. Her dark eyes opened and looked at him. That was what finally broke his trance.

His brothers. He needed to find his brothers. They would help him. He ran with the baby to the car, holding her to him as he sped back to the *fútbol* field. When he got close, he saw the flashing lights and knew they were gone, too.

* * *

"There was no one there," Father Martinez told Peel and Anna. "Only the bodies and the rest of the police department. Everyone else was gone. People ran as soon as the shooting started. They left picnics and toys scattered. Everything just left behind."

He took a deep breath before going on. "They killed my brothers and their wives. They killed three children. It was a massacre. Those kids, they were little and the bullets tore their bodies apart. Someone called my parents, and they came, but I didn't let them near. I didn't want them to see my brothers like that. When my mother saw the baby, she asked where Sonja was. I couldn't say it. I couldn't tell her. She knew. She took the baby and told me to go get her things.

"That's when I found this." He opened the desk drawer and handed Peel a plastic bag. Inside was a note on yellowed paper. She recognized the handwriting.

"I let the baby live for now. I'll be back for her, but I promise I won't kill her. I'll make her my whore. S."

"Oh my God." Peel inhaled sharply. "He's a monster." She handed the note to Anna, who read it silently then handed it back.

Father Martinez took the note and placed it in the drawer. "I ran to my parents' house and took the baby from my mother. I hid her, but I knew she would never be safe from him. Hiding her wouldn't be enough to keep her safe." He rubbed his hand over his face. "I'm not proud of what I did. My whole life I lived by God's laws, but that day I didn't." He fingered the large cross. "That's why I serve the church. It's my atonement.

"I knew about Eduardo's relationship with the Casalas family. I knew he was trying to expand his power. When Francisco Gutierrez married Dante Casalas's only child, Eduardo got what he wanted. After I buried my brothers, I came here and waited for Yolanda Casalas to appear. It was easy to take the boy from her. She was terrified I would hurt him. I handed her a note: 'Sebastien Gutierrez murdered my wife and my brothers. He threatened to make my daughter his whore. As long as my daughter is safe, your son will be.'"

"Father." Peel leaned forward. "Is she safe?"

There was no hesitation in his answer. "He can never touch her." They sat in silence, each with their own thoughts.

Suddenly, Anna straightened. Her tone soft, she asked, "Is she being watched over?"

He flinched at the question. He started to speak, but stopped. Then he looked at Peel. He was still fingering the cross when he seemed to reach a decision. He turned back to Anna. "Always."

Peel watched as the two held each other's gazes. Something significant had been settled between them. Anna stood. "Thank you."

He stood. "I believe you are a good friend to have."

"I hope so."

Peel looked between them. Father Martinez came around the desk and took her hand in both of his. "I'm sorry that I can't help you, Cousin." Then he looked over her shoulder to Anna. "But I don't think you will need my help after all."

They were almost out the door when he called out, "I will pray for you." They turned back at his words. He looked at Anna. "Both of you."

CHAPTER TWENTY-SIX

Neither spoke until they were off the base and back in Anna's car. Peel was vibrating with tension. When the car doors closed, she looked at Anna. "What happened back there? Do you know where they are?"

But Anna was already on the phone, and she put a hand up to silence Peel. After talking for several minutes, she hung up. "I'm going to take you to Juanita. Stay with her until I come back to get you."

"What? No. Anna, tell me what's going on. What do you know?" Anna didn't answer as she concentrated on her driving. The leisurely tour of Mexico City was clearly over. She accelerated out of the neighborhood, passing cars as she maneuvered through the narrow side streets. Once they were on a busy thoroughfare, Anna looked up and down the blocks, seeming to search for something. With an abrupt acceleration, she forced her way across two lanes. "Anna, slow down. What's going on?" Peel had one hand on the console and the other on the dash.

Anna ignored her and pulled next to a cab. She got out and spoke to the driver. They reached an understanding and she handed him three bills. "Peel," she called through the open car door. "Get in the cab. He's going to take you to Juanita. She'll meet you on the street." When Peel hesitated, Anna shouted, "Peel, now!"

Peel got out and walked over to the cab. "Anna," she started, but Anna put two fingers on her lips.

"There's no time. Go." She pushed her in and slammed the door. Without another look, Anna jumped into the SUV and sped off.

Peel sat in the back of the cab, stunned. The driver said something to her in Spanish. She shook her head and said, "English?" He shrugged and started to drive.

As promised, Juanita was waiting on the curb. Peel climbed out and looked at the other woman, unsure of what to do. Juanita pulled her into a hug. "Anna told me to take good care of you. Come in."

She led Peel into a tiny bright kitchen and pulled out a chair at the tile table. Warm colors surrounded her, and she relaxed some. The room reminded her of Rosita. Juanita opened an apartment-sized refrigerator and pulled out a salad and a Coke. "Is this okay? Anna said you hadn't eaten."

Peel blinked at her. The emotion of the morning, Anna's abrupt departure, now this woman's kindness in her tiny kitchen—all of it was overwhelming. She put her head in her arms and cried.

"Oh, *mierda*," Juanita swore. "I'm sorry. What did I say? Is it the salad? Do you want tea? I can make tacos. All Americans like tacos."

Peel sniffled and lifted her head. Her voice shook a little. "Everything is lovely. I'm crying because you're so kind."

"Okay, no more kind." Juanita gestured to a drawer by the two-burner stove. "Get your own fork. It's right there."

Peel laughed and got the fork. "I'm sorry. A lot has happened today. Actually, a lot has happened in the last couple weeks." Peel sat in front of the salad. "Thank you for letting me come here."

Juanita joined her at the table with her own Coke. "It's okay. Anna's a good friend. I would do anything for her."

Peel sniffled again. Juanita handed her a napkin from the holder on the table. "It seems like you're a good friend to her, too."

Peel gave her a watery smile. "Do you always find women for her?"

Juanita blushed and looked down. "It's a silly game we play. Anna likes the ladies from America. They make her feel like home."

Peel thought back on Anna's words. *"While you're in Mexico, you need to think about your safety. The men around here, especially Sebastien, don't need consent to fuck you."* At the time, she'd thought Anna was as dangerous as the men around her. Now that she knew better, she could understand Anna's need to connect with someone from home, especially not knowing if she would ever return.

"I have to leave for work. Anna said you like the telenovelas, so I turned the TV on for you in there." She lifted her chin, indicating the other room. Peel laughed again.

She stood when Juanita did and hugged the woman. "Thank you for being a good friend to her." She could tell Juanita was surprised by her words.

"Maybe you two come to the bar tonight?"

"Maybe."

* * *

Anna played the priest's words over and over in her mind. If she was right, she would take Sebastien and Casalas to the children today. If not, she could very well cost Peel her life.

She pulled over and dialed her phone. "Yes," came the polite answer.

"This is Anna, Sebastien Gutierrez's associate. It's urgent that I speak with Mr. Casalas."

"One moment, please." She sat for several minutes waiting for him to come on the line.

"Anna? Have you found him?" Casalas's voice contained a mixture of hope and trepidation.

"I believe so," she answered. There was silence. Anna knew he didn't want to ask the question that had been in his mind for thirty years. "Mr. Casalas, I need your help."

"Yes." His sigh was heavy through the phone. "I promised to make you a wealthy woman. I assure you, my word is good."

"Sir, I don't want money." She waited, wanting to give him a minute to absorb her words. "I'd like you to let the Devin woman go."

His response was what she expected: silence. She'd planned for it and waited for him to speak. She knew if she filled the silence with a rush of words, he would see her as weak. "Why?" he finally asked.

"She has no part in this." Anna unspooled her argument a little at a time.

"Neither did Eduardo." His voice held only sadness.

Anna was careful. "No, sir, but neither did the Devin baby." She held her breath. If she angered him now, it was over.

His sigh was the answer she hoped to hear. "Yes. The children should have never been part of this." His next words were also expected. "Sebastien will not like it."

"No, he won't."

"You're willing to go against him?"

"Not alone." She wanted to beg him to protect her, but knew it was futile. She was Sebastien's employee. He, alone, would determine the consequence of her betrayal.

"I see." The next block of silence stretched so long that Anna thought she had lost the connection. Then, "He's gone, isn't he?"

The change of subject didn't surprise her. That it had taken him this long to ask showed he'd known all along. "Yes, sir."

"How long?"

She paused. Giving him this information was a risk. "From the beginning."

His voice was full of sadness. "I don't know how I'm going to tell his mother. Yolanda always believed she would see him again."

"You can return him to her."

"Yes. That's all I can do now. What is your plan?"

"I'd like to take her to the embassy. Once she's safe, I'll call you with the information."

"Hmm. And you'd like me to contact Sebastien?"

"Yes," she answered.

"I'll expect to hear from you in two hours."

* * *

It was getting dark when Peel heard a car stop in front of the house followed by a knock on the door. "Peel, it's Anna. Open the door."

Peel unbolted the door and pulled it open. Anna stepped inside and pulled her close. The kiss was long and intense. Peel broke away first and was startled to see Anna had tears in her eyes. "Anna?" Peel's breath caught. She searched her face.

"You're going home."

"What? Anna, no. I told you. Not like this. I'm not exchanging your brother's life for mine. We still have time. Maybe Father Martinez will come around."

Anna shook her head. "No. I know where the children are. I spoke to Dante Casalas this afternoon. He promised to make me rich if I found Eduardo. I asked him to send you home instead."

"Why did you go to him and not Sebastien? Sebastien was going to send me home if we found Eduardo." Even as she said the words, she knew they weren't true.

Anna's look was gentle, and she pulled Peel tightly against her as she spoke. "No, he wasn't. He would never have let you live. You know too much. Think of the crimes he's admitted to you. He won't be happy, but he can't disagree with Casalas."

"What's going to happen to you after this? Won't he take it out on you? Do you even know for sure where they are? What if you're wrong?" Peel gripped Anna's arms.

"I'm not wrong." Anna kissed her again. "We have to go. I'll tell you everything in the car."

"Where are we going?"

"To the American embassy. I'll drop you off, and then I'll take them to the children. That's the deal I made."

"That doesn't make sense. What's their insurance if you're wrong?" Anna didn't answer. "Your brother? Right? That's what it is. They have your brother."

Anna grabbed Peel by the shoulders and looked in her eyes. "I'm not wrong, and my brother is safe. I sent him away before this." She slid her hand down Peel's arm and clasped her hand. "We need to go. I have to get back to them in an hour."

* * *

Once they were in the car, Anna started talking. "Little things bothered me about Father Martinez. His story didn't add up."

"Like what?"

"Like…" Anna paused. "What's the baby's name?"

Peel blinked. "Sonja was his wife." She was quiet for a time, then frowned. "You're right. He never used her name."

"Weird, right?"

"Maybe it made him sad to think about her."

"He was definitely sad, but I think he grieves for his wife and brothers. The baby was an afterthought to him. Think about it. He finds Sonja and then doesn't even check on his child? He didn't even remember he had a daughter until he heard her cry." Anna took a breath. "Then there was the mausoleum."

"The mausoleum? What about it? You said she was afraid of being buried alive."

"Yes, and I understand wanting to fulfill her last wishes, but she was gone. And he had a baby to take care of. Yet he gives his house to the church, and his only stipulation about the money was to have Sonja interred in a mausoleum in Mexico City. How was he going to take care of the child?"

"If he's going to give her up for adoption, he wouldn't need the money," Peel pointed out.

"He would need money to get her out of the country. You can get a lot done in Mexico, but you have to have money for bribes." Anna looked over her shoulder and changed lanes.

"What are you saying?" Peel crossed her arms over her chest.

Anna noticed her body language and reached over to put her hand on Peel's thigh. "What was his answer when you asked if she was safe?"

"Um…" Peel paused. "He didn't say yes, did he?"

"That's right. He said, 'he can never touch her.' Peel, how does he make sure Sebastien can never touch his daughter? How can he absolutely guarantee she will never be Sebastien's whore?" Anna waited for Peel to say something. When she remained quiet, Anna said, "There's only one way."

"No." Peel shook her head vehemently. "He wouldn't do that."

"He was a cop. He tried to follow the law, and look what happened." Anna glanced at Peel. "He told us he became a priest to atone for what he did. Kidnapping a crime boss's grandson and giving him to a loving family in the United States? Gabriel Devin would believe he saved the child. There would be nothing to atone for."

Peel put a hand over her mouth and stared out the side window. Eventually, she turned to Anna and whispered, "He killed her. That's what you're saying, isn't it?"

"Yes. I think he killed her the night he read the note. I don't know if he meant to, or if he was even in his right mind, but he killed her. He must have been overwhelmed by what he did and by the depth of his loss." Anna wasn't convinced Gabriel Devin felt the loss of the child, but she wanted to protect Peel. "Afterward, he needed justice for her, so he took Eduardo."

"And killed him, too." Peel looked like she was having a hard time processing what she was hearing. "Anna, I don't know. It's a big reach for a man who was a cop and is now a priest."

They stopped at a light, and Anna was able to fully turn and face Peel. "I wasn't sure until I asked him."

"What?" Peel shook her head in confusion. "You went back?"

"No. At the end of our meeting. I asked him if she was being watched over. He didn't answer right away. Do you remember that?" She looked over at Peel, who nodded. "He said, 'Always.'"

Anna watched as the pieces clicked for Peel. "They're with her. Sonja is watching over them. The mausoleum." She stared out the windshield. "It was so he could put the children in the casket."

"Yes."

They drove in silence. Peel reached for Anna's hand and put it against her cheek. "I don't know what to say to you. Thank you is not enough. Saying I'll never forget you is silly. How could I forget you?" She wiped a tear. "You saved my life, and you made me feel alive in a way I never have. You are an incredible woman, Anna Sandoval."

Anna scoffed. "Sandoval isn't my last name. I saw it a couple of rows above where I signed in." She brought their clasped hands to her lips. "I'm sorry for what you've been through. You are a beautiful, smart, and incredibly sexy woman. I'm glad I got to sleep with you." Anna grinned her cheeky grin, hoping it would make Peel laugh. It did.

Anna pulled into the drive of a Sheraton hotel. She pointed across the street. "That's it. The embassy is right there. Tell the guard who you are and what happened. They'll get you home."

Peel was crying now. "I won't tell them anything about you."

Anna tightened her grip on Peel's hand. "You have to. You need to tell them everything that happened to you. That includes me."

"You saved me. I'm not going to do anything that would harm you."

"Peel, please. Think about it. You have enough information to topple a cartel. If you leave any part of it out, you'll look guilty. You deserve to have your life back. I'll be fine. I know what I'm doing."

Peel unbuckled her seat belt and moved over the console separating them. She put her hands on either side of Anna's face and kissed her. "Promise me. Promise me you'll stay safe."

"I promise," Anna said, her eyes filling with tears.

"Will Sebastien hurt you?"

"No, I have something he wants." She kissed her one last time. "Go."

Peel hesitated, and Anna whispered, "Please." Peel ran her fingertips down Anna's cheek, then stepped out of the car.

Anna watched her fade in the rearview mirror as she drove away.

CHAPTER TWENTY-SEVEN

The same man answered, "Yes."

"It's Anna," she said simply.

This time it was Sebastien who took the phone. "Anna," was all he said.

She'd spent months watching and listening to him and knew his moods. His fury was palpable. "Yes." She kept her voice steady even though her heart pounded.

"You took Miss Primm to the embassy?"

"I did." Anna couldn't tell if Casalas was with him. She needed to watch every word.

His voice was clipped. "Where is he?"

She knew he meant Eduardo. "He's with Devin's wife, Sonja."

The silence was long. When he spoke again, there was sadness in his words. "Are you sure?"

"Yes."

"Where?"

"There's a mausoleum at Our Lady of Guadalupe Cemetery. That's where they all are."

"All of them? His daughter?" Then, as if speaking to himself, "Of course she is. It's what I would have done."

Rather than respond, she asked, "Do you want me to tell Casalas where they are?"

Sebastien's anger was back. "You should not have talked with him today. We have much to discuss after this. We will meet you at the cemetery. See that you are there." The call ended.

Anna's stomach lurched. It had been a gamble to involve Casalas, but it had been her only option. Sebastien's words after she killed Ojos had never been far from her mind: *"I hope you do as well with Miss Primm."*

* * *

The drive to the cemetery took forty-five minutes. For once, Anna was thankful for the evening traffic slowing her progress through the city. It gave her time to think. This morning, when she realized what Father Martinez was telling her, she'd only gotten so far in her plan as freeing Peel. What she hadn't done was negotiate her own safety with Casalas. It wouldn't have mattered, anyway. Anna's actions were a betrayal to Sebastien. Betrayals had to be answered. Even Casalas couldn't intervene in that.

She drove down the tree-lined road until she came to the spot where she'd been that afternoon. Two large black SUVs were parked off the road. In the gloom, she saw a group of men gathered around the mausoleum. A circle of light shone on the entrance. With a deep breath, she got out of the car. The sound of pounding, followed by the rip of metal, told her they were close to getting the door open. As she neared the entrance, she saw two men working at the door while another two stood back with Sebastien and Casalas. Both men heaved a final shove, and the door gave way. For a few minutes, they continued to wrestle with the opening. By the time the door was open, Anna stood beside Sebastien. He didn't acknowledge her.

Silently, they filed into the dank space. Sebastien lifted a lantern up high, and they all scanned the bronze plaques. "She's there." Casalas pointed to a name in the lower corner of the building. "Sonja Rosales Devin, Beloved Wife and Mother" was written in raised letters. There were no dates. "Remove the faceplate. Be careful with the stone. This woman deserves respect," Casalas ordered the men. This surprised Anna, and her respect for the man grew. She heard a grunt next to her as Sebastien registered the words.

The two men unscrewed the corners of the marble façade and lifted the heavy stone away, exposing a thin sheet of metal. They looked questioningly back at Casalas for how to proceed. "It's caulk," he told them. "Break the seal and pull the metal away." It took several minutes, but they did as instructed. When it was done, Sebastien lifted the lantern, revealing the coffin within. Casalas called to the two men waiting outside. "Pull it out and place it on the floor. Carefully. Keep it level." He gestured to the doorway, and looked at Sebastien and Anna. "I don't think there is room for all of us while they pull the casket out." Sebastien left the lantern on the floor and they stepped into the night.

Anna heard scraping as the casket moved along the concrete floor of the vault. After several minutes, the four men reemerged and wordlessly stepped aside. "Wait at the cars," Casalas ordered. One man handed Sebastien the lantern and a crowbar, and they all walked away. Casalas looked at him and nodded. Anna hung back, wanting to give them privacy. The two men disappeared into the darkness.

She'd just taken a step to the side when a hand clasped over her mouth and a gun was shoved into her back. "Not a sound," a voice said in her ear. She recognized it immediately. Gabriel Devin or Father Martinez? She wondered which persona was holding the gun. "Go inside," he ordered. She did. The scraping of her feet as she crossed the threshold caught the attention of the two men inside.

Sebastien was bending over the casket, preparing to open it, but he straightened when he saw Anna, a question in his eyes. His expression turned to fury when he recognized who was behind her. "Devin." He lurched forward, a crowbar clutched in his hand.

"Easy." Devin pulled the gun away from Anna and pointed it at Sebastien. He froze in place, eyes burning with rage.

Devin stepped away from Anna and farther into the room, the gun still pointing at Sebastien. He looked between the two men. "Dante Casalas." At Dante's nod, he said, "Your men massacred my brothers."

Casalas answered, "Not on my orders."

"So I heard." Devin stepped closer to the casket. "You killed the men responsible?"

Casalas shrugged. "That is my business."

"Still proud. Even at the moment of your death." A growl from Sebastien caused Devin to turn slightly. "Come now, Sebastien. You must have known we would come to this." He lifted a shoulder. "It was always going to be you and me in the end."

Sebastien stepped toward him, his fingers tightening around the crowbar." Devin laughed. "Drop it. I assure you, you will be dead before you raise it above your head." They stared at each other. At a sound from Casalas, Sebastien let the metal bar fall. It clanked against the stone floor. "Back up," Devin ordered. Sebastien didn't move. Devin sighed and pointed the gun at Casalas.

"Sebastien, step back." Casalas's voice had the unmistakable tone of complete command. Sebastien moved.

Now Devin's voice was almost gentle as he spoke to Casalas. "Would you like to see him before you die? Do you need to know for sure?"

Instead of answering that question, Casalas asked, "How?"

"How did he die? Are you wondering if he suffered like my wife did? Like those boys at the *fútbol* field? Like Tomás?" Casalas remained silent. Anna marveled at the older man's calm. No one breathed.

"Yes," he answered. "I want to know if he suffered."

"He didn't. I suffocated him in his sleep." Casalas nodded, accepting the answer. "Would you like to see him?" Devin asked again. He never looked at Sebastien.

"Yes," Casalas said.

Devin waved with the gun. "Stand next to Sebastien." Casalas moved into position and waited. There were tears in the old man's eyes. Anna looked back to Devin, hoping to see sympathy, but there was none. "Open it," he said.

Sebastien growled, but Casalas silenced him with a quiet, "Stop. I need to see my boy." Sebastien looked deflated. He reached for the crowbar.

"No," Devin said. "You don't need that. It's not locked. Just turn the clasp on the side." When Sebastien did, Devin ordered, "Throw the crowbar into the vault." Sebastien picked up the heavy piece of metal, looked at it, then tossed it into the opening. "Wise decision. Now you can lift the lid."

Sebastien bent down and slowly lifted the lid. Despite being closed for thirty years, it opened without protest. Casalas held the lantern over the opening. "Oh, my boy," he whispered. "My poor dear boy." He dropped to his knees in front of the open casket. Sebastien bent down, reaching into the opening, but a sob from Casalas stopped him.

Devin turned to Anna, a look of triumph in his eyes. "Run," he said. She looked at him, confused by the word. He gestured with the gun. She hesitated for a moment, then sprinted for the door. At the threshold, she tripped but managed to regain her footing without falling.

Rather than head toward the cars, she ran in the opposite direction, into the shadows. Whatever was going to happen, she knew this was her chance to escape. Behind her she heard Sebastien yell and Devin laugh.

The sound of the blast was deafening, but she didn't have time for it to register before she was lifted off of her feet. After that, there was nothing.

CHAPTER TWENTY-EIGHT

Even with Anna's entreaty, Peel didn't tell them everything. When she gave her name at the gate and said she'd been kidnapped by members of the de Oro drug cartel, the guard let her in immediately. Over the ensuing hours, she lost count of how many people she met. Each time she finished telling her story, one official would look at the other and agree that someone else needed to be awakened. The last person she spoke with introduced himself as a DEA agent. "Ms. Primm, we need your help," he told her. "You have information that is invaluable to our efforts to stop the flow of drugs into the United States."

Peel was exhausted and her head was pounding. "I know. I'll help you whatever way I can." She squeezed her eyes shut, willing away the pain. "Will you let me know what happens to them? When you arrest them? To Sebastien, Father Martinez, and Casalas? To Anna." She choked on her name.

The agent misunderstood her. "You will be kept updated at all times. But you don't need to worry. Sebastien Gutierrez will not be a threat to you ever again."

She didn't bother correcting him. What did it matter? "What do you need?" she asked.

"We need you at DEA headquarters in Washington, DC. Several agents are gathering there awaiting your arrival."

She blinked in surprise. "For how long? Will I be able to go home?"

"Three or four days at the most. Then we'll get you back to Denver." Someone walked into the room and handed him a printout. He read it, then looked up at her. "We can get you out in the morning." He glanced at his watch. "Actually, in a couple of hours." He looked back at the paper. "The director has made arrangements for you to stay in guest quarters on a military base in the DC area. It's for safety, and for access to medical services." His voice was kind. "You had a serious concussion, and from the looks of the headache you are fighting, you may still have symptoms."

Two hours later, Peel was taken by convoy to an airfield outside Mexico City. There she boarded a military transport plane for Washington, DC. She'd been able to hold herself together during the long night of debriefing, but now that she was leaving Mexico, leaving Anna, she started to cry. The woman seated beside her handed her a tissue and spoke in a low voice. "You're safe, now. They can't hurt you. You'll be home soon." She smiled her thanks to the woman but said nothing. How could she explain it wasn't her safety that worried her? Closing her eyes, she willed herself to think of anything but Anna.

The bounce of the plane on a runway woke her with a start. She opened gritty eyes to see her seatmate smile at her. "Feeling better?"

Peel blinked a couple of times and found that her headache was better. "Yes. Thank you. Are we in Washington?"

"Yes. As soon as we finish taxiing, you'll be met by a DEA agent who will escort you to the base hospital."

To Peel's relief, the drive was short. At the hospital, she was put through a battery of tests assessing her balance, hearing, vision, and cognitive ability. As she was being led into yet another room, Peel spoke up. "Can we continue this tomorrow?

I'm exhausted. I'm hungry. I need to shower and change my clothes. I don't think I can do any more."

The woman seated at the desk laughed. "Of course. We get a little overeager sometimes. Can we do one more test before I leave you alone for the rest of the afternoon?"

Peel groaned, mainly for effect. "Really? How bad is it?"

"It's a CT scan. All you have to do is lie still and breathe. You had a grade-three concussion and were in and out of consciousness. We'd like to do the scan to rule out any brain injury."

After the scan, she was taken to guest quarters where she showered and dressed in the clothes she'd had on the night before. With a sigh, she climbed into the bed and buried herself under covers. Sleep came quickly.

Sometime in the late afternoon she was roused by a knock. A woman in civilian clothes held up two bags and asked, "Hungry?"

"Yes." Peel stepped aside to let her in, a delectable odor trailing after her. "That smells really good."

"I'm glad. I figured most people can't resist good fried chicken and mashed potatoes."

"I certainly can't." Peel's mouth was watering.

"I'm Christina Simpson, one of the psychologists here on base. May I join you for dinner?"

Peel didn't think she had the option to say no, but found she didn't care. There was nothing to occupy her mind other than her constant worry for Anna. "I'd like that."

Dr. Simpson was good company. They made small talk over dinner, but eventually, as Peel knew it would, the conversation turned more serious. "Good news. Your scans are fine. There doesn't appear to be any damage to your brain. For a while, you may experience headaches when you're overtired or stressed, but that will go away in a month or so."

Then she leaned back, crossed her legs, and said, "How are you? Would you like to talk?" The questions were open-ended, allowing Peel to avoid answering if she wanted, but she found she wanted to talk to this kind stranger. Maybe because she didn't remember the kidnapping, she started by talking about

Sebastien. She described the house, his polite façade, the deaths of the Devin family. She talked about Gabriel Devin and how he became Father Martinez. She told her about the two murdered children buried with Sonja Devin. The psychologist took a lot of notes, but it didn't feel obtrusive. She listened, only interrupting with murmurs of shock and sympathy. Peel was sure Dr. Simpson had heard worse—she was a military psychologist after all—but she appreciated the other woman's acknowledgment.

Peel finished by telling her of the final drive to the embassy. There was no judgment or condemnation when Dr. Simpson looked at her and asked, "Do you want to talk about Anna?"

For the first time, Peel cried. She talked about the gentle way Anna had bathed her the first night and how she'd held the ice pack when her headache returned. She told her about Anna's relationship with her brother and friendship with Rosita. Just like at the embassy, she didn't talk about Anna's murder confession or their intimate relationship.

Peel expected Dr. Simpson to mention Stockholm syndrome or to recommend medication. Instead, she said, "It sounds like you were lucky she was there." All Peel could do was nod and wipe away tears. As the conversation wound down, Peel asked if she could call Linda. Dr. Simpson's eyes were kind and sympathetic. "Not yet. We need to fully debrief you, first. I know you told your story several times at the embassy, but the DEA needs to talk with you before you talk with anyone else. Is there someone I can call on your behalf?" Peel gave the psychologist Linda's name and number. "Now, who is she?" Dr. Simpson asked. "Your partner?"

Peel nearly laughed, thinking back to how Anna had claimed she had excellent gaydar. Apparently, where Peel was concerned, excellent gaydar wasn't necessary. "No, she's my best friend."

"Is there anyone else you would like me to call? Family?" Dr. Simpson probed gently.

She surely didn't mean anything when she asked the question. She wasn't pointing out the loneliness of Peel's life or the absence of meaningful relationships, but it felt that way. "No, just Linda." That wasn't completely true. She wished they could call and find out if Anna was safe. She wondered how long it would be before Anna wasn't in her every thought.

The psychologist had also brought her military-issue sweats, fatigues, a couple of gray T-shirts, and boots. Dr. Simpson apologized for the selection. Like everything in her life right now, they reminded her of Anna, especially her severe military attire. Finally alone in her quarters, she cried again.

The next morning a sharp knock awakened her. She stared at the ceiling for a few moments trying to make sense of her surroundings. At the second knock, she rose and made her way to the door. A woman dressed in military fatigues held two duffel bags.

"Good morning, ma'am. Dr. Simpson asked me to bring these to you." She lifted one bag. "Civilian clothes." Then held up the other. "Toiletries." She didn't move from the doorway.

Peel realized a response was required. "Uh, thanks. You can put them down wherever."

The soldier nodded and placed the bags on a utilitarian table inside the door. The move was reminiscent of her first mornings in Mexico when Elena and Anna brought her fresh clothes every day. She got lost in the memory and missed the next thing the woman asked. "I'm sorry," Peel finally said. "I'm a little out of it this morning. What did you say?"

She nodded her understanding, sympathy in her eyes. "Of course, ma'am. I'll return in ninety minutes to take you to the DEA. Is there anything else I can get you before then?"

Peel shook her head. "No, thank you very much. I'll be ready."

When the soldier left, Peel sank onto the couch. She had slept hard after her emotional evening, and her eyes burned and itched. All she wanted was to close them and drift back into the dreamless sleep of the night before, but she knew that wasn't possible. Her mind had already started thinking of Anna and it wouldn't allow her the peace of sleep. She shuffled to the bathroom and turned on the shower. And vowed not to think of Anna.

After breakfast Peel was driven from the base to a nondescript federal office building in the heart of DC. Her military escort stayed with her until the elevator doors opened on the fifth floor, where a receptionist thanked the soldier by name. Peel looked between them in surprise. Apparently, she mused, there were a lot of kidnap victims returning from Mexico. The receptionist led her down a hallway and opened a door on the left. Peel had expected an interrogation room like the one she'd been in with Detective Bellamy, so the corporate conference room was a surprise. After accepting an offer of coffee, she sat.

The wait wasn't long. Within minutes the conference room filled with suited officials carrying notepads and file folders, but no computers. Each person who entered murmured a greeting, but there were no introductions, and once seated, no one spoke. The last person to enter approached Peel with an outstretched hand. "Ms. Primm, I'm DEA Special Agent Mark Hettinger." She took his hand. He gestured to the people seated around the table. "These are members of various task forces investigating Mexican cartels. They are very anxious to hear what you have to say. However, if the number of people is too overwhelming, I will clear the room immediately and the two of us can talk alone." Hettinger was a thin-faced man with dark eyes. They were intense but not unkind. He seemed to care about her answer.

"I think I'm okay," she answered. "Just nervous."

"I understand. If at any point you want us to break or to move to a smaller group, please say so. You are helping us. Whatever makes you the most comfortable is what we'll do." At Peel's nod, he went on. "I'd like to start by having you tell us the events of the last couple weeks. It started with your grandfather's birth certificate? Is that right?"

Once again, Peel shared her story. She spoke nonstop for thirty minutes, only pausing to take a drink of coffee or answer clarifying questions from Agent Hettinger. While she talked, she looked at each of the members in the room. Some watched her intently, their gentle nods and sympathetic expressions helping her overcome her nerves. Others took detailed notes. When she recalled the three conversations she had with Sebastien, everyone picked up a pen and wrote. Twice she was nearly interrupted by people at the table, but a look from Hettinger stopped them.

When she finished speaking, Agent Hettinger excused everyone from the room with instructions to return in twenty minutes. When the last person left and the door closed, he looked at Peel intently. "I want you to know, everyone in this room is in awe of you."

She pulled back with a start. "In awe? I was kidnapped through my own stupidity. I would still be there now if Anna hadn't saved me. She figured it all out and she made the deal that got me here."

"Yes, but you kept your wits. You managed to befriend your captors. You kept your head about you enough to find a starting point. What you don't know is the starting point you found had a huge impact here in Washington. For years there have been rumors of moles in the DEA, but no one knew if it was true. The cartels often seemed to be ahead of us, but it was hard to know whether our organization had a leak or if it was happening on the Mexican side. Most of the time, we blamed Mexico because, frankly, every organization in Mexico has been infiltrated by the cartels." He tapped his fingers on a file in front of him. "When we got word to track anyone who searched for or accessed the Casalas file, we couldn't believe it would be so easy. Within hours, two high-ranking agents in two different departments asked about the files. The person who finally managed to access the file was in line to become a division head." He smiled at Peel. "Believe it or not, you're a hero around here."

She laughed, not knowing how else to react. His praise made her uncomfortable, but she couldn't deny she was proud. "Thank you for saying that."

He gave her a fatherly pat on her hand, then leaned back, preparing to stand. "Do you need a break? Restroom? More coffee?"

"Water would be great, and would you point me to the restroom?" He stood, and she followed him out. Once in the bathroom, she leaned against the sink and looked in the mirror. Her eyes were puffy and shadowed. Worry lines creased her face. With a sigh, she washed her hands and splashed water on her face. She felt marginally better until she turned and found no paper towels, only hand dryers. Groaning, she toweled herself off on the sleeve of her T-shirt, then made her way back to the conference room.

Hettinger greeted her with a bottled water. "I'm going to bring everyone back in again," he said. "They're going to ask you about the people you came in contact with while you were there. They'll focus on one person at a time. Anything you can think of, say it. You've already proven that every detail is important. Okay?" At her murmured assent, he stood and opened the door.

For another two hours, she was asked to recall every detail of her interaction with Sebastien and, eventually, Anna. Last night she'd agonized over how to answer these questions. She knew she would not reveal their relationship. She had gone back and forth over including Rosita and Juanita in the debrief. What about the women from Denver? They, too, had been innocent. Should she mention them? During breakfast, on the drive, while waiting for the meeting, she vacillated.

And then when the first question about Anna came, the answer was easy. She told all. Everything. She looked at each person in the room when she told them they had become friends and eventually lovers. She wanted them to see her sincerity and her complete sanity. Anna had saved her, and Peel would do anything to help her. She'd been wrong to think withholding information would protect her. She had to trust that Anna's goodness would come through to these people.

When the meeting was nearly over, Agent Hettinger asked her if she had any questions. Yes, she had questions. "Have you arrested Sebastien?" She wasn't ready to ask about Anna. The room was silent, and every agent found something to write.

For the first time that day, Agent Hettinger looked away from her. He stood. "Thank you all for coming," he said with a nod. The dismissal sent the other agents scurrying for the door. Peel read the responses and her heart fell.

When he met her gaze, she narrowed her eyes. "You're not planning to arrest him, are you?"

He held up a hand. "No, it's not that. Let's go to my office. There have been some developments, but I wanted to share them with you in private." At the question in her eyes, he continued. "They are all aware. I'm not concerned about the integrity of the people in that room." They walked in silence through a room of cubicles to an office in a far corner. The agent gestured for her to sit at a table, then joined her. He clasped his hands in front of him. "The night you arrived at the embassy, there was an explosion in a cemetery in Mexico City. Although there was extensive damage, we believe it was centered in a mausoleum." He watched Peel carefully. "We've confirmed that Sonja Rosales Devin was interred there." Pausing, he waited for Peel to absorb his words. When he started again, his voice was quieter. "At least three people are believed to have been killed. The Mexican coroner is doing his best to identify victims." He cleared his throat awkwardly. "They're still trying to separate the recent dead from interred bodies. The task is difficult because the blast was intense and focused in a small area."

Peel remembered this feeling. She'd had it just a few days ago when she'd heard Sebastien say Anna was dead. Was it possible that Anna could have survived the shooting only to be killed in an explosion? She stared down at the polished surface of the table, wondering how hard it would be to clean if she vomited. Her ears buzzed. Agent Hettinger was still talking. She looked up, watching his mouth move. He had such kind eyes. Why were his words so hurtful?

"Peel?" He touched her hand. "I need to ask you a couple more questions if you feel up to it." She looked at his hand. She had a question for him, too, but she wouldn't ask it. As long as she didn't, Anna was still alive. "Peel, here's what we know. Since that night no one has seen Sebastien Gutierrez, Dante Casalas, Father Martinez, or Anna. There was a car parked nearby. It was registered to Sebastien Gutierrez—a blue SUV." Peel felt the blood drain from her face. He noticed. "Yes, we believe it is the one Anna was using." Hettinger leaned close like he expected to have to catch her from falling off the chair. "Peel, do you think Father Martinez was capable of setting the explosives?"

She blinked several times. This wasn't the question she expected. She squeezed her eyes shut and strained to make her mind start working again. Was Father Martinez capable of blowing up the other two men? Of course he was. She opened her eyes and looked at him, steady and sure. "He killed his own baby. If he could do that, he's capable of anything."

He nodded, contemplating her. "That's what we thought, too." He continued to hold her gaze. "Take a minute to think before you answer my next question. Was Anna capable of setting the explosives?"

"Anna?" she asked in surprise.

"I know this is hard for you, but there were only two people who knew the children were buried with Sonja Devin. Only two people knew Gutierrez and Casalas would be there that night. We know one of those people disappeared for most of that afternoon. In fact, you could argue that Anna could have set the entire situation up, including framing Father Martinez. No one knows for sure the children were buried there. It's possible we never will."

Peel listened. While he talked, Anna's words haunted her: "*I killed a man last night…Shoveled dirt on his face until he suffocated… Don't fool yourself into thinking I'm a good person. I'm not.*"

"I-I don't know. I guess what I learned in Mexico is people are capable of anything if it means protecting their family." It was the most honest answer she could give him. She couldn't bring herself to say what was really in her mind. Yes. Yes, Anna might have killed Sebastien to protect her brother.

"Thank you for being honest. I know she means a lot to you." Peel looked at him then, but the judgment she expected wasn't there. Only sincerity. "Would you like some more water?" he asked.

"No, I'm fine." She took a deep breath. "So, what now?"

"Would you be willing to stay one more night in DC? I know you must be anxious to get home, but we've been conducting raids for the last two days based on your information. The teams will be processing those sites and the information they've gotten from you. It would be very helpful if you were available for further questions."

"Is it safe to go home?"

"Yes. The Mexican organizations are in disarray after the deaths of Casalas and Gutierrez. As for the Disciples of Gold, they've either been arrested or scattered."

"Okay." She pushed her hair back. "Could I go back to the base now?"

"Of course. I'll have someone take you right away."

Peel wanted out of this building, but she didn't think she could face sitting alone in the institutional room on the base. "Actually, do you think I could talk with Dr. Simpson? Is there some way to contact her?"

"I'll make sure she's available."

* * *

Dr. Simpson was waiting for her. "Agent Hettinger called and filled me in." Peel was grateful she didn't have to give voice to her worst fear, but she broke down at the woman's words. Dr. Simpson handed her tissues and waited. When the tears ebbed enough for her to begin speaking, she looked hopelessly at the doctor. "How can I feel so much for someone like her?"

The psychologist gave Peel another of her gentle smiles. "Like what? What was Anna like?"

Peel took in a shuddering breath and whispered her answer. "Loving."

Dr. Simpson slowly nodded her head. "What else?"

"She was funny. Quick, you know? And so gentle. When I was hurt, she was careful with me, always checking to make sure I was okay. Protective. Even when she was upset with me, it was because she was trying to protect me from myself." They sat in silence for a full minute, Peel staring miserably at the wadded tissue in her hand.

"Peel, how do you feel about Anna?"

She found the answer was easy to say. "I think I love her." She silently implored the doctor to understand, to not judge. "I'm afraid to tell you that. I'm afraid you'll think it's Stockholm syndrome or some other break from reality."

The doctor laughed. "First, Stockholm syndrome is not a break from reality. It's a response to people being in an intensely emotional experience. Second, I don't believe you are suffering from it. From your descriptions, Anna was just as much a prisoner as you were. Sure, she had more control over her fate, but look at how she used that control." She leaned forward to impress her words on Peel. "She used it to save you. Anna's actions were heroic."

Fresh tears began and Peel let go. Anna had been her hero. She looked at Dr. Simpson, trying to convey a depth of gratitude for the psychologist's understanding. All she could say was, "Thank you."

CHAPTER TWENTY-NINE

The next morning, the same soldier knocked on her door. This time Peel was awake. "Ma'am, a message from Agent Hettinger. Also, Dr. Simpson is available this morning if you would like to meet with her." She handed Peel a printout of an email.

She read it carefully, then looked to the soldier. "I would like to meet with the doctor again. Do I have time for a shower and breakfast?"

"Of course, ma'am. Would an hour be enough time?"

"Yes, thank you." She started to turn away, then looked back. "Uh, what's your name?"

"Sergeant Jones, ma'am."

Peel shook her head and asked, "What's your first name?"

The woman smiled. "It's Kristin."

"Thanks for taking care of me, Kristin."

"You're welcome, ma'am. I'll be back in an hour."

Peel dropped back on the bed. Overwhelming grief had kept her from sleep the night before. Even the very real possibility that Anna was responsible for the explosion didn't dim her feelings of loss. She stared at the ceiling, unable to move. She let her mind drift to what would happen after the DEA was done with the debrief. Right now, Peel couldn't picture her life in Colorado. She knew it in the abstract, but she couldn't see herself back and actually living it.

An hour later, Peel stumbled through her feelings and worries, including the fact she'd forgotten to ask about the phone call to her best friend. The psychologist nodded. "Let me say this back to you. You were kidnapped by a Mexican cartel, given two weeks to solve a thirty-year-old disappearance, escaped, then found out an explosion may have killed your kidnapper and the woman you love. Now, you feel guilty because you didn't immediately ask about a friend, and you're unsure of how you fit back into your old life?" She paused for effect, and Peel liked her for it. "Does that sound ridiculous when I say it back to you?"

"Yes." She laughed. "Thank you." She looked at her hands. "But, what am I going to do? What if I can't go back and live a normal life?"

"Honestly? I think you're expecting too much too soon, but let's work on the question you asked. What would be normal to you?"

"Working at the library, living in Denver, hanging out with Linda."

"And what parts of that do you feel you can't do?"

"I don't know. All of it. Any of it? When I think about going back, I just feel…" Peel was struggling to put her thoughts together. She shook her head in frustration.

"What was the first word that came to your mind when you started to describe your feeling. Don't judge yourself. Just say it."

"Empty."

"Empty. And what's causing the emptiness?"

Peel knew the answer as soon as she had said the word. "Anna. I don't want to go back to a life that lacks so much…" Again, she struggled to find words for her feelings.

This time it was Dr. Simpson who supplied the word. "Love?"

Peel looked at her with watery eyes. "Love," she conceded.

"Anna gave you a gift when she saved your life. She also helped you realize you haven't been living your life. How will you repay her?" There was an unmistakable challenge in the doctor's words.

"Aren't you supposed to let me draw my own conclusions?" Peel teased.

"Pffft. I don't have much time with you, and this is too important."

"I'm going to stop waiting for love to walk in the automatic doors of the library."

Dr. Simpson threw her head back and laughed. "That's a great start, and a very vivid picture. I think you have to be open to allowing more people in your life, too. Broaden your circle of friends. Allow people to know you."

Peel nodded. "Could you come back to Denver with me?"

"I've been looking into a therapist for you in Denver but haven't had much luck." She paused. "I have a proposal. We could do a weekly video appointment, if..." Again, the dramatic pause. "If you also agree to attend a weekly trauma support group meeting."

Relief washed over Peel. Once again, she felt her eyes starting to tear. "Yes, thank you, yes." She wiped the tears off her checks and laughed ruefully. "Can we work on the crying?"

"We'll work on anything you need, but I approve of the crying."

That afternoon, in the same conference room as before, Peel waited for the parade of agents to begin. They filed in and seemed to naturally land in the same seats. Agent Hettinger took his seat at the head of the table. "Ms. Primm, thank you for staying an extra day." She nodded. "A new area has come up in our investigation. We've been surveilling the Disciples of Gold since you were taken. In the last week, its leader, Ojos Gutierrez, was supposed to have flown to Mexico. We believe it was to meet with Sebastien Gutierrez. Ojos has not been seen since. Did you see either of these men while you were at the estate?" He pulled two mug shots out of a file folder in front of him and handed them to her.

As the agent spoke, Peel was sure she knew what happened to Ojos Gutierrez. She took the pictures carefully, relieved when she didn't recognize either man. "No. I didn't see them."

"You said that Anna had been shot while in Mexico City. Did she ever say who shot her?"

"No, but when I overheard Sebastien that night, he said it was a mugging or an angry lover." Peel needed to be cautious.

"What night was she shot?"

"Wednesday. I saw her Thursday morning."

"Could there have been anyone at the estate you didn't know about?" Hettinger pressed.

Peel kept her face neutral. That must have been the meeting Anna didn't want Peel to hear. "Absolutely. I spent most of my time in an upstairs bedroom. It's a large estate with several buildings."

"The timing of the hit on Anna and the disappearance of Ojos is too coincidental not to be connected. We believe Sebastien had him killed for ordering the hit." Hettinger studied her for a reaction.

Peel didn't know if she should agree with him or just stay silent. She decided to try to protect Anna. "If someone tried to kill Anna, I believe Sebastien would be very upset. He seemed impressed by her."

"Impressed?"

"Yes. He respected her. I don't know what Anna did for him, but whatever it was, it was important."

The agent looked around the room. "Other questions?" When there was no answer, he excused the agents from the room. "Will you join me in my office, again?"

"Of course." Like the day before, they wandered through the cubicles in silence. Once in his office, they sat at the table.

"Peel, I haven't been completely honest with you. Within a day of your kidnapping, we knew you were being held at the Gutierrez estate."

Peel was dumbfounded. "You did? How?" Then a rush of anger hit her. "Why didn't you rescue me?"

"We talked about it, but we couldn't come up with a plan that would guarantee your safety. Even when Sebastien was not there, too many men guarded the estate. It became less urgent when we heard how you were being treated. Then, you started to be a source of valuable information." He shrugged. "We knew about the deadline. We would have gone in before that day."

Peel stared at him. Her mouth was hanging open and she snapped it shut. She didn't know what to say. Then, with dawning understanding, a tiny flicker of hope started in her heart. "You had someone there at the estate."

"Yes. We raided the estate yesterday. That created the opportunity to get this person out. She's here and she's asked to see you."

Peel's heart pounded, and her hands started shaking. "She's alive?" she asked in a small voice.

Hettinger was already making his way to the door, but he turned back to her, cocking his head to the side. "Yes. Of course she's alive. I'll go get her."

Emotion began to overwhelm Peel. She was having a hard time catching her breath, and the shaking in her hands progressed to her legs. The door opened behind her and she turned slowly.

Rosita stood in the doorframe, a broad smile on her face. "Peel," she called out, her arms outstretched.

Peel rose, trying to cover her despair. She crossed the room and threw herself into the other woman's arms and started to cry. Rosita held her close, rocking slightly. She patted Peel's hair and whispered, "Hush now, you're safe. He can't hurt you."

Peel could barely hear her because she was sobbing. All the emotion that had come to the surface when she thought she would see Anna rushed out. She clung to Rosita. After several minutes, she pulled back from the embrace. "You were watching over me," she said in wonder.

"I was watching over you," Rosita said. "You were very brave."

Peel stopped and shook her head hard. "Wait. You speak English? Why didn't you tell me? Why didn't you talk to me?" Peel put one hand on her hip and used the other to wipe her face.

Rosita's eyes had the familiar twinkle. "Because it was entertaining to listen to you try to speak Spanish." At Peel's sound of outrage, she held up her hands. "Sebastien never wanted anyone to know I spoke English. He believed people would talk in front of me when he was out of the room."

"Did they?"

"Not often. Everyone in Sebastien's business is paranoid. I'm sure they tried the same thing with their housekeepers." She chuckled.

"Did Anna know about you? About this?" Peel gestured around the room.

"No. Anna worked for Sebastien. I would never dare tell her, but I think she suspected."

Hettinger had moved to sit at his desk while the women reconnected, but now he leaned forward. "You never told us. What made you think that?"

Rosita walked farther into the room. She carried herself with confidence. She was the same housekeeper Peel had known, yet somehow she was even more in charge than she had been on the estate.

Rosita sat in one of the chairs in front of the desk while Peel took the one next to her. "I wasn't sure. At the end, it seemed she was telling me more than she had ever before. It wasn't just a friend sharing gossip. It was someone sharing information she hoped would be passed on."

Hettinger looked at her. "Do you think Anna was looking to get rid of Sebastien? Did she want to take over the cartel?" He looked surprised when both Peel and Rosita burst out laughing.

Peel let Rosita answer. "No. Anna hated those men. I think she wanted to destroy the cartel."

Peel thought of something. "Agent Hettinger, did you find Anna's brother? Is he safe?"

"As I said, we've been watching the Disciples. Sometime in the last week or so, the man we suspect to be her brother, Miguel

Flores, disappeared along with his parents. He reappeared a few days ago. He's in no danger."

"Flores?" Rosita asked.

"Yes. We believe that's Anna's last name, too."

Anna Flores, Peel thought to herself. It was a beautiful name. Anna Flores. Rosita was asking another question, interrupting Peel from fantasies about hyphenating her last name. "The boy who was killed was Tomás Flores."

Hettinger looked confused. "Casalas's grandson?"

"No, the little boy whose death started all of this bad blood. His name was Tomás Flores."

"You don't think…" Peel started.

"No," Rosita answered. "His whole family was killed. Maybe it's God's way."

"What is?" Hettinger was watching them intently.

"Maybe it was God's way of making the family pay. A Flores returns to Tierra de Oro and gives all of their secrets away." Rosita wasn't looking at either of them now.

"Did you know him?" Peel asked her.

"Yes. It's a small town. All the children knew each other. We never talked of it."

Hettinger let the silence go on for a few moments. Then he looked to Rosita again. "Did you see these men at the estate either Wednesday or Thursday?" He passed the photographs over to her. She looked at them and then handed them back.

"Yes. Ojos and Mute. Ojos is Sebastien's cousin, but there is bad blood between them." Hettinger nodded as Rosita spoke.

"Did you see them leave?"

"No. When they got to the estate, they went down to the pool to drink. I had food already set out for them, so Sebastien didn't need me. When men like that come, I lock myself in my rooms."

"Do you think Sebastien would have killed Ojos if he found out he put the hit on Anna?"

Rosita didn't hesitate. "Yes."

Hettinger pressed. "His cousin?"

Rosita made a sound of disgust. "Sebastien didn't consider him family. That man was a pig."

"Surely Ojos was more important to him than Anna?"

"No. I never knew why Anna was there, but Sebastien seemed to trust her more and more. If Ojos tried to kill Anna, Sebastien would be furious. He probably buried him."

Peel's sharp intake of breath brought their attention to her. "Buried alive?" Instantly, she regretted her question.

"Sebastien's signature killing. It had some connection to the family's history as mine owners," Hettinger explained.

Peel didn't respond, but now she knew Anna had not lied to her. Again, her words came back to Peel: *"I shoveled dirt on his face until he suffocated. Still think I'm not like that?"*

Rosita seemed to sense Peel's distress, and she reached out to place a hand on her knee. "Anna is a good person. Whatever she was caught up in was out of her control. I'm sure of that."

Peel had always felt that way about Anna, too, but she didn't know how to reconcile that feeling with the truth that faced her. Then, as she had so many times in the last weeks, the last hours, she teared up as she said, "She may be gone."

Rosita nodded. "They told me about the bomb." She leaned forward and took Peel's hand. "We need to have faith and believe she survived." Rosita's face was calm, and Peel let herself hope. There was nothing to base it on other than Rosita's faith. For now, she'd take it.

"Where are you staying?" Peel asked.

"I'm staying on the base until they can find me a place to live."

"You're not going back to Tierra de Oro?"

Hettinger answered. "We believe Ms. Sanchez is safe in the United States, but her returning to Mexico is not advisable."

"Safe in the United States?" Peel asked. "Like witness protection?"

"No. We have no reason to think that anyone is aware of the help she has provided us. But, to be certain, we have offered her asylum in this country."

An idea flickered in Peel's mind. "Can she live anywhere?"

"Yes. We are working on arrangements for her now," Hettinger answered.

Peel's heart leapt. "Can she live with me? In Denver?" She turned to Rosita. "I inherited my house from my parents. It has plenty of room for both of us. And if you wanted to live alone, we could find you your own place, but at least you would know someone."

Rosita was silent, and Peel suddenly felt embarrassed. On the estate she'd felt close to Rosita. Maybe the other woman didn't feel the same way. She was just doing a job—actually two jobs, Peel realized.

Rosita must have seen her face redden, and she spoke quickly. "Peel, I'll be a reminder of a bad time in your life. You feel close to me now, but it won't be the same when you get home." Her tone was gentle, sympathetic.

"It's not like that. I feel connected to you. You're not the housekeeper of the man who kidnapped me. You're the friend who took care of me and helped me survive. If it doesn't work out, you can always go someplace else, right?" Peel cringed at how desperate she sounded.

Agent Hettinger was watching them closely. "I think that's an excellent idea. Ms. Sanchez will need help acclimating to life in the US. You are the only person who understands what she's been through, and she understands what you survived. We can make this happen if it's what you both want."

Peel looked at Rosita with her eyes full of hope. "Please? Come home with me?"

Rosita huffed out a breath, then broke into a wide smile. "Thank you, *mija*." At the sweet word, Peel's tears spilled.

CHAPTER THIRTY

Three months later

Peel and Rosita had fallen into an easy life together. Rosita took control of the house and Peel's life, and Peel loved it. The emptiness she'd feared had been filled by the bustle of the small Mexican woman and her boundless energy.

Her friends fell in love with Rosita, too. It started when Peel invited Linda to dinner so they could meet. Two nights later, Linda was sitting at their kitchen table when Peel got home. "Did we have plans?" Peel asked as she tossed her purse on the table.

"Nope," Linda said. "Rosita invited me."

"I knew I shouldn't have added her to my phone plan," Peel grumbled. Since Rosita still cooked for an army, Linda now ate with them at least twice a week. Between Rosita and Linda, the emptiness she feared never materialized. She felt the loss of Anna, but it didn't overwhelm her like she'd thought it would. Somehow, Rosita's presence kept Anna alive.

The first time Peel took Rosita to the library with her, she won the staff over with her pasties. They were charmed, and begged her to make them for the little coffee shop in the lobby. Within weeks, Peel's kitchen was a makeshift bakery, and she shopped in bulk—with Rosita in tow, of course.

The school year was about to start, and with it came the return of the Anime club. All of the kids had been by the library to see her, most several times, but the club had been on hiatus for the summer. She was excited to see them, but she was especially looking forward to introducing Rosita to the group. She laughed every time she thought of how Rosita would react to American teenagers.

The first week, she listened with joy to their summer adventures and welcomed the normalcy of their craziness. At the end of the meeting, she called for their attention. As usual, they didn't hear her until Jenn shouted, "Shut up, you guys!"

Peel nodded her thanks at the immediate silence. "I know I told most of you that the housekeeper from the place where I was held in Mexico is now living with me." Nods all around. "Would you guys be okay if I brought her to meet you next week?"

"Your Mexican Mama? Yes! Bring her," one of the kids yelled.

"That's racist," someone scolded.

"No, it's not," another argued. "She's from Mexico. That makes her Mexican. There's nothing racist about saying 'Mexican.'"

"You're supposed to say, 'Hispanic.'"

"No, she's Latina."

Peel looked at Jenn, who obliged her silent request. "Shut up, you guys."

"Rosita is very proud to be from Mexico. She would be honored to be identified as Mexican, however, I'm not sure she would be honored to be called my mama." They laughed, and Peel continued. "She's old-school, so no swearing."

Predictably, someone called out, "That's a bunch of shit."

Peel laughed with the rest of them. "Just be nice to her. She is a special person who's getting used to a new life."

A chorus of, "We will" followed her request.

The next week Peel was late picking up Rosita, so the kids were already in the community room when they arrived. Peel was cautioning Rosita to not show fear when the door burst open. A Mexican flag hung on the far side of the room next to a poster that said, "Welcome to Denver." Bags of tortilla chips and a couple of jars of salsa lay open on a table. There were no plates or napkins, and it appeared someone had tried to jam chips into the mouth of the jar, but Peel didn't care.

The teenagers lined up to introduce themselves to Rosita and give some form of welcome in Spanish or English. When the introductions were over, Peel looked at them. All she could think to say was, "You are the kindest group of people in the world." Then, predictably, she teared up.

"We know," they said in unison. Rosita laughed and patted Peel's arm.

"Can we ask questions?" As always, Jenn was the spokesperson.

"Of course," Peel said, looking at Rosita. "Rosita likes to talk." Peel got the expected disapproving tsk and stepped away before the older woman could swipe at her.

The kids chattered away at Rosita, and she chattered right back. They asked about telenovelas, and she tried to understand Anime. Peel cringed, hoping there would be no mention of her fondness for heaving breasts. Mostly she sat back, munching chips and marveling at her new life. Toward the end of the night, one of the quieter girls raised her hand. "Jenn, you said you'd ask her." Peel tensed, ready to jump in.

"I forgot." Jenn grimaced and checked her phone. "I think we still have enough time." She turned to Rosita. "They need help with their Spanish homework." Peel relaxed, and Rosita clapped her hands in delight. Within minutes she was holding a textbook, a group of chairs circled around her. Peel heard her grunt then whisper something in Spanish to the kids, who burst out laughing.

One student turned to Peel. "I thought she didn't cuss!"

"She cussed?" Peel was shocked.

"She said our homework was…" Hearing a sound from Rosita, she stopped. "Um, she thinks it's stupid."

The two women drove home laughing and chattering about the kids. Peel felt good. Rosita fit seamlessly into her life and filled the void left by the death of her parents. She stopped at the bank of mailboxes and pulled out the usual stack of circulars and glossy postcards. Since Rosita loved looking at the ads, Peel tossed them in her lap.

Once in the house, Peel headed for her bedroom and called over her shoulder, "I'm taking off my bra and putting on sweats."

"There's a card for you," Rosita told her when she returned to the kitchen.

"Who's it from?"

"I didn't look."

"Liar." Peel laughed. "You can't help yourself." The postcard showed a pink circular lifeguard stand on Miami Beach.

Rosita was indignant. "I had to see if it was for me."

"Mm-hmm," Peel was only half listening. She flipped the card over and read the handwritten note.

> 6 PM, August 31st
> Ogden Hotel Bar
> Sandoval. Steed Sandoval

She read it again, not understanding. Flipping the card over, she stared at the beach, trying to make sense of the bright photograph. When she turned it again, the name "Steed" stood out to her. She gasped, then screamed. Rosita jumped at the sound. "What's wrong?"

Peel held the postcard out to her. "Anna."

Rosita read it. She looked at Peel with a combination of confusion and pity. "You think this is from Anna?"

"She's alive." Peel could barely speak. "Oh, Rosita, I didn't want to hope, but I couldn't help it."

Rosita wasn't convinced. She pointed to the words. "Why do you think Sandoval Steed Sandoval is Anna?"

"No, it's not all one name. She's alluding to a line in every James Bond film. When he introduces himself, he says"—she paused, lowering her voice and affecting a British accent—"Bond. James Bond. He says his last name first. Then he says his whole name."

"Uh-huh." Rosita continued to look at Peel with pity. "Why would Anna do that?"

"She knows I like spies. It's a code, so only I will know it's her." Peel snatched the card from Rosita and looked at it again. "It's not just that." She looked up to Rosita, desperate to make her understand. "When we went to see Father Martinez, we had to sign in at the military base. She signed her name, 'Anna Sandoval.'"

"Then what is this other name? Steed?" Rosita clearly remained unconvinced.

"Steed is the partner of Mrs. Peel." She touched her chest. "My Mrs. Peel. It's Anna."

Rosita gasped and put a hand over her mouth. "Our Anna is too strong to die." She wrapped her arms around Peel. "She wants you to meet her at this hotel?"

"I think that's what it means. Oh, Rosita, she's alive." They hugged again, then Rosita pulled back. She sat back down at the table, wiped her eyes, and picked up the wineglass. "What will you wear?"

Peel laughed hard. "I don't know. Shorts? It's still hot. Maybe jeans."

She waited for one of Rosita's many sounds of disapproval, but none came. Instead, she said, "You need a sexy bra."

Remembering Anna's manipulation of her wardrobe in Mexico, Peel agreed. She laughed happily. "We'll go tomorrow, and you can help me pick out a new one." Tonight, she would agree to anything. "Rosita, she's alive."

"I know, *mija*." Rosita didn't use the endearment often, but every time she did, Peel felt a surge of warmth. She leaned over and hugged the older woman again.

* * *

The house was awash with the smells of Anna's favorite foods. Peel greeted Rosita with a hug. "I'm going to shower and get dressed."

"Wear the shirt that shows your *tetas*." This, too, had been the subject of several long discussions. Peel feigned outrage every time Rosita suggested it, knowing full well she would be showing her *tetas* to Anna. When she appeared downstairs, fully dressed with cleavage on maximum display, Rosita looked her over and gave an approving nod. "Go get our girl."

That's what she intended to do.

In the hotel lobby, she looked around for the bar. When she spotted it, the butterflies she'd had all day turned to panic. What if it wasn't really Anna? What if Anna wasn't who Peel thought she was? The distance between the reception area and the bar seemed both too long and too close. She took deep breaths as she walked, trying to steady herself. Once she stepped into the darkened room and turned the corner, she saw her.

Anna was at the bar, a draft beer in front of her. A Rockies baseball game was on, and she seemed to be watching. Peel stared at the long glossy hair trailing down her back and the fingers tapping against the glass. Emotion overwhelmed her. "Anna." She practically breathed the word. She didn't think she'd spoken aloud, but Anna turned.

She was beautiful. Dark eyes met Peel's and held for a long moment. As Anna stood, Peel saw her uncertainty. Her plan had been to play it cool, to let Anna set the pace. Stupid plan, she thought. She rushed forward and threw herself into Anna's arms. "I thought you were dead," she whispered. Peel felt the ever-present tears start to rise but refused to let them fall. "I'm so glad you're here. And you're safe." She pulled back and looked into Anna's eyes. "Are you safe?"

"Yes." It was the first word Peel had heard from Anna in months, and the sound of her voice thrilled her. She grabbed Anna again and held on. She felt the chuckle in Anna's chest. "Maybe the bar wasn't a good idea."

"It wasn't," Peel said into her chest. "Have you paid?"

"No. I was going to drown my sorrows if you didn't show up."

"You doubted me?"

Anna leaned in and whispered, "Well, there was the whole kidnapping thing to overcome."

"I'm a sucker for a bad girl," Peel teased. Then she winced. "That sounded really cheesy. Pay your tab. We'll go to your room..." At Anna's grin, she held up a hand. "To pack your bag. You're coming home with me."

Anna's grin widened. "Is Rosita cooking?"

Peel started, then eyed her. "How do you know about Rosita? It was supposed to be a surprise."

"We have a lot to talk about," Anna said. "And I'll tell you everything. Just not here." The grin returned. "So, has Rosita been cooking?"

"All day. There's food everywhere." Peel rubbed Anna's arm. "She's really excited to see you."

Anna's eyes were soft. "I'm really excited to see her." She motioned to the bartender for the check. "How is she?"

"Exactly the same. She's taken over my life, and I wouldn't have it any other way."

"It's great, isn't it?" The bartender placed the bill in front of Anna, and she put ten dollars in the folder. "Let's go," she said, wrapping an arm around Peel.

Outside the bar, Peel hesitated. "If I get the car, do you promise you won't disappear?" She didn't mean to sound pathetic, but she couldn't stand the thought of Anna being out of her sight. At the same time, she knew if they went up to the room, they wouldn't leave. It was tempting, but she'd made a promise to Rosita.

Anna was surprised. "You're not coming up?"

"No. I don't trust you. We'll never get out of here."

Anna grinned. "You mean you can't control yourself around me?"

"Really? You're starting already?" She tried to sound exasperated, but all she could feel was elation. "Go. I'll be right there," she said, pointing to the door.

Twenty minutes later, Peel pulled out into traffic. She glanced over at Anna. "I can't believe you're here. I thought we lost you."

Anna reached across the console and put her hand on Peel's thigh. "I came as soon as I could."

Peel looked sideways at her, then reached down to place her hand over Anna's. "You're not a gang member, are you?"

Rather than answering, she said, "Did you like Steed Sandoval?"

"I did. Very cute. I really liked the James Bond reference. So, are you saying you're a spy?" She squeezed the hand under hers. "You know, if you're MI6, I won't be able to keep my hands off you."

"How would that be different from when you thought I was in a gang?"

"You know, I think I've actually missed your ego. I don't know why, but I find it endearing. Probably because you try so hard." When Anna started to speak, Peel interrupted. "No, nope, don't even go there. You're all talk, aren't you?"

"Maybe I'm a little talk," Anna mumbled.

"Not believing you." Peel's voice took on a serious tone. "Who do you work for? Can you tell me?"

"I can't tell you exactly, but I do work for the government."

"Which government?"

"United States."

"And you were undercover in Mexico?"

"Yes."

"Are you still undercover? Are there people looking for you?"

"Not really."

"Not really, what? You're not really undercover, or no one's looking for you?"

"Both."

Peel gestured at her impatiently. "Start explaining."

"Where do you want me to start?"

Peel considered the question. "Is your name really Anna Flores?"

"It is, and I really did grow up in the neighborhood run by the Disciples of Gold."

"Do you really have a brother?"

"Yes. Miguel. And Sebastien was using Miguel to keep me in Mexico."

"Is your brother a spy, too?"

"No, he's not," Anna replied. "He's does auto body."

Peel thought for a minute. "I'm not sure I understand. They put you undercover in your own neighborhood?"

"My mother had a heart attack, and the doctors told us she had to have an expensive surgery. Before I could stop him, my brother borrowed money from Ojos to pay for it. I was still in college at the time. After the surgery, I told my handler I couldn't work for the agency because I had to help my brother get out of debt."

"You already had a handler?"

"Yes. They do tend to recruit early. Anyway, when I told her what happened, she thought it was an opportunity to infiltrate the Disciples." Anna looked out her window. "She went to a big meeting in Washington about it. When she came back, we set up a money laundering scheme and I convinced Ojos to hire me."

"What were you doing in Mexico if you were going after the Disciples? Were you laundering money for Sebastien?"

"No." Anna shook her head. "I was selling guns."

Peel looked over to her. "Guns? How did you go from money laundering to guns?"

"I saw an article in the paper," Anna said. "Did you know most of the guns in Mexico come from the United States?"

They stopped at a light, so Peel turned to Anna. "Really? All we ever hear is how violent Mexico is. Those guns come from the US?"

"Not all of them. About seventy percent."

"Seventy percent?" Peel was incredulous.

"Yeah. So, I talked to the agency and they decided to expand my operation. I convinced Ojos to buy and smuggle guns for de Oro." Anna had been looking at Peel as she talked, but now she looked away. "I was actually excited when Sebastien wanted to meet me. I thought it was a big break, and I had him." She looked back at Peel. "Then, he wouldn't let me go home."

"Did he threaten Miguel?" Peel reached for Anna as she looked up to see the signal turn green. She turned her attention back to the road.

"Yes. I couldn't leave." Anna put her other hand on top of Peel's. "If you hadn't come, I would still be there."

"That last day you told me Miguel was safe. Is he?"

"He is. We had a plan to get my parents out of Chicago. That happened while you were there. Then when everything happened with Ojos, I called Miguel and told him to disappear. He did."

"Anna?" Peel's voice was tentative. "What happened with Ojos?"

Anna stiffened, then took a deep breath. "I killed Ojos."

Peel still held Anna's hand. "He tried to kill you?"

"Yes. He ordered the hit. It was Mute who shot me."

"Mute?"

"He's the new leader of the Disciples. Mute told Sebastien that Ojos ordered the hit. Sebastien called me that afternoon. He sent me to Casalas to get a Kevlar vest. There was another guy with Mute, so he had to actually shoot me to make it look real." She grimaced and rubbed her chest. "But the asshole didn't have to shoot me twice."

They stopped at another light, which gave Peel the chance to look at Anna. "Is that who you met that night? When you told me not to leave the casita?"

"Yes. Sebastien convinced Ojos to come to Tierra to talk about a replacement for me. They were at the pool. Ojos was getting drunk and started insulting Sebastien. Sebastien sent someone to get me from the casita. When I walked out, Ojos lost it."

"Anna, I don't understand. How can you just kill someone? Aren't you supposed to uphold the law?"

"In my line of work, 'upholding the law' is nebulous. If I hadn't played my role that night, Sebastien would never have trusted me. I could have tried to get out of it, but he would have been suspicious. In the end, I decided that protecting Miguel, and you"—she squeezed Peel's hand—"was more important."

Peel was quiet. She knew they were at a crossroads. If she couldn't understand the choice Anna had made, there was no going forward for them. When she spoke, it was with conviction. "You didn't have a choice."

Anna let out a loud breath that sounded like relief. "I didn't see one."

They drove in silence for a few blocks. Finally, Peel asked the question that had been weighing on her since the DEA meeting. "Anna, what happened at the cemetery?"

Peel listened as Anna recalled that night in the cemetery. At the end, she said, "I've never seen so much hatred between two people. Gabriel lived his whole life for that moment in the mausoleum. I'm still not sure why he let me live."

"He knew you're a good person."

"I don't know if there was a good person there that night."

"Anna, you can't believe that. I don't, and neither does Rosita." Peel knew there wasn't anything more she could say, so she switched to a teasing tone. "Not only are you sexy as hell, but you're also, funny, smart, and an amazing person."

Anna went along with the change. "Sexy, huh?" She made a low sound in her throat. "Why didn't we stay at the hotel? We'd be in bed right now."

"Patience." Peel laughed. "Rosita is waiting to see you. No sex until after the reunion."

Anna groaned. "So many rules."

They fell into an easy silence even though they were both aware there was much more to say. "Were you hurt?" Peel asked after a time.

"Not really. I was knocked unconscious, but it couldn't have been for long. When I woke up, I could hear the sirens approaching, but no one was there yet." She tightened her grip on Peel's hand. "There was nothing left. The trees and grass were on fire, but all that was left of the mausoleum was a crater. All around it were pieces of stone and dust, but they weren't very big, you know? No one could have survived that." Peel glanced at Anna when she heard the pain in her voice. "He let me live," Anna said.

Peel pulled Anna's hand to her lips and kissed it. She didn't know how else to convey her support. "How did you get out?" she asked.

"I walked away. I turned my back on all of it and just walked away."

Peel couldn't decipher Anna's emotions. Guilt for living? Grief? The latter possibility frightened her. She tugged Anna's hand onto her lap, forcing the woman to turn to her. "Anna, what are you feeling? You sound so…" Peel left the sentence unfinished.

"I know. That's what I've been struggling with since that night." Anna shook her head. "It was my first time undercover. I wasn't prepared emotionally for it. I don't think anyone could be. I despised Sebastien, and I've convinced myself that both Devin and Casalas were evil, too."

At Peel's sound of protest, she held up her hand. "He killed two children, Peel. What else can you call him?" She shook her head. "But that's my problem, too. I felt sorry for him. I could rationalize, even understand his actions."

"So, what? You feel guilt for leaving the cemetery that night?"

"No. I feel like I walked away and nothing was better." Before Peel could protest, she said, "No, I know the cartel is destroyed, and the Disciples are in disarray—"

"And Rosita and I are alive," Peel interrupted.

"Thank God," Anna said, smiling. "I always pictured some grand moment of justice. Handcuffs, or a guilty verdict and long prison sentences. I wanted to watch it all get dismantled." She pulled her hand free with a pat on Peel's thigh and raked her hair back, lifting it off her neck. "Do you understand?"

Peel thought she did. "They got to determine the justice. You feel like they still had control?"

"Yes. And there I was, slinking through the cemetery like I was the guilty one."

Peel's mind whirred, trying to channel Dr. Simpson. "It's been three months. What have you figured out?"

"Ooh, you're good. Therapy?"

"Yep. I also know that when it comes to you, I did not suffer Stockholm syndrome."

"Good to know," Anna said. "Are we getting close to your house?"

"About ten minutes. Plenty of time." Peel gave her a sideways look. "But we can continue later if you like."

"Yes. Let's talk about something else."

"You really are a spy."

"I'm an undercover agent."

"That's sexy as hell."

"It's a burden I live with."

Peel laughed. "I'm so happy you're here."

"Me too."

They pulled into Peel's garage a few minutes later. Rosita ran to Anna, gathering her in her arms. Peel teared up as she watched the reunion between two people she loved. Loved? There was no doubt she loved Rosita, but Anna? The last hour proved she knew nothing about her. Maybe not love, but her heart definitely felt something.

Anna spoke to Rosita in Spanish as Peel led them into the house. "You don't have to speak Spanish to her. She's known English all along." Peel tried to sound irritated.

"When did you tell her?" Anna asked Rosita.

"You knew?" Peel's voice went up an octave.

"Of course I knew." Anna pointed at Rosita. "She doesn't have much of a poker face. If you'd watched her carefully, you'd have seen the smirk."

"Argh. You spies act so superior."

"We are," Rosita and Anna answered simultaneously.

"I'll get the wine. You two talk," Peel said. "Or would you rather have beer? Rosita bought everything you ever mentioned liking."

Rosita patted Anna's cheek. "It's so good to see you, *mija*."

"Hey, I thought I was *mija*," Peel protested.

"Don't be jealous. You are both my girls. Go get the wine. Don't forget the snacks on the counter." She made a shooing motion toward Peel and took Anna into the family room.

Peel smiled at the bossy little woman who had transformed her life, then hurried to obey. In the kitchen she took her time, wanting to give the two friends privacy. She leaned against the counter sipping her wine and admiring the new bright paint and the shelves of herbs planted in colorful pots. In the last week her focus had been on seeing Anna again, not what would happen next. Now that she was here, Peel knew what she wanted. Having Anna and Rosita in her home felt right. Rosita's voice carried into the kitchen. "Where is the wine? Are you drinking it all?"

They talked for hours. Anna told them a tip from a Catholic priest ensured that hundreds of archaeological treasures from the Gutierrez estate were sent to Mexican museums rather than back to the black market. "Padre Benito," Rosita mused. "He was a good friend."

"And contact," Anna added.

Peel looked between the two of them. "Padre Benito? He's a spy, too?"

"He's not a spy. Just a go-between. It's easy to share information in confession." Rosita shrugged.

"What about you?" Peel looked at Anna. "You never went to church."

"It's easy to share information in the bedroom."

Peel gasped. "All those women at the bar? You slept with your contacts?"

Anna pretended to be indignant. "No. I didn't sleep with my contacts." Then she gave Peel that familiar grin. "But sometimes I accidentally picked up the wrong woman. I couldn't blow my cover, so…"

"How often did you pick up the wrong woman?"

"Every once in a while."

"You did it on purpose!"

"God and country, Peel. It was all for God and country." Anna grinned.

Rosita frowned at Anna and scolded her in Spanish. Anna tried to look contrite. "Rosita says if I don't attend mass, I can't use God as an excuse."

Around midnight, Rosita stood and announced she was going to bed. Anna stood, too, and gave her friend a long hug. Rosita patted her on the cheek and left the room. Anna sat back on the couch. She picked up her empty wineglass, twirling the stem in her fingers. Peel could see the hesitation and knew she had to be the one to break the silence. She reached for Anna's glass and placed it on the table. "Come to bed with me."

In the bedroom, Peel wrapped her arms around Anna's neck. "No more talk. Tonight, I want you to make love to me." She kissed her, and the arousal she'd tamped down all night rushed through her. Anna pulled her close, leaning into the kiss.

"I've missed you," Anna whispered. "I want you so much."

Peel stepped back and unbuttoned her blouse. Anna caught her breath when the new bra was revealed. "Rosita told me to wear a shirt that shows off my boobs."

"Rosita is a very wise woman. I've been looking down this shirt all night."

"I noticed."

"This is a very sexy bra. I thought you didn't wear sexy bras."

"I do for you."

Anna kissed her again, and they undressed each other. They made love slowly this time. The passion was still there, and at times so was the urgency, but there was more tenderness. More love, Peel thought to herself. After, they lay in each other's arms, neither speaking.

More to keep her emotions at bay than anything else, Peel asked, "How did the agency approach you? I mean did someone just come up to you on campus?"

"I didn't know it at the time, but I was targeted as a potential recruit in one of my classes. The agency didn't approach me until later."

"Really?" Peel sat up. "I tried to get recruited in college. I took classes I thought they would be looking at."

"Like what?"

"Studies in Spy Novels."

Anna laughed so hard and so long Peel was afraid she would wake Rosita. Finally, she put her hand over her mouth. "Okay, smart girl, what class did you get recruited in?"

"Um, Intro to Criminal Justice."

Peel flopped back down on the bed pouting. "It seemed too obvious."

Anna rolled over on top of her. "I'm crazy about you, Peel Primm."

"I'm crazy about you, too." Peel's face was serious as she caressed Anna's cheek. "What are we going to do?"

"We're going to make love again." Peel was prepared to argue until she felt Anna moving against her. They could talk tomorrow.

* * *

They were both sound asleep when Rosita knocked on the door and entered with coffee. "Get up!" she called. "Breakfast is almost ready."

Peel lifted her head off Anna's shoulder and glanced down at their bodies. Thankfully, she'd pulled the sheet over them before they fell asleep. "I'm getting a lock," she told Rosita. "Do you know how to install a lock on a bedroom door?" she asked Anna, whose eyes were still closed.

"I'll learn," she muttered.

"Ten minutes." Rosita placed the coffees on the bedside table and strolled out.

"Did she even shut the door?"

"Nope." Peel rolled over Anna and off the bed. "She knows better." Peel headed to the bathroom, then looked over her shoulder to check Anna's response. "Don't even think of going back to sleep. You know she'll be back."

Twenty minutes later, the three of them were gathered at the kitchen table with massive plates of food in front of them. "Uh, Rosita?" Anna pointed at the food. "Did you think I hadn't eaten in three months?" Anna earned a stern look and the expected tsk. She laughed.

After they'd eaten their fill, Peel started to clear the plates. Anna jumped up to help, but Rosita pulled her down by her forearm. "Sit, we need to talk." Anna did as she was told. "What are your plans?"

Peel could have kissed Rosita. She tried to act nonchalant as she walked back and forth from the table to the sink. "I'd like to talk to the two of you about that." On Peel's next trip to the table, Anna grabbed her wrist. "Sit for a minute." When Peel did, she continued. "It took a few months to finish everything with Sebastien, but it's done now. I have a lot of vacation time, comp time, whatever you want to call it, owed to me. I'm going to visit my parents and Miguel, but after that I'd like to come back here for the rest of my time off. To be with you." She looked at both Rosita and Peel but held Peel's gaze. "I'd like to see what we can be."

"I'd like that, too." Peel intertwined their fingers.

"I'm not inviting myself to stay here. I can rent a place close by. I'd just like to be able to spend time with you."

Peel looked at Rosita. "That's ridiculous. You'll stay with us." Rosita nodded. "If you'd like your own space, we have another bedroom. Rosita and I can fix it up while you're gone. We want you here."

Anna's smile was wide. "I'd like that."

Once again, it was Rosita who asked the hard question. "What about your work, *mija*? Are you still working for them?"

Peel held her breath. She didn't know if she could handle Anna going undercover again. From her face, Peel could tell Rosita felt the same.

"The Disciples think I died in the explosion, so I have to lay low while the raids are happening. When I go back to work, it will be as an analyst. I can't say I'll never go undercover, but it would have to be something major, something no one else could do."

"Where will you live?"

"I wasn't sure I wanted to keep doing the job. When I told the agency I was thinking of leaving, they offered me my pick of locations."

"And?"

"And I haven't told them, yet. I was waiting to talk to you."

"Is Denver a possibility?" Peel didn't dare hope.

"Yes."

"Then I think you should tell them you're coming to Denver." Peel slid onto Anna's lap and gave her a long kiss. Then she leaned back and stared into Anna's dark eyes. "Is it safe for you to work for them?"

Anna ran her hands from Peel's shoulders to her hands. She clasped both of them in hers. "I promise you. From now on, my job will be analyzing data, maybe planning operations. My time undercover is over."

Peel nodded. "Analyzing data, you say?" At Anna's confused look, she said. "Think they'd hire me?"

Anna lifted Peel off her lap, grabbed her hand, and turned to Rosita. "Peel has always wanted to be a spy." She lifted her eyebrows. "I think I should take a look at her résumé."

She pulled Peel toward the bedroom, stopping when Rosita called out, "The office is the other way."

Anna grinned at her friend. "Do you really want us to use the office?"

They both laughed at the older woman's snort.

Bella Books, Inc.

Women. Books. Even Better Together.

P.O. Box 10543
Tallahassee, FL 32302

Phone: 800-729-4992
www.bellabooks.com